Frankly, My Dear Clara

FRANKLY, MY DEAR CLARA

KRISTI ANN HUNTER

Oholiab Creations
Georgia, United States

To the One who has purpose for us all
Galatians 6:4-5

And to Jacob, for helping me learn what "living for Jesus" truly meant

ONE

Miss Clara Woodbury was in possession of the customary solitary head which could only reasonably wear one hat at a time. This condition made the procurement of a third walking bonnet an irrational and unnecessary expense. This observation, which Clara had offered up in fifteen various phrasings over breakfast, had been thoroughly dismissed by her aunt. The viscountess insisted that young ladies participating in their one and only chance at a London social Season needed a minimum of three walking bonnets.

So Clara had dutifully joined her mother and aunt at the milliner where they'd ordered a bonnet with a startling resemblance to the one she'd plopped on her head as they'd left the house an hour prior.

Unfortunately, she was now back down to owning only two serviceable walking bonnets, as Clara's oldest hat was being crushed along with her head, her body, and her dignity. The hundreds of hairs, two ears, and single nose that she also possessed were being equally assaulted.

Clara didn't know what had caused her current predicament or even what that predicament actually was. All she knew was it had left her pressed tightly between her mother, who was screeching like an out-of-tune violin, and her aunt, who seemed to have forgotten every word in the English language aside from "oh, dear."

She attempted to turn her head so that at the very least her nose could stop trying to spear its way through the shoulder of her aunt's fine woolen pelisse but was hindered by the bonnet Clara could only assume was a lost cause. The headwear was caught on something. Every shift caused it to yank painfully at the coiffure beneath it.

And there was a lot of shifting.

The brim of her askew bonnet and its collection of decorative blue feathers filled Clara's vision. Her best guess, from the brush of fabric along her neck that accompanied every jerk of her hair, was that her mother's sleeve was somehow to blame for the constant pulling of the hat.

Mother's lungs were certainly to blame for the screaming that pierced Clara's ears as sharply as her aunt's boot heel was pressing into her little toe.

"Oh, my heavens, get it off, get it off, get it off!" Mother squealed.

"Unhand me at once," Aunt Elizabeth declared in a frantic yet haughty tone. She had not only remembered there were more words than *oh, dear* in the English language, but her wits had gathered enough to remind her that she had married into the aristocracy and was therefore a lady who could issue imperious orders. The thread of shaky panic running through that order was enough to increase Clara's concern.

Who was her aunt attempting to order about? They were in the middle of a London square, hardly a location known for mid-afternoon assaults or robberies.

Admittedly, Clara hadn't been giving her surroundings or her companions a great deal of attention, but surely the approach of an assailant would have been different enough to break through her moroseness over having to spend yet another afternoon shopping.

Then again, this was hardly a normal assailant. The silent figure had thus far managed to do nothing but press the trio together into a sandwich of social opulence that was not likely to endear Clara to any of the potential marriage matches her aunt insisted London would provide.

As much as Clara wanted to return to the country where she belonged, doing so because she'd been laughed out of London as an utter failure wasn't exactly the way she wanted to do it.

The harsh, strong wind that had plagued them all day grabbed at her skirts and flung her loosened locks of dark hair into whatever small cracks of sight weren't blocked by woven straw and feathers. Pressed as she was between her aunt and her mother, she at least didn't have to worry about her fluttering skirts flying about enough to create an indecent show. That would send her home in shame as well as failure.

"I've got it. I've got it."

A steady masculine voice cut through the feminine distress just before her mother jerked forward, pressing Clara even tighter between her female relations.

The movement had at least dislodged her mother's arm from her bonnet, though the freedom was accompanied by a sharp tug of her hair. Her eyes were watering with the stab of pain but at least she could now tilt her head enough to uncover one of them.

Framed between one errant curl and her own blue pelisse was a man. Or at least, part of a man. She could make out the brim of a black hat, a man's shoulder draped in a black coat, and the edge of a . . . kite?

Clara blinked rapidly and attempted to scrape her curl against her aunt's shoulder to get it out of the way. This catastrophe had to have been caused by something more nefarious than a child's toy.

It appeared, though, that their attacker had indeed been made of fabric, twigs, and twine. A long, sturdy string looped around the women at least three times, binding them together in this tableau of hysteria.

The wind that had apparently turned the toy into a weapon of social destruction caught hold of Clara's loose curl and shifted it until she was once again all but blind.

"You have our thanks, good sir." Aunt Elizabeth's breathless voice was shaky, likely due to the trembles working through her body and rubbing against Clara's. "Your quick thinking saved us."

"Saved us?" Clara couldn't keep the flatness from her voice. Since her aunt declared them rescued, the assailant must have been the kite. That was beyond humiliating. Her irritation had her muttering, "How much saving did we actually need? We've hardly been attacked by a runaway carriage or an unruly dog."

"Don't be ungrateful," Mother whined.

Clara winced. Where had her hearty, practical mother gone? This was the same woman that had taught her how to cross a stream while carrying a parcel and not get her hems wet. This was the same woman who had fed a screaming toddler with one hand while comforting a grieving widow with the other.

And now, after four days in the company of her older sister, she was simpering helplessly because of a kite.

Clara would rather not spend enough time in London to discover if the condition would eventually affect every woman in her family. Namely, herself.

Aunt Elizabeth sighed and sent her elbow digging into Clara's ribs. Was she attempting to wriggle out of the cage of kite string or correct her niece's behavior? Either way, Clara was finished with the entire uncomfortable business. It would be a minor miracle if their spectacle had not attracted a crowd, but whether or not God had blessed them with momentary anonymity, the sooner she was extricated from this predicament, the better.

And it seemed her fastest way out was at the hands of the unknown man.

"Apologies, kind sir." Clara flailed one hand about, attempting to grab one of the loops of confining string. "I'm certain we would have survived the final impact of such a dastardly foe as a kite, but it is nice not to be required to do so."

"Of course." He cleared his throat, but the sound seemed more to cover the beginnings of a chuckle than out of physical need. "If only I'd arrived here sooner and prevented your current entanglement."

Another wiggle, an accidental stomping of her mother's toe, and a jerk of her head to further dislodge the bonnet, and Clara could finally see past her aunt's shoulder.

Their rescuer was no longer wearing a hat and the violent wind danced through the strands of brown hair that were a little too long to be fashionable.

He had one arm secured around a paper and twine wrapped package while the other fought awkwardly with a broken kite still trying to ride the strong gusts of wind.

Clara tried to twist so she could look about the square. "Who does that thing belong to, anyway?" There wasn't a child about that she could see. Not many Mayfair residents either, which was fortunate.

The man made a show of looking about the green, but if his greater field of vision yielded any clues, he didn't give it away. "I believe the owners have made themselves scarce, my lady."

"I am not a lady," Clara instinctively corrected.

"Honestly, Clara." Mother sighed.

"Er, my apologies," the man said with a quick glance at Clara's aunt, who stood at the front of the unfortunate little trio, looking every inch the lady she was. Of course their would-be rescuer was more than a little confused. "I, er, meant no disrespect."

Neither had she, but her mother and aunt would consider it impolite, regardless. It wasn't that Clara had a problem with the peerage individually. She'd grown up happily playing with her cousin and had enjoyed visiting her grandfather's barony until he died, and the estate passed to some distant relation.

It was being counted among the class as a whole she had a problem with. She wanted to help people. She wanted to make a difference in their lives. That would be harder to do if she was seen as inaccessible or if people assumed she considered herself better than an average person.

What she wanted to do right in that moment was fold her arms across her middle and stomp her foot in frustration, because it wasn't fair for her family or anyone else to make her feel bad for simply wanting to be normal. Since she could do neither, she stuck her nose in the air and tried not to feel any more ridiculous than she had a few moments earlier. "It is the truth. We should seek truth without hesitation."

"Refusing it shows we value men's esteem more," the man said quietly.

If she wasn't being held in place by her aunt and her mother, Clara's knees might have given way in shock. She stared down at the man, her mouth slightly agape.

He lifted his attention from the string and met her gaze, a grin now fully evident on his face. "Not an exact quote, I'm afraid, but the idea is there."

She blinked at him several times in silence.

"It's Blaise Pascal." His tone was less confident as he gave her a small nod before setting the paper-wrapped package carefully on the ground to free up both his hands to work on the kite.

"Yes," she blurted out. Could she get away with blaming the slight breathlessness in her voice on her attempts to get free? "*Pensées.* Have you read it?"

"Of course he's read it." Aunt Elizabeth shook her head, sending the feathers of her uncrushed bonnet brushing against Clara's nose. "It's hardly a popular enough book to be quoted as dinner conversation."

Clara twisted to free her face from the feathers and her leg brushed the man's arm. She looked down. He looked up. Then he gave her a quick wink before turning his attention back to his efforts to lower the loops of string to the ground.

"I'll have you free in a moment." He grunted as the wind tried to throw the kite back into the air. After tucking the object securely beneath his knee, he cast a look around the square. "No one else seems inclined to lend anything aside from eyes and ears to the situation."

He tugged on the string and Mother knocked into Clara's back once more, making her head smack against Aunt Elizabeth's shoulder. This time the bonnet feather went into Clara's mouth.

She sputtered inelegantly, trying to force the downy bits from her tongue.

Aunt Elizabeth sighed. Again.

Mother shrieked. Again.

Clara wished she could close her eyes and wake up snug in her little room at the rectory in Eldham. Again.

The quick, sure steps of a running man approached from Clara's other side and before she could lift her chin and turn her head in the direction, the person had joined in the rescue efforts, bringing more tugging and jostling to the string.

"Ah, finally." Aunt Elizabeth's tone was everything gracious as the loops of string were worked to the ground. She stepped forward, her movement as graceful as it would be in a ballroom.

Clara pushed her ruined bonnet back into place atop her head and shoved her errant curls behind her ears. Her cleared field of vision now included her grinning older brother, Marmaduke.

His grin widened as he extended his hand. As much as she would like to glide forward as her aunt had done, she didn't trust herself not to trip over the lowered string or even her own hemline. She slid her hand into her brother's and prepared to step free of her prison.

"Thank you for your assistance, Duke."

Aunt Elizabeth's words had the man who'd snagged the kite jumping to his feet. Unfortunately, the string was still in his hand and Clara's foot was in the air outside the circle while the rest of her remained within it. The loop caught around her knee, finally completing the kite's mission to knock her off her feet and ruin her London Season before it had even begun.

Except she didn't get a humiliating face full of grass and dirt.

Instead, the stranger's arm wrapped around her waist. For a moment, the situation was awkward, filled with a tension she couldn't identify.

Then the abandoned kite caught a gust of wind and flew up to knock solidly against the man's back.

He winced as giggles threatened to spill from Clara's mouth. She gritted her teeth. Lady or not, she could not be so rude as to repay the man's chivalry by laughing at him.

With Marmaduke's assistance, it took only a moment to free all entrapped feet and skirts and wrap the string securely around the remains of the broken kite.

Clara's mother took a deep breath and straightened her bonnet, pretending for all the world that she hadn't been near hysterics mere moments earlier. "You can't say such things, Elizabeth."

Aunt Elizabeth was far more concerned with straightening her skirts and pelisse than her sister's views of propriety. "It was merely a jest, Miriam. We've done it for years."

It took Clara a moment to realize the sisters were referring to the family's habit of ironically shortening Marmaduke's name to that of a high personage. The unknown man's startled reaction to thinking he was among a top-ranking peer only supported Clara's desire to not be counted among their ranks.

The man slowly retrieved his parcel, his bright golden gaze bouncing from one person in their little group to another. Was he trying to decide who among them was actually a person of consequence? Was he hoping for some kind of reward?

Clara's relief turned bitter at the edges. Why wasn't it enough for people to simply accomplish a good deed?

Well, she could disavow him of any anticipatory notions he was holding. Aunt Elizabeth might be a viscountess, but there was no one so illustrious as a duke in their little circle. "I believe, Aunt, that it is a jest more suited to private excursions in the country than a populated square in the middle of the city."

Aunt Elizabeth pouted. "No one is close enough to hear, Clara. You're being far too serious."

"She has but one Season in London," Mother said as she moved to stand shoulder to shoulder with Clara. "We can't afford to be anything but serious."

Where had this strong woman been ten minutes ago? Clara's ears were still ringing.

Marmaduke clapped his hands together. "While you three debate the correct time for a joke we've all been bandying about since I was in the nursery, I shall introduce myself to No One."

"No one?" Aunt Elizabeth frowned. "What on earth are you speaking of?"

Marmaduke pointed to their rescuer. "You said no one is close enough to hear and unless this man is incapable of it, he most definitely heard."

A tinge of red worked up the man's neck, reinforcing Clara's idea that he'd been of a mind to gain something tangible after his good deed.

Aunt Elizabeth had not an ounce of shame, though, as she merely frowned at her nephew.

Marmaduke gave the other man a bow. "Mr. Woodbury, at your service."

"I am Mr. Lockhart. How do you do, Mr. Woodbury?" Despite the common pleasantries, Mr. Lockhart didn't look at all satisfied with the exchange. If anything, he looked more confused.

Mother sighed, but Clara couldn't find it in her to feel sorry for the woman. She'd given her son the ridiculous name in the first place.

Marmaduke grinned, seemingly unconcerned and clearly happy to dwell in the middle of confusion. "Oh, I'm well. It's a lovely day, a catastrophe has been humorously averted, and I am presently annoying the women in my family by holding strictly to the letter of the good manners I have been taught."

It was Mother's turn to frown at the exchange. "What good manners are you exhibiting?"

He puffed out his chest and placed a hand over the middle. "You were the one who told me it simply wasn't done to introduce a woman to a man she'd given no indication of wanting to meet."

Marmaduke grinned at Mr. Lockhart. "You should know though, in case you happen to hear this lovely woman referred to as Mrs. Woodbury, that she is my mother, not my wife." He waved a hand about. "Wouldn't want anyone confused about anyone else's identity here."

The man dipped his head to examine the package he'd been carrying, but it wasn't enough to disguise the wide, laughing grin that split his face. Apparently, he wasn't so put out by the lack of monetary gratitude that he couldn't appreciate the ridiculous.

Clara just wished she wasn't the ridiculous in question. Even if she could feel her hair sticking out in four different directions while the brim of her bonnet dipped low over her ear, she did not take kindly to being laughed at. She gave the bonnet a jerk, attempting to center it back on her head, and ending up entirely dislodging the bow beneath her chin.

The man coughed in a failed attempt to disguise his brief chuckle.

And that was enough embarrassment for one day.

Clara knew what sort of behavior was expected of her as a member of London society. Any moment since her arrival in London that hadn't been taken up with shopping had been filled with her aunt's lectures on society's rules. Prime amongst those rules had been to never walk anywhere on her own.

Every rule had extenuating circumstances, however, and Clara was of the mind that being viciously attacked by a kite counted as such. Despite wanting to stomp away from the encounter, taking out her frustrations for the entire day—no, the entire past week—on the grass beneath her boots, she walked gracefully and sedately away from the group.

Clara made her way across the square, past a scruffy dog with judgy, beady eyes, two openly curious women—three if she counted their maid—and a delivery boy who turned away so briskly when she frowned at him that he nearly toppled the stack of boxes in his arms.

Indignation robbed her of the last of her decorum, and she stomped up the stairs to her cousin's front door. Clara went to shove the door open only to have it whisked inward by the very attentive butler.

Only her years of walking rough trails in the countryside kept her from falling on her face as she stumbled through the opening, arm outstretched like she was chasing an errant child. The indignation was truly the final straw.

"I beg your pardon, milady," the butler, Hodges, said stoically, "but I've taken the liberty of sending word downstairs that Sally should meet you in your rooms to, er, see to your hair."

Clara glanced in the mirror beside the door. It was even worse than she'd feared. The bonnet was half crushed, curls draped lopsidedly over one shoulder, a feather from her mother's hat was sticking upright out of the neckline of Clara's bodice, and a bruise was already forming on the cheekbone that had connected far too rapidly with her aunt's shoulder.

With nothing more than a groan to acknowledge the butler, Clara abandoned any remaining good form and slumped up the stairs. London was turning out to be a bad egg indeed.

TWO

M r. Hugh Lockhart's prayers that morning had included his oft repeated request that this would be the day he had the opportunity to meet an aristocrat or two for an extended encounter.

Perhaps he should have been more specific in his request.

In his mind, such an encounter would lead to a possible stepping stone to having his own business. It was why, whenever possible, he delivered repaired clocks to London's elite himself. So far, none of the timepiece owners had been inclined to indulge in an extended conversation, but all it would take was one to help him get started.

While the encounter in the park could fit as an answer to his prayers, it had not been quite what he had in mind.

Now that the excitement was over, the scattering of people around the green went back to their own business. Not that he blamed them for stopping to watch the earlier farce. The absurdity of the women being set upon by the errant kite was a memory that was likely to make him laugh for days to come.

At the moment, though, any urge to laugh was being smothered by the awkwardness of the little group now standing around a broken, subdued kite.

At least, Hugh felt awkward.

Mr. Woodbury or Duke or whoever the man was, grinned as if he hadn't a care in the world. The two remaining women wore expressions of far less happiness, appearing to wish they were anywhere else but not willing to traipse away as the youngest lady had done.

No, the youngest woman. Because she was not a lady.

Even the discomfort of the moment wasn't enough to keep his lips from twitching at that recollection, so he busied himself with collecting his fallen hat and paper-wrapped package. Once he was confident his face had returned to an appropriate expression, he stood and gave his momentary companions a respectful nod.

"It was my honor to be of assistance, my ladies." He stumbled over the word ladies, but it seemed only their absent companion had issue with the honorific. "As I have business to attend to, I will leave you in the care of your, er, Mr. Woodbury."

"Have no fear," the affable other man said. "I shall see them home and keep a close eye out for any more wayward toys."

Hugh glanced about the green, where the day's hearty wind was dallying with more than just the kite. Several ladies held their skirts in a tightly wrapped configuration and nearly all the men had a hand on their hat or had given up and chosen to carry it.

Even now the twirls of problematic breeze were threatening to send Hugh's hat toppling back to the ground. He shoved the object further down onto his head, hoping it would secure it without pushing it too far out of shape. He'd need to keep an eye out for more flying objects as he crossed the green.

With a last nod to the trio who didn't seem to know quite what to do with themselves, he walked off.

As he crossed behind a tree that temporarily blocked the wind, a scraping sound emanated from the package in his arms, bringing him to an abrupt halt. He'd tried to be careful with the box while aiding the group of ladies. The outer wrapping bore no visible damage, but that didn't mean the delicate contents hadn't suffered from his dash across the green.

He tucked himself further into the protection of the cluster of trees and shrubs, then used his body to block whatever wind remained as he knelt and set the package on the ground.

The tails of his coat flipped about as he untied the string and peeled away the protective wrappings to reveal the nearly 100-year-old table clock.

He leaned over to peer in the glass window on the side of the wood casing. The spring he'd realigned and the verge escapement he'd had to replace appeared undisturbed. He couldn't check the striking mechanism without turning the clock over and opening the back, but it was less likely that element had been disturbed by the shaking. Possibly the winding key had become dislodged and now sat in the bottom of the casing.

Satisfied all was well, he replaced the protective wrappings and secured the twine. Taking a deep breath, he shook his head and rose to his feet once more with the clock securely clasped in his arms.

Though he knew his focus needed to be on the lord he was en route to see, he looked back to see if the ladies and Mr. Woodbury were still standing about. They were nowhere to be seen. Most likely they lived in one of the homes lining the square. He hadn't been able to see where the younger woman flounced off to, but the lack of concern from the women meant she must not have needed to walk far.

As he was on his own, he allowed the memory of the moment to inspire a chuckle.

He was still smiling when he reached his destination, as it, too, was one of the fine townhomes at the edge of the square. Four layers of windows stretched above him as he eased down the six steps from the street to the servant entrance. The windows stretched four across as well, indicating there was certainly money within these walls. There was also a viscount with a penchant for fine timepieces.

Was there any chance he'd be willing to invest in the opening of a new chronometer shop?

Despite Hugh's daily prayer, he sighed in anticipation of defeat. Aristocrats rarely involved themselves in trade, preferring investments that were less directly connected to the acquiring of their friends' money.

There was always a chance, though. The world was changing rapidly, and some titled gentlemen were becoming more and more interested in the technological advances of the day. One day, Hugh would encounter a blessed benefactor. Until then, he'd do as he'd done for the past three years and attempt to garner the attention, respect, and recognition among the wealthy so they might see him as a master clockmaker and desire to work with him directly.

If he could gather a little clientage along the way, he could save up the funds for his own shop. It would be slower than he'd like, but at least he'd be moving forward. Today his job was to impress the aristocratic owner of this lovely clock.

Two footmen, three maids, and one butler later, he was shown into the study of the Viscount Eversly.

The man stood from the desk, a genuine smile crossing his face as he rubbed his hands together and came around the furniture to meet Hugh in the middle of the room. He didn't appear much older than Hugh's twenty-six years, but he was obviously excited about the clock.

"This is it, then? Johns was able to fix it?"

And therein lay the problem with Hugh's grand plan. As long as everyone assumed it was Mr. Johns working on their clocks, they'd continue to ask for the shop owner. Despite his limited eyesight that wouldn't allow him to work with the smaller elements anymore, the older man refused to bring Hugh on as a partner instead of the employee he'd become at the completion of his apprenticeship.

Mr. Johns had never even looked in the casing of this clock. It was Hugh who had gotten the mechanism ticking along better than it had when it was new.

But it wasn't Hugh's name on the door, and he couldn't outright correct the assumption. He needed the steady job, and it was Mr. Johns' name on the invoice. He was the one with the reputation as the man who could handle the more exacting repairs. That might have been true once, but Hugh had long ago surpassed his teacher's abilities.

Shoving aside the sinking feeling of despair, he put on a smile to assure the clock owner his expensive repair had been completed correctly.

"A few of the gears and interior workings had to be replaced. Most of it was a matter of cleaning and rebalancing everything." He nodded toward the desk and raised the wrapped package. "May I?"

Lord Eversly waved toward the door. "Why don't we take it to the drawing room? That way you can set it in position, and we'll know everything is at it should be."

"Of course." Hugh fell into step behind the viscount and exited the study. He glanced discreetly around at the furnishings and decor. He'd seen the interior of many of London's finer homes as he performed the task of resetting a repaired mechanism. Clocks of great worth or sentimental value stopped keeping time even with weekly calibrations and he—or rather Mr. Johns—was called upon to make them new again.

Normally he walked the rooms in stiff silence to the accompaniment of a butler who always seemed to think Hugh was going to abscond with the silver. Occasionally, like now, he was accompanied by the gentleman of the house, but either way, he always fell into his place two paces behind his escort.

This situation didn't seem to be to Lord Eversly's liking, though, as he fell back to walk beside Hugh as they walked through the house.

And he chatted the entire way.

"My grandfather taught me how to tell time by that clock. It sat in my room at the country estate for years, but I'm almost never there anymore."

Hugh nodded. What would an appropriate response be? Clearly the man expected this chat to be a conversation and not a monologue with an audience of one.

Fortunately, if there was one topic Hugh could confidently speak on, it was timepieces. "Did it stop working after the relocation?"

Lord Eversly tilted his head in thought as he took them up a flight of stairs. "Not right away, no. But it stopped keeping accurate time after that." He shrugged. "Then it stopped working entirely."

"The move might have dislodged the piece that finally broke." Hugh nodded toward the package. "One gear was in three pieces down in the well of the clock."

Lord Eversly gave Hugh a crooked grin as he placed a hand on the latch of a door. "Mr. Johns tell you that?"

"Ah . . ." Hugh tried to avoid telling anyone an outright lie, but some people got very upset if they thought their project had been handed off to a lowly lackey and not seen to by the perceived master craftsman. He should have known better than to be lulled into easy conversation by the viscount with the charming reputation. All of London knew of Lord Eversly's silver tongue.

"Not to worry," the viscount said with a chuckle. "I shall simply thank *you* for my working clock." He pushed the door open. "Oh, hello there!"

Hugh followed the aristocrat into what appeared to be a family parlor and was glad he'd not yet removed the clock's protective wrappings. The package bobbled in his arms, and he hugged it to his chest to keep it secure.

Seated on the couches throughout the casual sitting room were all the participants of the earlier kite spectacle.

And only Mr. Woodbury appeared happy to see him.

THREE

Clara gulped down the remaining swallows of tea from her cup, hoping the bracing bite of the bitter brew would clear her vision. She had to be hallucinating. That man could not possibly be standing in her drawing room doorway.

And yet . . .

She glanced around the room. Everyone else seemed able to see him as well. He was apparently all too real.

Clara had lived in the country all her life. She'd stumbled into mud puddles, snagged her skirt on wayward twigs and rocks, and been chased down more than one lane by an angry goose. Never had she endured a greater humiliation than the encounter twenty minutes ago in a London square.

Maybe it was the indignity of her appearance, her mother's hysterics, her aunt's snobbery, the delicacy of her current situation, or the fact that the entire business had been the fault of a child's toy, but the why didn't matter. What did matter was that she'd coiled her hair into a simple low bun and ordered tea be brought to the family drawing room to pretend the entire afternoon had never happened.

And now, the man who'd witnessed it all was standing in front of her.

The only positive note was the stranger appeared as uncomfortable as she was by the surprise encounter.

Mother's cheeks were tinged with pink as she continually lifted and lowered her teacup. Aunt Elizabeth was blinking rapidly, looking from her son, Ambrose, to the newcomer and back again. She had been rather insulting to the man earlier, and he was obviously friendly with the viscount.

What if he was someone important? Would anyone notice if Clara slid to the floor and hid under the skirted couch?

Marmaduke, of course, had not a single misgiving as he rose from his seat with a wide smile, arms outstretched as if he were welcoming a friend home from a years-long journey to India. "Mr. Lockhart."

Ambrose looked from his cousin to the package-carrying man with confusion. "You know each other?"

Mr. Lockhart cleared his throat and adjusted his hold on the parcel. "We had a recent encounter. It was of little consequence."

God bless the man, whoever he was. Unfortunately, Clara's brother was not as inclined to save her from embarrassment as this stranger.

Marmaduke laughed and moved to stand behind Clara. When his hand landed heavily on her shoulder, she allowed her eyes to slide closed as if not watching would stop what was soon to happen.

It didn't.

"Our mothers and my poor sister were brutally attacked out on the green." Marmaduke's voice was filled with an overabundance of horror. "Mr. Lockhart saved them from certain doom."

"I do believe you've missed your calling," Mother said dryly as she collected the used teacups onto the tray, her cheeks still flooded with color. "Such dramatics cannot possibly be to your advantage on the cricket pitch."

"Clearly you haven't been to many cricket matches," Marmaduke muttered.

Aunt Elizabeth rose from the settee and straightened her skirts. "Our family does not need a professional performer among our ranks."

Marmaduke's grip on Clara's shoulder tightened again, but this time Clara lifted a hand and gripped his fingers in support. Aunt Elizabeth might not have said having a professional athlete in the family is bad enough, but there'd been enough discussion about it over the years and the message was more than implied.

As if Aunt Elizabeth needed an outlet for her displeasure, she frowned at her sister and the tea tray she was holding. "Honestly, Miriam, you aren't in the country anymore. The servants will see to that."

Clara winced. Mother frowned at the tray in her hands and then the low table as if trying to decide whether returning the tray to the surface or carrying it from the room was more embarrassing.

Aunt Elizabeth wasn't waiting for her sister to decide. She turned away from the table, straightened her shoulders, and tilted her chin a little more into the air. "I believe I shall go check with Mrs. Turner about dinner tonight. She was going to see if the market had any good fish."

Ambrose's eyebrows lifted as he stepped aside so his mother could leave the room.

A tense silence filled the room as her the last echoes of her footsteps drifted away.

"Mr. Lockhart, allow me to belatedly present my mother, Lady Eversly," Ambrose said flatly as he gestured to the empty door.

"A pleasure, I'm sure," Mr. Lockhart murmured.

The entire room seemed to exhale a sigh of relief as the moment slid away.

Clara's ease was short-lived, though, as Marmaduke had not forgotten that he had an opportunity to torture his little sister.

"As the package is apparently yours, Ambrose, I'm doubly glad Mr. Lockhart was able to keep it safe while he rescued our relatives in distress."

"We were hardly in distress," Mother said as she set the tea tray on the table and rearranged the dishes on it as if that had been her plan the entire time. "'Twas a trifle inconvenient but hardly a loss of composure."

Mr. Lockhart coughed and seemed to find the toe of his shoe of sudden intense interest. Was he remembering how Mother had screamed and flailed about, knocking Clara's bonnet askew? She certainly was.

"I saw you from the window, Mother." Marmaduke didn't bother to hide his laughter. "There was most definitely a loss of composure."

Mother snatched up the tea tray once more, sending her carefully rearranged cups clattering against each other. "Tea? Yes. Tea. More tea." She strode toward the door. "I'll have some sent in."

Ambrose once more waved a hand toward the empty doorway. "My aunt. Mrs. Woodbury." He turned his brown eyes to Clara and Marmaduke. "Would either of you like to mysteriously exit the room?"

"I'm not going anywhere," Marmaduke said with a laugh. "Clara might wish to flounce out though."

Clara frowned at her brother. She'd be the absolute last person to leave this room now.

"The young lady, er, woman has nothing to be embarrassed about," the stranger said in a calm voice. "She maintained her composure the entire time."

What was she meant to say to that?

"Are you certain?" Marmaduke stepped to the side and leaned down to cross his arms on the back of the settee his aunt had recently abandoned. It brought his eyes down to Clara's level. "Not even a squeal when you were attacked?"

"Would one of you please tell me what happened?" Ambrose strode into the center of the room and faced down his cousins, arms crossed imperiously over his chest.

Clara fought the urge to roll her eyes. While he was her cousin, he might as well have been her brother. Growing up, he'd spent more time in their home than his own. All his school holidays had been spent at the vicarage, and when he decided to retreat from London these days, he was as likely to visit his uncle as return to his own country estate.

In the past few years, Clara had actually come to view the situation with a measure of pity, that her cousin seemed so rootless in his life despite his duty and title. At the moment, though, she felt nothing but frustration. Ambrose was doomed to join Marmaduke in being an insufferable idiot once he learned about the kite.

"I'll just set up the clock then, shall I?" Mr. Lockhart strode across the room in a long, awkward path that gave the little group a wide berth.

Ambrose nodded toward the fireplace. "It fits nicely on the mantle."

Mr. Lockhart's gaze connected briefly with Clara's as he crossed to the fireplace. The glimpse of such a unique, golden shade had her tilting her head for a second look, but he steadfastly gave his attention to the package he was unwrapping.

"What happened on the green?" Ambrose was clearly not distracted by the man with the clock. "Were you truly attacked?"

"No," Clara said decisively.

"Yes," Marmaduke said with equal confidence.

Ambrose looked from one to the other and back again. "Well, which is it?"

"It was a kite." Clara sighed. Maybe if she told the story, they could all admit it was nothing and move on with their lives. "It got away from some children, and we got a bit tangled in the string. It was nothing."

"They were imprisoned by the string," Marmaduke corrected. "Bound together into a six-legged monster."

Clara closed her eyes. A monster? Truly?

"The kite whipped about them, intent on ravaging their coiffures in a fit of jealousy of the fabric of their skirts—"

"What?" Clara's eyes popped open as she turned to look at her brother.

"—but just before the angry kite could devastate its final target, our hero, Mr. Lockhart, swooped in to restrain the beast and save the day."

"You really did miss your calling," Clara muttered. "Do you intend to take to the stage when you can no longer swing a cricket bat?"

"Don't even speak such a thing. I shall always be able to swing a cricket bat."

Ambrose extended both his hands, palm out, toward his cousins. "May we return to this beast of a kite?"

"Ah, yes, where was I?" Marmaduke stood and turned to lean one hip on the sofa so his arms were free to gesture about as he told his story. "There they were, held captive by the kite's dastardly string, slowly being choked to death by its tightening hold."

A muffled snicker came from the direction of the fireplace, but when Clara glanced that way, Mr. Lockhart appeared to be going solemnly about his business while paying no heed to the room's dramatics.

"Mr. Lockhart snatched the kite from the air mere inches from your mother's face—one handed, mind you, since he was still carrying the clock."

Clara had to admit that part, at least, might be true.

"Had he been but a moment later, our family would have been the first scandal of the season, forced to retreat to the country until the gossip had receded. The tale would have been in all the papers, and my dear sister would be forced into a life of spinsterhood because no one would want to marry a woman who'd been disfigured by such an attack."

Clara had the sudden urge to find every child in London and ask them to fling their kites toward her face.

"Fortunately, Mr. Lockhart was there, to rescue our sister, who clung to him as he dragged her to safety—"

"I beg your pardon." Clara jerked from the chair to poke a finger toward her brother. "There was no clinging."

There was also no mistaking the quiet laughter now coming from the man near the mantel.

Marmaduke lifted his hand, index finger and thumb bent to form a curve with a slight gap in between them. "There was a little clinging."

He sighed and sent Ambrose an exaggerated look of sympathy. "I can't blame her, though. She'd just come through a life-threatening experience. I'd cling to a handsome gentleman as well."

"I did not cling." She crossed her arms and faced Ambrose.

Ambrose grinned. "So you agree the gentleman is handsome."

She would not dignify that with an answer. Nor was she going to admit her cheeks were heating.

"Yes, there was a kite and, yes, Mother, Aunt Elizabeth, and I were trapped in the tangled sting. Mr. Lockhart came to our aid but we would have managed without him."

"Hmmm." Ambrose scratched his chin as he looked from Clara to Marmaduke. "Who should I believe?"

"Honestly, Ambrose, you can be as vexing as he is." Clara turned to her brother. "And what possible scandal could have occurred?"

"The kite could have knocked you off your feet and cast your skirts up in front of half of London."

"Not if the string was tying our skirts down." Clara stuck her nose in the air. "If you're going to make up stories, at least keep all your pieces straight."

"What we need here," Marmaduke said with a sly grin, "is an impartial third party."

So help her, if he'd taken account of everyone who'd been on the green so he could discuss this little incident with them, she'd break his cricket bat over his head.

But, no, Marmaduke had no need to scour London. He merely turned his attention to the fireplace.

"What say you, Mr. Lockhart?"

FOUR

Hugh paused in the act of winding the newly placed clock. If the viscount and Mr. Woodbury thought Hugh was going to say anything about the incident, they were touched in the head. Whether or not the lady wanted to be termed one, he was going to treat her as such.

He finished winding the clock, set the pendulum swinging, then closed the casing with a satisfying clink. Giving the clock a nod, he turned to face the room's occupants. "I say your clock appears to be working perfectly, but let us know if you notice an issue with its calibration."

Silence greeted his statement, broken only by the light ticking of the newly repaired gears. Moments later, the small bell rang in the half hour. As the chime faded, Hugh fought to keep his expression stoic and his gaze off Miss Woodbury.

If he offered them nothing but blandness, they would hopefully drop the subject. Like the moment in the square, this was not the sort of interaction that was going to gain him anything.

A crooked grin slowly spread across the viscount's face. "Glad to hear it." His eyebrows rose. "Now. If you please, whose version of the kite attack story corroborates with your own telling?"

Hugh's gaze cut to Miss Woodbury before he could stop the instinct. She was twisted in her seat, peering at him over the back of the couch. What was his best path forward here?

The young woman groaned. "Why couldn't Aunt Elizabeth have had a daughter? Then I wouldn't have to spend so much time with the two of you."

"Come now, darling cousin. If I'd had a little sister, there'd simply have been two of you toddling along after us boys. And if I'd been born a girl, well, this entire house would now belong to my far more beastly cousin, George."

Miss Woodbury looked rather like she wanted to have the whole lot sent to this beastly George now but would settle for bashing her cousin in the head with a cushion.

Hugh rather wished she would. The distraction would allow them all to forget his presence, or at least that they'd asked him a question.

She didn't lob a cushion at the man, though, and soon three pairs of questioning eyes were turned back onto Hugh.

"Frankly," he said slowly, measuring his words so as to appease his influential audience, "I believe the truth lies somewhere in the middle."

There. That should be diplomatic enough.

Lord Eversly's grin widened into a full-blown smile as he considered Miss Woodbury. "So there was a little bit of screaming."

"Must we continue this discussion of kites? I grow weary of it." She sighed and shifted to sit straight in her seat once more, giving Hugh her back.

He should probably feel slighted by the move, but his lungs were too thankful for the return of easy breathing to care.

Lord Eversly dropped onto the seat beside his cousin. "We can discuss Mr. Lockhart instead. How long was this clinging? Do I need to call him out? Kites at dawn, perhaps?"

Hugh tried not to laugh, truly he did. But with most of the attention no longer directed his way, his guard had relaxed too much, and a light snicker escaped. He got it under control quickly, but probably not fast enough to escape the notice of this particular group.

"Oh, bother," Miss Woodbury said with a sigh. "Please come join us, Mr. Lockhart. If you're going to be a part of this conversation, we can't have you lurking about."

Hugh opened his mouth to defend himself, but snapped it shut again as he moved to round the settee and stepped into view. These people apparently had no concept of letting a professional man go about his work in peace. "I meant no disrespect, milad—er, I mean, miss."

Pink slashed across Miss Woodbury's cheekbones and slowly deepened until the splotches were nearly red.

The other two men watched her with varying degrees of amusement. Hugh wanted to come to her defense because she did seem terribly outnumbered, but he could hardly reprimand a viscount, and even if Mr. Woodbury was a mere gentleman and not the heir-presumptive to a dukedom, he still outranked Hugh.

"You corrected him, didn't you?" Mr. Woodbury asked.

Lord Eversly chuckled. "I thought Mother had convinced you to accept the respect while in London."

Miss Woodbury opened her mouth, closed it, opened it once more, then seemed to melt into a flop against the back of the settee.

Suddenly, Mr. Woodbury jerked to a standing position, one finger jabbing mightily toward the ceiling. "I'm the commander!" His hand turned until the finger was pointing toward Miss Woodbury. "And I have a question."

"We have company," she replied in a desperate-sounding rush.

"I have it on good authority that this man is no one."

Lord Eversly frowned at Hugh. "You called yourself no one?"

"Actually, Lady Eversly referred to me as no one, if we want to put a fine point on it." Why, oh, why had he corrected the aristocrat?

The maybe-someday-might-be aristocrat grinned. "And he had a right fine sense of humor about it." He looked at his sister. "Now. Question. Can you honestly tell us you weren't just the tiniest bit frightened by the kite attack today?"

Hugh couldn't stand by anymore. This exchange had already passed propriety, so what did it matter if he kept going? He didn't have a sister, but he had a cousin of a similar age that he was close to, and he knew well the teasing such relationships endured. He could not consider himself a gentleman if he didn't at least attempt to come to Miss Woodbury's aid. Lady or not, she wasn't *his* sister or cousin and participating in this farce, even as a spectator, felt wrong.

"I believe," he said with his heart pounding mightily in his chest, "that anyone would be at least momentarily afraid until they knew precisely what it was that was wrapping about them." He pressed a hand to his chest. "I know I would be."

Mr. Woodbury frowned at Lord Eversly. "Do we have rules about allowing someone else to answer a question for you?"

Lord Eversly shrugged, but his grin was wide. "I think it's grounds for issuing a command."

Miss Woodbury sputtered. "That's not fair! I didn't ask him to answer for me."

"So you were afraid?" Mr. Woodbury pressed.

"As he said, it was a startling experience and as my vision was limited by Mother and Aunt Elizabeth, it was some time before I could ascertain that it was a kite."

Mr. Woodbury tapped his chin thoughtfully. "I'm still issuing a command."

"Of course you are." Miss Woodbury deflated with a sigh.

Hugh took an involuntary step toward the group. "I beg your pardon, but are you playing Questions and Commands?" He'd heard of the game, of course, had even played it a few times as a child, but he'd always considered it something more for the schoolroom than the drawing room, unless of course the party intended to court a scandal or two.

"Yes," Miss Woodbury said as she glared at her brother. "The game has been going on for years. We rotate the role of commander each month, and I haven't been forced to perform a command in over two years."

Lord Eversly shrugged. "'Twas an accomplishment that had to fall sometime." He reached out a finger and tweaked her nose. "Living such an open book life means you need a little excitement, anyway."

"Perhaps London will remove my inhibitions. It certainly has done so for—"

"As the commander," Mr. Woodbury announced, drowning out the end of his sister's sentence, "I declare that you, my dear sister, have to fly a kite." The man looked immensely proud of himself.

Lord Eversly laughed. "That's brilliant."

"Need I remind you two that we are in London? And quite near to Mayfair? Even a child flying a kite, like one was today, is an anomaly in this part of town. We are no longer children frolicking carefree about the countryside."

Lord Eversly shuddered. "You sound like my mother."

Hugh had already become too familiar with this family and absolutely should have kept his mouth shut so as not to embroil himself any deeper into their squabble.

Despite this resolve, it was his own voice that filled the room as a response. "You could go a little ways north or east."

"North, I understand, though the sheep herders might have something to say." Lord Eversly frowned. "But why east? That's further into London."

Hugh swallowed. In for a penny . . . "At this time of day, most of the residents won't be home if you can get into a place such as Bloomsbury Square. The residents are primarily professionals. There's also Lincoln's Inn fields."

Hugh all but held his breath. It didn't matter how friendly an aristocratic family seemed to be. They would still consider themselves too far above Hugh's station to allow him to truly participate in a private conversation, particularly one as personal as this seemed to be. He should make his professional goodbyes and get out of here.

Yet he didn't. He stayed, watching as Miss Woodbury glared at the two grinning men.

"Perfect!" Mr. Woodbury clapped his hands together and rubbed them with glee. "Have we time to go now? Ambrose, call for your carriage."

Hugh winced in sympathy as Miss Woodbury rose to her feet with a beleaguered sigh. Obviously, she knew when to fight with her brother and when to give in.

Hat dangling from one hand, Hugh stepped closer to her. "Please accept my apologies, Miss Woodbury. I wasn't thinking when I offered the suggestion. I'm certain it would still be inappropriate, as there is no guaranteeing access or privacy."

She shook her head, mouth pressed into a thin, resigned line. "Do not trouble yourself. They are too stubborn to let this go now and will have me on the green outside if we do not let them try elsewhere. Normally, they bandy their ludicrous commands at each other, but I suppose they couldn't resist the novelty of tossing one my way."

"Ah." Hugh shifted his weight from foot to foot. This was uncharted waters for him. "Might I be of assistance in another way, then?"

"This is hardly your doing." She frowned up at him. "Marmaduke's retelling would only have been worse if you'd not been in the room. He probably would have attempted to reenact the entire thing. The man truly should have considered the stage instead of the pitch."

"I . . . see." Hugh glanced over at the men. The Duke reference from earlier must have been a familial shortening of the name Marmaduke. It was a nickname that could cause a great deal of confusion, but a family playing Questions and Commands for years on end was hardly conventional. He'd remember this day for a long time. "I should take my leave."

He moved toward the door but stopped when Miss Woodbury stepped up beside him. "Thank you, by the way."

All resentment seemed to have melted away, and she wore a soft smile that brought a spark of beauty to the simplicity of her current appearance.

The imbalance Hugh suddenly felt had to be evident on his face as he asked, "What for?"

"Why, saving me from that dreadful kite, of course."

Of course. She'd hardly be thanking him for his part in forcing her to fly a kite in the middle of London. The events of a mere hour ago felt days old, though.

"It was my honor." He executed his most courtly bow. He may not spend a lot of time in ballrooms, but he knew how to respect those that paid his bills. The urge to gently lift her hand and kiss the air over her knuckles nearly sent him tumbling headfirst to the carpet, and he swung himself upright so fast that spots momentarily danced in his vision.

What was wrong with him? This wasn't a dance at an assembly room, and he hadn't been invited over for tea. The strange behavior of the viscount and his cousin must have addled Hugh's mind.

He strode for the door, intent on removing himself from the situation.

"Where are you going?" Mr. Woodbury asked as Hugh reached the exit of the room.

Helplessly, Hugh gestured toward the space beyond the open door. "Ah, I was—"

"You should come with us." The viscount was talking to Hugh, but he was grinning at Miss Woodbury.

Mr. Woodbury slung a companionable arm across Hugh's shoulders. "When was the last time you flew a kite?"

"I . . . don't rightly know."

Hugh had moved from uncharted territory to a place that wasn't even marked with a *Here there be dragons* on the map. What was happening?

"Yes, you should join us," Miss Woodbury added, her voice dry enough that Hugh couldn't tell if she meant the sentiment or not.

Mr. Woodbury leaned in to speak in a low voice. "It's been years since she flew a kite. She might need saving again."

"And you two would simply let it take me to the ground?" Miss Woodbury shook her head. "How chivalrous."

"You can show us the way," Lord Eversly added. "Don't know that I've ever been to that part of London."

Hugh stared at the viscount, attempting to assess the true intentions behind his seeming friendliness. Was Hugh meant to treat him as if they were equals? He tested the waters by saying, "Isn't that the job of your coachman?"

Lord Eversly grinned. "I'm rather adept at pretending otherwise when it suits me."

Ten minutes later, after witnessing more teasing banter than he'd been privy to since his own childhood, Hugh found himself tucked into a black carriage next to Lord Eversly as they rolled through London. Miss Woodbury sat directly across from him, her expression fluctuating between emotions so frequently that he couldn't begin to guess what she was feeling.

Annoyed? Interested? Excited? Maybe a little of all three? They were going off to fly a kite in the middle of London, after all. That was hardly a daily occurrence.

At least, not in his world.

He'd not have expected it to be part of her world either. She seemed a little too straitlaced for such frivolity. Despite her seemingly serious demeanor, though, she'd been playing an ongoing game of Questions and Commands with her brother. What did that mean?

He shook his head. All it meant was that she was a human with all the complicated nuances that came along with being such.

The deep cushions and well-maintained springs of the viscount's carriage cushioned him from all the normal bumps and jostles of London's roads. The shades that were partially lowered didn't possess a tear that sent sunlight spearing directly into a passenger's eyes. Never had he realized a carriage could provide such a comfortable journey.

When had he last ridden in a private carriage? Had he ever done so? A hired hack, yes, and an occasional post-chaise, but he couldn't recall a single privately owned carriage.

His three companions spoke comfortably as they rolled down the road, though the men were more jovial than Miss Woodbury. Whatever myriad of emotions she'd been feeling earlier, she seemed nothing but perturbed when they came to a stop.

London was calmer and quieter out here, away from the bustling social maneuvering of Mayfair and the shopping districts. In the evening, the residential square beyond the carriage window would fill with gentlemen, solicitors, and the wealthier tradesmen, all returning home from their daily labors. Now it was nearly empty, with only a handful of people from the nearby residences going about their business.

It was hardly dismal or disheveled, but that scattering of people on the street still craned their necks at the sight of a fine, private carriage, particularly one bearing an aristocratic coat of arms.

Miss Woodbury slid down into the seat and away from the window. "Why didn't we bring your unmarked carriage?"

Lord Eversly gave her a blank-faced look. "Because my only unmarked conveyance is a two-man curricle?"

"Our cousin likes to feel important." Mr. Woodbury bumped his shoulder against hers. "You know that."

Lord Eversly rolled his eyes. "That importance is what is going to get us into this square."

"So you intend to impress a gentleman, not charm a lady?"

"Why would I do that?" Lord Eversly grinned and swung the carriage door open before jumping out to land lightly on his feet. He tossed a mischievous look over his shoulder to his carriage companions. "Charm is ever so much more fun."

As Miss Woodbury was still huffing in offense—though Hugh wasn't certain how genuine it was—Lord Eversly went to chat with a couple of women near the locked square gate.

Mr. Woodbury also exited the carriage and set about extracting a kite from beneath the vehicle's seat.

That left Hugh to climb out and offer the unattended Miss Woodbury assistance in exiting the vehicle. While he was somewhat offended on her behalf to be slighted by the two higher-ranking gentlemen, she didn't seem at all surprised by the way events were playing out.

Instead, her focus seemed to be on the area around them. "It's quiet here. Who lives in these buildings?"

Hugh stood beside her, looking around at the simple but elegant homes and the clean but quiet streets. "Solicitors. Architects. A few second and third sons making their livelihoods in business. Not anyone you're likely to encounter during a Season."

He couldn't read her features well enough to know her thoughts on the matter. She might be disdainful of the lower surroundings, curious about people who had to actually work for a living, or bored because the adventure had worn thin and now she wanted to go home.

Or maybe her face just looked like that.

"A penny for your thoughts."

She blinked and jerked as if she'd completely forgotten he was there.

"Apologies," Hugh said with a nod. "I didn't mean to startle you." He took a half step away from her. He needed to remember his place in this little group, which was convenient interloper. He was not a part of their friendship, nor a player in their outing. He was simply the man who knew where a woman of gentle breeding could fly a kite and not ruin her reputation.

In this area of town, anyone who saw them was far more likely to shake their head and mutter about aristocrats than seek out the writer of the local gossip rag. Especially for someone as socially insignificant as the cousin of a viscount.

"Come along then! Let's fly a kite." Lord Eversly stood at the entrance to the square, holding open the gate as the two ladies walked on, occasionally glancing back over their shoulder at him and giggling.

Mr. Woodbury shook his head and walked into the square, but Miss Woodbury stopped in front of the viscount. "What did you say?"

Lord Eversly frowned. "I said you wanted to fly a kite."

Her eyes narrowed. "That's it?"

He used a hand to turn her toward the square and ushered her inside. Hugh followed behind, easing the gate nearly closed behind him, but not shutting it since they didn't have a key to let them out when they were finished.

"Do you think I'm walking around promising to marry women in return for small favors and then breaking their hearts when it's over?"

"I hadn't thought that, but now I am. However did you come up with such an idea?"

He sighed. "Your father. He's almost as disapproving of me as you are." Lord Eversly put his hands on Miss Woodbury's shoulder and pushed her into the square. "Now go fly a kite."

She walked to the middle of the grass and took the fabric and sticks from her brother. "I shall remind you lot one more time that we are no longer children. We would do better to find more elevated conversation and activities to occupy our time."

"Have you intentions of being a governess one day? Because that was a perfect imitation of one." Lord Eversly took the kite from her hands and handed her the string instead. "Off you go now. A command is a command."

Hugh leaned his shoulder against one of the trees scattered about in a corner grouping and watched as the little family cluster walked to the center of the green space.

For several long minutes, they looked from the kite to the air and then about the square as they spoke in hushed tones. Were they coming to their senses? That was something of a shame, as this had been certain to be one of the most entertaining spectacles Hugh had seen in a while.

Finally, Lord Eversly turned to Hugh. "I say, Mr. Lockhart. Have you any remembrance of how to actually fly one of these?"

FIVE

I t was difficult to say which was worse—determining to fly a kite in the middle of London or realizing that she couldn't remember how to do it. Actually, the worst part was probably that this entire episode was being witnessed by a complete stranger. A stranger who had already seen Clara at enough of a disadvantage for one lifetime, not to mention a single day.

"Why are you involving him? If you don't know how to do it, I shouldn't have to continue." Clara crossed her arms over her chest and restrained the urge to stamp her foot.

She'd just declared herself not a child. She needed to act accordingly.

"Dear cousin," Ambrose said with a grin, "there are many things you do that I am incapable of."

"Name one."

He blinked at her for a moment, his face a picture of bland arrogance.

Marmaduke laughed. "It would be easier to list the things you do that Clara is capable of not doing."

"Aha!" Ambrose pointed at his male cousin before turning his grin back to Clara. "I've got one. I am incapable of pleasing your father while you do it masterfully."

Clara lifted her gaze to the clouds riding the wind through the sky and pleaded for God to grant her patience. "As Duke said, that is more a matter of not doing than doing. If you wished to please my father, simply stop philandering about."

It was a common argument, one Clara knew was about far more than her cousin's tendency to socialize with women of easy virtue and frequent the gaming tables at his club. Still, she couldn't help but advocate for less vice in his life. If he weren't constantly embroiled in inappropriate actions, he might be in a better state of mind to hear more important truths.

"Maybe I'll consider it," Ambrose said with a crooked grin, "if you successfully fly this kite."

This too, had become an all too familiar exchange. Ambrose would promise to consider listening to her about the benefits of a more moral lifestyle in return for her acquiescence on some matter or another.

She would give in. He would conveniently forget, or, in his words, consider the option and come to the conclusion of no. Once she'd even commanded him to spend a week away from his usual entertainments. She'd neglected to put enough parameters around which week it would be, and he'd used a week spent in bed with a raging head cold as his fulfillment.

If she were to simply toss the kite into a tree, she could declare this entire matter complete, but she wasn't willing to stoop to that level of trickery. Clara frowned at the kite. Actually, perhaps she was.

Marmaduke cleared his throat. "Come along, then. I'll help you sew clothes to take to the workhouse tonight if you fly the kite now."

Clara's eyes widened as she looked to her brother. The man was actually a very good stitch. "Truly?"

He narrowed his gaze. "You have such strange ideas of fun. But yes, I truly will." He shoved the spool of kite string into her hand. "Get to it."

She considered the kite for a moment and then tossed it into the air. They all three watched it plummet straight to the ground.

A low chuckle sounded to her left. She'd forgotten Mr. Lockhart was there. Well, almost forgotten. Tried to forget might be the best wording.

He had moved closer at Ambrose's beckoning, and now he leaned against a tree, watching them and trying to smother his laughter at her attempt.

"I suppose you can do better, then?" She stuck her nose in the air, trying to emulate her aunt's haughty nature instead of cowering in embarrassment as she wished to do.

He cast a look at the two men before striding over to her and picking up the kite. After giving it a considering look, he turned his gaze to her. "Run."

She blinked at him. "Run?"

With a nod toward the grassy expanse behind her, he said, "Yes. Run."

What did more humiliation matter at this point? As he'd pointed out, any witnesses weren't likely to be people she'd encounter at the gatherings her aunt was taking her to. There would be no one to tell this tale but her brother, her cousin, and a tradesman she would never see again.

She started to run.

Mr. Lockhart jogged behind her for a few steps before giving the kite a toss. It wobbled in the wind, tugging at the string in Clara's hand before catching a breeze and floating up above the trees.

A light hand on her elbow pulled her to a stop. He gestured toward the sky. "Your kite, miss."

Clara couldn't help the smile that stretched across her face as she watched the brightly colored fabric dance in the sky.

"I daresay that's a right proper revenge," Marmaduke said as he came to her side and admired the kite.

She tugged at the string once more, trying to steer the kite away from a tall tree, but instead of veering, the kite dipped. The tree blocked the breeze the toy had been riding, and the kite came plummeting down.

Directly toward Clara.

Mr. Lockhart jumped in front of her and snagged the edge of the kite before it could collide with her nose.

Ambrose bent over, bracing his hands on his knees as he let out a laugh that echoed off the buildings to fill every corner of the square. "You know, Clara, I'm starting to think kites really do have something against you."

"Twice in one day, Lockhart." Marmaduke chuckled as well. "I think that makes you a hero of some sort."

The glimmer of happiness vanished as Clara tossed the spool at her brother. "What are you then? I do believe you witnessed both attacks and did nothing to stop either."

Ambrose laughed louder. It would serve him right if he fell over and got grass stains on his breeches and had to suffer the displeasure of his valet.

"I flew the kite. Now I suspect both of you will drop your end of the bargain and behave as a proper gentleman."

Ambrose's laugh faded to an unrepentant grin. "It was a command, after all. Nothing further should be required."

Why did the man have to be so frustratingly correct all the time? It made it difficult to help him in spite of himself. "I need to return home. Mother is likely searching for me so we can prepare for tonight's party."

She moved purposefully toward the gate, a trail of men in her wake.

Ambrose jumped in front of her to swing the portal open. "Where are you off to tonight?"

She waved a hand in the air. "I haven't the slightest idea. A musicale maybe? She said the balls start next week, and we'll begin our hunt in earnest."

Her stomach turned at the idea. Practically speaking, she knew she needed to marry. Her father's living and pension couldn't support her forever. Still, she'd rather not upend her entire life's work and meaning simply to keep a roof over her head.

"Come now, you'll enjoy a ball or two." Marmaduke gave her hand a conciliatory pat before guiding her up into the waiting carriage.

"Yes, I would, but Mother would have me go to twenty or thirty of them. Whatever it takes to find me a suitable husband."

"What signifies a suitable husband?"

Everyone froze in the act of settling back into their seats to look at Mr. Lockhart. The man himself appeared stunned to have heard his own words.

The pause was but for a moment, and soon Ambrose was knocking on the roof to indicate they were ready to proceed.

"Noble," Clara muttered.

Marmaduke winced. "He doesn't have to be noble, just . . ."

Clara glared at him until he sighed in defeat. Their mother and aunt could say what they wanted, but everyone in the family knew they intended to find her a man of higher birth. She was, after all, the granddaughter of a baron.

"She just wants you to marry well so you're taken care of," Marmaduke said, trying once more to convince Clara that this entire London business wasn't a horrific tragedy. "The easiest way to do that is to utilize the connections you have to reach a slightly higher level of society."

Ambrose shrugged. "If it helps, you can consider it a favor to my mother. She's delighted about the entire business." He grinned. "Her only regret in life is not having a daughter to dress up and parade about London."

"And now she has you," Marmaduke added with a matching grin.

"I live to please," Clara said in a flat voice as she glared from one man to the other.

Across from her, Mr. Lockhart watched with a considering eye. "What would you choose?"

The air in Clara's lungs thickened. No one had ever asked her that, so she'd never voiced it aloud. Oh, she'd come close, but never really said the words.

Marmaduke snorted. "Her choice would be to not marry at all."

Clara jerked her head around, staring at her brother with wide eyes. That wasn't true. Not entirely. She wasn't against the idea of marriage. She just wanted . . . more.

"Truly?" Mr. Lockhart asked, surprise evident in his voice and features.

"Yes." She sighed. "Well, no, but also yes." Her fingers gripped her skirt and then smoothed it back flat. "It's not that I don't want to marry, it's that I hate that I *have* to marry." She glared at her brother. "Marmaduke gets to go on about his business, hoping that one day he'll simply stumble into a relationship. And all he does is bat a ball about."

"Your respect of my career is overwhelming." Marmaduke smiled at her, but there was a tightness around his eyes that made her wish she could take the words back.

"The point is," she said, pressing on since she couldn't go backward, "I am not allowed to go about my service to the church and hope to one day find someone. No, I have to put aside my charity work and be frivolous for a few months and hope that somehow that will find me a man who shares my priorities." She smoothed her skirts and muttered, "'Tis frustrating."

"There's no reason to give up your charitable works." Ambrose shook his head. "Mother would be happy to have you join her society. There's no need to make yourself a martyr to good connections."

Clara glared at her cousin. Did he really equate the work she did with her father every day to his aunt's weekly gathering of . . . of . . . well, Clara wasn't entirely certain what they did, because she was to be attending her first meeting of the Virtuous Ladies Society for the Care of Wounded Soldiers this week, but she didn't think they'd be spending their time delivering food baskets to the poor.

Mr. Lockhart continued to quietly consider her. He even opened his mouth once before closing it, shaking his head, and giving his attention to London passing by outside the window.

She was grateful for his silence. He'd interrupted her life enough today.

As soon as they returned to Eversly House, Clara left the men to their own interests and retreated to her room. She wanted to blame the unsettledness in her chest on a belated reaction to the day's close calls, but the stirring felt more like an itch to do something.

If only she knew what that something was.

Ever since her mother had declared she would have a Season in London, Clara's life had not been her own. She'd blindly gone along with the suggestions of her mother and aunt because Clara didn't know the first thing about participating in high society—or any society really—for the purpose of finding a husband and not to enjoy the company of friends.

Her mother was walking down the corridor when Clara crested the top of the stairs.

"Good gracious," she said, pressing a hand to her chest. "What happened to your hair?"

Clara lifted a hand to discover that even her practical bun had been no match for the conditions outside. "You of all people know how windy it is today."

She entered her room and set her bonnet on the end of the bed before sitting at her dressing table to release the rest of the bun and brush out her hair. The maid would have needed to start over for tonight's coiffure anyway.

"I didn't know you were venturing out again." Mother perched on the edge of a chair and twisted her hands together. "Did you take a maid?"

"No. I took my brother and my cousin." Mr. Lockhart's presence didn't signify so Clara kept it to herself. Mother was nervous about every little encounter of late, and there was no reason to risk sending her into conniptions over a tradesman.

"I suppose that's proper enough." Mother sighed as her shoulders slumped forward. "I do wish you'd take this Season more seriously though."

How much more seriously could Clara take it? She hadn't complained about the schedule—at least, not much. She'd been cooperative at the modiste, well, except for the number of ball gowns because some things were simply too extravagant. She'd even agreed to having a dedicated lady's maid for the Season, though that was more out of practicality than anything else.

If Clara had to care for four outfits a day and twist her own hair into these different styles, she'd never leave the room.

Clara placed the brush on the table and folded her hands in her lap before facing her mother. "What is it you would have wished me to do this afternoon?"

"What other young ladies do. Embroider, sew, read, practice the pianoforte." Mother flitted a hand about. "Not gallivant across the City, traipsing along behind your brother like you did in the country."

Clara refrained from rubbing at her suddenly pounding temples. "You would have me dedicate my time to solitary indoor pursuits when the entire purpose of our being in London is to meet people?"

"Not just any people. Particular people."

Clara frowned. "Father would have you kneeling for confession if he heard you."

Mother frowned right back. "That's not what I meant, and you know it."

Did she? A month ago, Clara would have said yes, she knew her mother had meant nothing derogatory toward a person of any rank, but now, since seeing her in London, Clara wasn't so certain. Of course, Mother was concerned about Clara living a comfortable life, but why did that mean parading about in ballrooms and drawing rooms and allowing her aunt to spend a small fortune on an entire wardrobe?

Mother sighed. "You're young and ideal, but you don't know as much about living as you think you do."

"I'm twenty-two, Mother. Hardly fresh from the schoolroom."

Mother's lips pressed into a thin line. "If you are so worldly and wise, then you know you must marry or take on a profession. As your care and comfort are far more dependable if you marry well, I highly suggest you take advantage of this opportunity your aunt has provided."

Mother had fallen in love with Father while attending a country fair and had willingly married down and adjusted to a less lavish lifestyle than she'd been born to. Did she regret it? Was that why she was so determined to give Clara the opportunity she'd foregone?

Her statements were also far too similar to the ones she'd heard in the carriage this afternoon. Did no one see her point? "I intend to marry, Mother. We both know I'd be a dreadful governess."

Mother stood with a sigh and shook out her skirts before walking toward the door. Before leaving, she turned to give Clara a considering look. "It would be different if you were in love," she said softly. "A true love match is the most precious and rare commodity a woman can find on earth. But if one must marry for practicality, there is no reason to make it a more difficult union than it has to be. God has given you the connections to allow you to marry well. Don't waste them."

On that quiet judgment, she left the room, leaving Clara to clean up more than just her mussed hair.

Clara returned to brushing out her hair, her mother's last statements repeating through her mind. Mr. Lockhart's words from the carriage worked their way into her mind as well. What did she want?

There had never been a question of Clara's getting married. It was what gently born women did. And while Clara might not want to be lumped in with the ranks of nobility, she had to admit she hadn't lived a hardscrabble life either.

Marriage had always been a step to take in the future, though. She didn't spend time imagining what it would be like or dreaming of her future husband. It had simply been an expectation, like learning her maths or dispensing alms to the poor.

Despite growing up in the shadow of a love match, Clara had never considered if that was what she wanted for herself. She'd just sort of assumed a husband would appear one day. That was a ridiculously unpractical notion, and Clara hated being impractical.

She abandoned the hairbrush and crossed to the writing desk for a pen and paper. It was time she attacked this like she did everything else in life and created a plan. The *how* was well in hand, considering the social schedule Mother and Aunt Elizabeth were crafting.

All that remained was for Clara to determine the *who*. The sooner she lined up a suitable husband, the sooner she could return to her life and focus on things that truly mattered to her.

What did she want?

She wanted a husband that would appease everyone—including herself. What qualifications were required of such a man? After some consideration, she put pen to paper and started her list.

1. Ready to marry. Preferably actively in search of a wife.

Convincing a man to marry her would be far easier if he was already looking to marry in the first place. Someone like Ambrose, who was determined to put off settling down for as long as possible, would only extend her time in London.

2. Of good family

Clara frowned for a moment and then scratched it out.

2. Of titled family

That was honestly what her mother wanted, or they wouldn't be in London. Mother's father had been a baron and while Mother never seemed too concerned with the idea that she'd married "down" by society's standards, that past played in to what she would accept for her only daughter.

3. Interested in charity and the church

She nibbled on the end of her pen for a moment before writing again.

Clergyman?

Being a vicar's wife would suit her well. She'd adored working alongside her father, after all.

She sat the pen on the desk and frowned at her list. Three things. It should be simple, yet she had her reservations. Could such a man be found while cavorting at parties or musicales or whatever other invitations Mother had procured?

She hadn't the slightest idea, but she knew someone who did. Whipping her hair back into something that slightly resembled a bun, Clara grabbed her list and headed once more for the stairs.

SIX

S even minutes later, Clara was grumbling to herself about wasted space and the benefits of her family's simple, twelve-room vicarage when she finally located Ambrose and Marmaduke in the billiard room.

"I require your assistance." Her announcement sounded almost panicked to her ears, but she attributed that to being slightly out of breath from running all over the house, grumbling.

Neither man seemed particularly concerned, though, as they finished watching a red ball bounce around the bumpers before giving her their attention.

Marmaduke arched an eyebrow while Ambrose hid a smirk behind his hand. "Oh?" Marmaduke drawled. "Whatever for? We've already forced you to enjoy life a little." He raised his eyebrows. "Nice hair, by the way."

She lifted a hand to find her hastily twisted bun had fallen halfway out. No matter. The maid would redo everything anyway.

Clara lifted her chin. "I require your assistance in selecting a suitable husband."

Ambrose lost the battle and let out a bark of laughter.

"Do try to take me seriously," Clara said with an exasperated sigh. "This is a very important matter."

"I'm certain it is." Ambrose lined up the balls for a new game. "But I have a certain reputation and Duke, here, all but shuns good society as a whole, so I fail to see how we can help you trap the hapless fellow you've targeted."

"I haven't a target at all." Clara deflated and sagged against the side of the doorway. "That is the problem."

Ambrose sighed. "Very well, then. How high are we reaching? Riverton, perhaps? He's young, known to be more than a little stodgy, and loves his family." He frowned. "No. Wait. He got married last year."

"Can you honestly picture her as a duchess?" Marmaduke leaned over the table and sent balls scattering across the green baize with a crack of his cue.

"I still picture her as a lass in braids tagging along as we climb trees, so imagining her married is a bit beyond me."

"How very encouraging," Clara mumbled.

Ambrose had the decency to look somewhat abashed, even as he gave a nonchalant shrug. "Apologies, cousin, but it's true. Still, I'll help as best I can. What do you need?"

"Whether the two of you want to admit it or not, Mother would prefer the man I marry be at least connected to a title." She pulled out her list, short though it was, and reread it to maintain her focus. "All I require is a man with enough means to keep me comfortable, so my parents need not worry, and enough faith that we agree upon life's important works."

"The means should be easy enough." Marmaduke grimaced. "Faith, however, isn't a quality as easily measured or discussed."

"Nonsense." Ambrose smiled as if his horse had just won a race. He pointed his cue at Clara. "You need a younger son."

Marmaduke leaned on his cue, a thoughtful frown on his face. Then he nodded slowly. "That might do it. One bound for the church?"

"Precisely." Ambrose pointed at Marmaduke as if congratulating him on coming up with the idea in the first place.

Clara pulled her lip between her teeth as she considered the notion. She had considered a man of the cloth herself, but she had forgotten the fact that many of those positions were filled by younger sons of the aristocracy. It was where many third and fourth sons found their purpose, since the freedom gained by access to means with no inherited responsibilities left them free to pursue higher personal callings.

It was the perfect solution.

Ambrose was too far away as he stood on the opposite side of the billiard table, but Marmaduke was within reach and Clara threw her arms around him as she smiled broadly. "You're both brilliant!"

"Would you tell my mother that?" Ambrose asked, as he lined up a new shot.

Clara waved him off as she ran from the room and to the nearby library. Moments later, she was back in the billiard room with a thick, leather-bound tome in hand. She plopped the book onto the table, sending balls rolling and bouncing against bumpers.

"That doesn't count," Marmaduke said.

"Yes, it does." Ambrose grinned. "The interference came from neither of us. I win."

Clara ignored them both as she flipped through pages. Lineage after lineage stared up at her. There were plenty of younger sons and first cousins, but how could she know which ones were intent on acquiring a living and which were buying a commission in the army?

Or, even worse, going into some form of business.

"What are you doing?" Marmaduke finally asked.

"Isn't it obvious? She's flipping through Debrett's *Peerage* like my mother peruses the latest furniture catalog." Ambrose racked his cue, then leaned against the table to nudge Clara's shoulder. "You can't choose a husband from a book."

"Why not?" Clara flipped another page.

Ambrose looked to Marmaduke, but the other man simply shrugged. The viscount sighed. "He might be stingy or dumb as a post."

"Or incapable of riding a horse," Marmaduke added.

Both Clara and Ambrose frowned at him until he crossed his arms and frowned back. "You have to admit, it would be a strange thing."

Clara shook her head. Ambrose placed a hand over the book page. "He could be a stick in the mud. Or bracket-faced."

Unable to flip more pages with Ambrose's hand in the way, Clara straightened and looked from one man to the other. "I care not for his outer appearance, as it is the life we will build together that matters."

Ambrose let out a disbelieving snort. "You'll want to fancy the man at least a little."

Clara attempted to pull off a haughty look, but it was difficult when her eyes didn't even top her cousin's shoulder. "I will fancy a virtuous heart."

"If you say so." His tone implied he didn't buy it for a moment. "I've yet to find a heart so virtuous that—"

"Do take care," Marmaduke cut in, though it was unclear if his warning was for Clara or Ambrose. He cleared his throat and looked at his sister, placing a heavy hand on her shoulder. "Clara, do not let haste cloud your judgment."

He meant the words and gesture as a comfort, Clara knew, but it felt like he was holding her back instead of helping her move forward.

"You should feel something for your husband," Ambrose said. "Respect, at the very least. Some form of affection would be better. You aren't destitute."

Clara swallowed. "We can't afford another season, and Mother's worry for my future may soon start causing her health to decline."

Marmaduke choked on a laugh. "Her constitution is better than that, I should think."

"Very well then. It is my constitution that could not survive another year of this." She stabbed a finger at the book. "Now, would you both please focus?"

The two men sighed but gave their attention to the pages. Marmaduke wasn't much help, as the only gentlemen he knew were the ones that played alongside the professional players in the cricket clubs. Ambrose, however, knew at least a little bit about everyone.

For thirty minutes, they reviewed the lines of England's finest families. They came up with discouragingly few possibilities.

As in none.

There were a limited number of livings in the country and while many would one day be assigned to younger sons and cousins, very few had already been earmarked. It would be a gamble to marry without assurance that the man would be assigned to a parish that provided a parsonage along with a salary and pension.

Clara turned the page and found the next option, a sense of desperation making her drag her finger down the page in a way that nearly caused it to rip. "Mr. Lewis Pitt. Third son of the Earl of Blitzmoor."

"He recently finished his schooling," Marmaduke said with a tilt of his head. "I've played cricket against him before, and he seemed a decent sport."

Both siblings looked to Ambrose who had been freely offering information until that point.

"He's due to inherit a living," Ambrose said slowly, as if he didn't want to give Clara the information.

Clara brightened. Finally, she had a promising candidate. He was a young, educated, and in direct line for the church. "When?"

Ambrose's eyebrows lifted. "When the current vicar dies or retires. That's how it works, you know. It's been promised to him, though."

Clara beamed and clasped her hands together. "He sounds perfect."

"I rather doubt it," Ambrose mumbled.

"Nonsense." Clara slammed the book closed. "We've been looking at names for the past thirty minutes and his is the only suitable situation we've crossed." Sometimes God made the path clear by providing only one door. Clara wasn't about to despair over a lack of options. She only needed one husband, after all.

"Just . . . promise me you'll consider the actual man before doing something rash." Ambrose frowned at the book but turned away to retrieve his cue.

"What do you know of marriage prospects? When was the last time you even spent time with a respectable lady, cousin?" Clara picked up the book and clutched it to her chest.

Ambrose tossed her a grin, seemingly unaffected by her censure. "This afternoon. I took you to the park."

She cast her eyes to the ceiling. "That is not what I meant." She lowered her glare to meet his gaze once more. "I love you dearly, cousin, but even you must admit that I would be a fool to listen to you on matters of virtue and prudence. You do not exactly walk the path of morality."

"Clara," Marmaduke said in a low warning. "I don't think—"

"Let her speak," Ambrose said with a thread of stone beneath the light tone. "We've gone more than an hour without her giving me a lecture on my immoral behavior or declaring me a squandersome wretch. I'm sure she's near to bursting with the restrained words."

Clara's cheeks heated as she watched her cousin strike the billiard ball hard enough to send it careening off the table.

She'd fed hungry children, comforted mourning widows, kept vigil beside a multitude of sick beds, but here amongst her own family was the humbling reminder that she had accomplished but a modicum of the mission God had given her.

It didn't matter how many lessons she shared from her father's sermons or how many verses she tried to remind him of, Ambrose claimed nothing of God but a regular seat in church on Sundays.

"Let it go," Marmaduke whispered as he turned Clara gently toward the door.

Clara glared at her brother through narrowed eyes. They'd had enough conversations over the years to know Duke's theology was sound and his heart devout. Despite his seemingly frivolous career, he viewed his life as a sort of ministry. Was he truly ready to give up on the man who was practically a brother to them both?

"How can you say that?" she whispered.

"Because." Marmaduke practically sighed out the word. "It isn't that he doesn't know what you want to tell him. It's that he doesn't believe it. He never has."

Never? Clara blinked, trying to remember the years before he'd gained adulthood. Childhood ramblings don't lend themselves to discussions of sermons and ethics. She'd thought him a man who'd strayed away soon after finishing his schooling, but if Duke was right and the divide was even greater, the matter was more pressing than she'd realized.

"But—"

"Why don't you go get Aunt Elizabeth's opinion of Mr. Pitt?" Marmaduke pulled her gently from the room. "It's got to be worth more than ours, anyway." With a thin smile, Marmaduke returned to the billiard room.

Clara stayed, hidden out of sight, waiting to see if Marmaduke would say something without her present. Maybe he had a different way of stating things that Ambrose would only listen to in private.

The only sounds to drift from the room, though, were the crash of billiard balls and a groan of disappointment followed by a laugh of triumph.

Finally, Clara stalked off to prepare for the night's event. She would discuss Mr. Pitt with her aunt that evening, and then at least one area of her life would be moving in the right direction.

Then, tomorrow, she could see about putting other areas on the right path.

For the first time, Clara saw this trip to London as a God-given opportunity instead of a familial obligation. Where else would she meet a man with the intentions and connections to take a position within the church? She'd been thinking a ministry-minded gentleman might be the best she could do, but this was even better.

She'd had her few days of self-pitying melancholy, but now it was time to get her head on straight. She was going to build the perfect future for herself, save her cousin from a life of depravity, and make sure her brother remembered what was important in life.

Clara's maid was nearly beside herself with concern by the time Clara returned to her room, but her toilette was completed in plenty of time and Clara was still in the drawing room before her mother and aunt.

The ride was too short for her to broach the subject of Mr. Pitt with her aunt, but Clara wasn't concerned. She would find a time at the musicale or after the event.

As the daughter of a vicar, Clara had been in and out of many fine homes. She took tea with charitable-minded ladies, was invited to all the gatherings of the lower gentry in the country, and often got selected to even out the numbers at a dinner party.

She'd seen nothing like the rooms they walked into that night.

They weren't in a ballroom, but doors had been thrown open to allow the party to flow through the front hall, the dining room, the music room, and two large drawing rooms. Every corner seemed to drip with near gaudy opulence.

Clara tried not to gape as she followed her aunt, who didn't seem to even be glancing at the surrounding decor. Were all homes in London like this?

Eversly House was certainly exquisite, but it wasn't decorated to this level. Of course, that could be due to it being Ambrose's primary residence as much as anything else.

"Now then." Aunt Elizabeth folded her hands in front of her and gave the room a long look. "The prospects might still be slim as we are somewhat early in the Season and, well, frankly speaking, the bachelors we are considering do not always flock together as regularly as the upper tier ones do."

A twinge of irritation tickled the back of Clara's throat. She wanted to remind her aunt that all were equal in God's eyes and all had value, but they could have that discussion later. For now, Clara, too, had a goal in mind and it wasn't to gain the eye of a top-tier anyone.

"Do you know if Mr. Lewis Pitt will be in attendance?" Clara stretched her neck, looking about as if she'd be able to know if the man was here.

She didn't know what her future husband looked like, though. He was a name in a book, a short list of practicality. Not that it would matter if she could identify him. Etiquette required that she be introduced, anyway.

"Mr. Lewis Pitt?" Her aunt's voice rose above her earlier whisper and threatened to draw the attention of the people around them. "Whyever would you pull that name out? He's certainly within your reach, but we can do better than a third son."

Clara resisted the desire to roll her eyes and express how nonsensical she found that statement. "I see no difference between a second son and a third."

"Aside from the number of hunting accidents standing between you and a title?"

Mother cleared her throat and spoke over the end of her sister's observation. "There's also low-ranking gentry and several gentlemen to consider."

Clara couldn't keep from looking at her aunt with a measure of horror. Had she really talked so casually about a man's potentially tragic death?

Aunt Elizabeth waved away Clara's outrage. "I'm hardly wishing doom on anyone in particular. Merely pointing out that certain credence is given to spares just in case. Death is a fact of life, you know."

Clara closed her eyes and silently counted to ten. Around her, Aunt Elizabeth and Mother discussed potential suitors as if they were selecting fish at the market.

"I do believe," Clara said, "that a third son bound for the church would be a more than adequate fit for me. That being so, Aunt, do you know if Mr. Lewis Pitt is in attendance?"

"Yes, yes." She sighed and nodded toward the music room. A young woman sat playing the piano while several people looked on and murmured among themselves. "He's over there. In the green waistcoat."

He was of average height, if the people gathered around him were anything to go by, with thick auburn hair waving back into a short queue. It was impossible to make out any more intricate details, aside from the fact that he seemed very quick to smile.

That was an excellent trait in a vicar. Clara gave a small, decisive nod. "I should very much like you to make an introduction."

"Of course." Aunt Elizabeth smiled at Mother. "We'll simply make our way in that direction."

Making their way meant introducing Clara to every man they encountered on their meandering path through the joined rooms. There was Mr. Thompson who owned a home out in Cornwall and only came to London for the first month of the season to discuss the political happenings.

Then she met Mr. Russell, who would one day be a baronet, unless he met with one of Aunt Elizabeth's untimely deaths before his father did.

After that there was Mr. Payne, who would be purchasing an officer's commission at the end of the Season, and Mr. Morris, who owned something having to do with shipping, and finally Sir John Hayes, a knight who had to be older than Clara's father.

Each and every one of them spoke kindly to Clara, but it was evident they were far more concerned with impressing Aunt Elizabeth.

Before they actually reached Mr. Pitt, dinner was served. As the crowd could not begin to fit around the dining table, smaller tables had been grouped throughout the rooms and seats had been left unassigned.

Aunt Elizabeth tried to maneuver their little trio to a table with the elderly Lady Hawkins, Mr. Morris, Mr. Russell, and a man she'd yet to meet, but Clara had other ideas. She might not be as subtle or crafty as her aunt, but she was just as—if not even more—determined.

A short delay, a quick dart through the crowd, and she and her aunt were taking the last two seats at Mr. Pitt's table. She wasn't sure where her mother ended up.

Introductions were made and dinner eaten. If Mr. Pitt gave the other young ladies at the table more attention than Clara, it was simply because he didn't know her yet. She had to admit, though, that he was a very affable man. Not only was he quick to smile and laugh but his companions were as well.

That was a good quality in a vicar as well, wasn't it?

Clara chewed her fish thoughtfully as she observed her potential husband. As he expressed grave concern over the health of Miss Davis's father and offered to come by the house and entertain the man with a game of chess, a peace settled in Clara's mind. Yes, Mr. Pitt was going to be a fine choice, indeed.

SEVEN

Hugh deftly polished his fingerprints off the bezel before giving the hands of the clock a test wind. The smooth, satisfying glide was rewarding, but the fact that Mr. Johns would get the gratitude was anything but.

When Hugh had been an apprentice, Mr. Johns would praise his work and talk about making him a partner when he was older. Within a year of his transition from apprentice to employee, those statements had turned into eventually selling Hugh the business, as if he had the means to save enough without receiving a slice of the profits. Lately, if anything was said at all, Hugh wouldn't be getting the business until Mr. Johns died.

That was, of course, unless the man suddenly remembered some long-lost nephew who deserved it more.

In those early years, Hugh had thought of Mr. Johns as a mentor and then possibly a friend. Now, he knew that to the older man, Hugh was nothing more than a business acquisition similar to every tool, bench, and spare part stocked in the workroom.

One day Hugh would be the man known for making the best clocks in all of England. He'd have his own shop, his own clientage, and his own reputation. Likely he'd have his own apprentices, too. And while Hugh knew better than to say he'd treat them like family when he hadn't yet been in the position of mentor, he vowed to himself that he'd never make them a false promise.

Unfortunately, the bank account in which Hugh was stashing the funds for that day was not growing as much as he'd like. He wasn't going to be hanging out his own shingle anytime soon, unless God sent an investor or an opportunity or both his way.

Hugh made a note on the invoice and slid it to the side of the desk before setting the repaired pocket watch on top of it. Then he pulled out his uncompleted sketches for a new chronometer design. He was all but certain his idea would work, changing the quality of timekeeping devices around the world and improving the preciseness of ship navigation.

If he couldn't find the time, money, or location to build it, though, no one would ever know about this change but him.

He could gamble everything he'd saved so far to secure the supplies and a space to work, but if he failed to gain attention or opportunity quickly, he'd be right back where he'd started at the end of his apprenticeship. Maybe even worse off, because Mr. Johns might not keep him employed if he learned about it.

Hugh took a deep breath and slid his notes back into their hiding spot. Patience was a virtue, and he'd do well to ask God for a little more of it. It was best for him to keep the job that paid enough to prevent his having to beg his uncle for a bed in the vicarage. One day, God would provide another path forward.

Mr. Johns walked into the back workroom, ignoring the other clocks and watches awaiting repairs, the gears in need of labeling and storage, and the tools that hadn't been put away. The place was clean—dust wasn't good for the interior mechanisms after all—but the general clutter created a different environment from the elegant showroom at the front of the shop.

Squinting even through his glasses, Mr. Johns picked up the watch and looked through the notes Hugh had made on the paper.

Several nods and a few mutterings of springs and latches later, Mr. Johns gave Hugh a smile. "Well done, lad."

Lad? Was Mr. Johns' eyesight and memory so far gone that he didn't know Hugh was a man of six and twenty? Or did he think treating Hugh like he was still an apprenticed child would keep him content at his back room bench?

"Thank you, sir," Hugh grumbled because the reality of his situation dictated he do so.

The bell on the front door clanged, and Mr. Johns nodded toward the showroom. "Go on out and help that customer." The old man grinned as he slid the pocket watch and invoice into a leather satchel. "I think I'll see to this delivery myself."

Of course he would. The pocket watch belonged to Lord Lindbury. The viscount Hugh had visited yesterday wasn't enough to garner Mr. Johns' attention, but a marquis was.

Hugh couldn't stop a slight grin from forming as he remembered the events that followed the clock delivery. Never would he have guessed he'd spend the afternoon chasing kites.

Never would he have guessed that more than once today he'd have found his mind wandering away to think about a certain young lady.

In his moments of desperation Hugh could almost convince himself he had enough money to strike out on his own, but not even in his dreams did he have the funds or position to consider courtship of a woman. Particularly if—lady or not—she was accustomed to the comforts that came from living in a fine townhouse in Mayfair.

Hugh shook his head and rose to move to the front room. The chances of him seeing any of yesterday's brief companions were small, so thinking of them was a waste of his time.

Except one of them was standing in the clock shop.

It wasn't the intriguing young lady or the personable viscount, but Mr. Woodbury standing in the shop with his hat in his hand as he examined a large case clock in the corner of the store.

"It is a pleasure to see you again." Hugh stepped up to the man, curious but also cautiously optimistic about his presence.

Mr. Woodbury grinned at him. "Is it? Even if I don't come bearing significant business?"

Surprisingly, Hugh wasn't disappointed. The afternoon had been the most enjoyable one Hugh could remember in a long while. He returned the smile with a nod. "Even then."

"Excellent." Mr. Woodbury nodded toward a clock on the wall. "Do you make these?"

"Some of them. I don't carve the wooden ones, but I've placed the gears inside."

"Makes sense." Mr. Woodbury gave the intricate clock one last look before turning to Hugh. "Do you play billiards?"

The abrupt change of topic sent Hugh's head momentarily reeling before it fully comprehended the question. "I . . . well, yes, I suppose. I know the activity, but I haven't played much." Billiard tables weren't common furniture in the rooms men like him could let. Nor was he spending his limited funds on club memberships, even if there was one that wanted him to join.

Hugh lived in a small set of rooms in a nearby side street, not the spacious apartments like the ones that surrounded the square they'd trespassed in yesterday. His evening entertainment was limited to books from his uncle or cards with one of his neighbors.

"As long we I don't have to explain the rules, you're invited." He scrunched his nose up for a moment. "Actually, I'll invite you even if you don't know the rules."

"Invite me where?" Hugh said carefully.

"To dinner."

"Dinner?"

"Yes. You know, mealtime, occasionally a ridiculous number of removals, often used to socialize, at least here in the city."

"I am aware of the concept, yes, but—" Before Hugh could clarify whether he was being invited to the viscount's house by his cousin or meeting the man at a restaurant later, another gentleman entered the shop.

He was older, with white hair pulled back in a low queue and a captain's jacket slung over his shoulders. After glancing quickly about the room, he barked, "I'm looking for Johns."

Hugh snapped his spine straight and turned to face the customer, forcing the confusing social encounter he was in the middle of to the back of his mind. "I'm afraid he's on a delivery at the moment. Might I be of service?"

The man gave Hugh a long look. "You're not an apprentice here."

"No, sir." Though Hugh wasn't certain what he was.

The man thought a minute before reaching into his pocket and pulling out a pencil and notebook. He scratched out a few lines, ripped the paper from the book, added a card from a silver carrier tucked into his other pocket, and extended the papers to Hugh.

"See that he gets this. My wife got a watch from Johns last Christmas, and it's kept time better than anything I've seen. I only have to set it once a month as long as I keep it properly wound."

The piece the man pulled from the tiny pocket of his waistcoat was one Hugh immediately recognized. He'd been quite proud of that piece and had been hoping to submit it to the Royal Observatory when Mr. Johns had up and sold it.

Hugh glanced at the paper and nearly let out a shout of excitement. The Royal Observatory was seeking a new chronometer for more accurate maritime navigations. The selected maker would also get the order for a Standard Astronomical Clock for the new tower being built in Greenwich.

It was the sort of opportunity that could make a name for a man.

Hugh swallowed hard to regain his ability of speech. "Of course, sir. I'll see that the maker of that watch learns of this opportunity."

"See that you do."

Then the man was gone.

And Mr. Woodbury was laughing as he read the note over Hugh's shoulder. "Maker of the watch, hmm?"

"Well, Mr. Johns doesn't trouble himself with innovation much these days." The old clockmaker had been good several years ago, but anything he submitted now would be a replica of what the Observatory already had in their possession.

Mr. Woodbury bumped Hugh's shoulder with his own. "Bring that same technical precision to the billiard table and we'll win for certain."

"We'll win?" Hugh folded the note and stuck it in his pocket. He'd copy down the information before passing it along to Mr. Johns. "I'm sorry, but why am I playing billiards?"

"Because Ambrose and I tire of playing only each other and my cousin only has one friend that's willing to shoot with me." His lips twisted into a wry grin. "They'll pay me to join them on the pitch but can't stand to share a room with me." He clapped his hands together. "So. Dinner? Six o'clock? At Eversly House, of course."

Of course. Hugh's mind was spinning at the rate he was receiving possible answers to prayer. This wasn't exactly what he'd asked for, but it was a far more realistic turn of events than the aristocrat himself waltzing through the door with aspirations of being a silent partner in a new store.

And now that he had it, he wasn't sure what to do with it.

Beyond accept the invitation, of course. "I would be honored."

"Remember that when you're losing." Mr. Woodbury plopped his hat on his head.

"I thought you said we were going to win."

Mr. Woodbury shrugged one shoulder. "I suppose I lied, then." He grinned. "The question is which time?" Then he tipped the brim of his hat in Hugh's direction before sauntering out the door of the shop.

Clara's tea had gone cold ages ago, but still she stared at it, as if the very force of her attention would heat the cup again. The alternative was to gape in horrified astonishment at the women around her.

She was attending her first meeting of the Virtuous Ladies Society for the Care of Wounded Soldiers and not once had they said anything about the plight of soldiers coming home with missing limbs and terrorized hearts. They'd had plenty to say about the appearance, manners, and prospects of the people pouring into London for the coming Season, though.

If this was what passed for charity in London, she could well understand why her father hadn't wanted to accompany them for any portion of the Season.

How could Mother stomach it? Clara glanced in her direction, but the woman who'd taught Clara how to properly fill baskets for the poor, keep a visit to the ill short but meaningful, and remember the names of every parishioner didn't seem particularly bothered by the current conversation. Not that she was participating much. Was that because she didn't care to gossip or because she hadn't the slightest idea who the people under discussion were?

Three weeks ago, Clara would never have allowed such a traitorous thought to occur to her, but Clara didn't recognize the woman her mother had become since arriving in London. Instead of being capable, confident, and steady, she was screaming at kites and fretting over lace and tea.

Aunt Elizabeth presided over the gossip from her seat to Clara's right. There had been little interaction with Aunt Elizabeth over the years, but Clara had once thought her fascinating. She would bring exquisite chocolates and parade about in smiles and fanciful dresses when she came to the parsonage to leave her son in his aunt's care or take him back to school.

The prolonged exposure was making her far less fascinating.

Where was the resolve she'd gained yesterday to use this time in London to craft the best possible future for herself? It had crumbled under the prospect of enduring afternoons such as this one for the next three months. Perhaps being a spinster wasn't such a bad option. Yes, she would be something of a strain on her parents and yes, her future would be very uncertain, but it had to be better than this.

She could make her gowns stretch a little further, let her room grow a little colder, and leave her plate a little emptier. Then, when her father passed on, there was sure to be a widower or two around that would marry her for her caregiving skills.

It could work. She could make it work.

One glance to her left had her abandoning the fleeting dream. Such a future would devastate her mother. She'd circled right back around to making the most of her time in London.

She just didn't know if this was anyone's best.

With a sigh, Clara leaned toward her aunt. "Shouldn't we discuss more pressing matters?"

Aunt Elizabeth frowned. "Such as?"

"Er, well, the wounded soldiers?" Clara glanced about the circle of women. That was what this group was about, wasn't it?

A frown of confusion puckered Aunt Elizabeth's forehead. "But we've already discussed that, dear. Weren't you listening? We're going to ask the attendees of Lady Bertram's ball to purchase flowers for their lapels or hair. The money will go toward feeding those living in the encampment."

That was it? "But . . ." Clara took a deep breath as she gathered her thoughts. "Who does that feeding?"

Aunt Elizabeth waved her hand about, genuine confusion on her face. "Someone from the church near the river." She gave a tense laugh. "You don't expect us to go do it, do you? We'd be attacked or robbed if we ventured into that area of Town."

Clara couldn't refute her aunt's words, as she didn't know enough about London to say whether or not it was true, but she couldn't stomach the idea that the only way to help people was to adorn herself even more and dance and socialize just as she would do on any other night.

Her gaze dropped back into her teacup. "I see."

Aunt Elizabeth nodded and gave Clara's knee a light pat. "Listen and learn, my dear. If you make a decent match this Season, you'll be expected to spend at least some of your time in charitable works. 'Tis the duty of the blessed, you know."

"Yes, of course," Clara mumbled.

Shouldn't charity be more than a social obligation? Visiting her father's parishioners was hard, heartbreaking work, but she'd always found it a source of encouragement as well.

Mr. Pitt was likely of the same mind, since he was bound for the church. As he was in a position of waiting, though, he had to be viewing his time in London similar to how she saw hers. Once their marriage was situated, they could both leave the city and focus on serving somewhere. Maybe they could even be traveling missionaries until they made their permanent home when his living became available.

The sound of her name pulled her from daydreams to reality. Mother was smiling now as the ladies discussed which events should have Clara's name added to the guest list. They seemed far more interested in making her their pet project than anything related to the wounded soldiers.

She set her teacup aside and murmured a vaguely worded excuse about needing to see to something—she didn't really care what they thought it was. Then she rose from her chair and slipped out of the room as quietly as possible.

In the hall beyond, she took three deep cleansing breaths. To her right, the front door beckoned as a means of ultimate, if impractical, escape. She could find a mail coach and make her way home. Father would understand that she couldn't stay in London.

Taking the mail coach by herself was reckless and irresponsible, though, and she wasn't quite that desperate.

Yet.

Resolutely, she turned her back to the door and strode deeper into the house. Her cousin and brother were likely upstairs in Ambrose's study, hiding from the gaggle of women in the drawing room. Maybe she could join them.

Her mind churned between ideas that would help her gain a speedy courtship with Mr. Pitt and ones that would allow her to abandon the entire business and return home. Lost in her struggling thoughts, she almost collided with a man at the top of the stairs.

An arm slid quickly around her waist and pulled her away from the stairs.

The shock of the contact was almost more disturbing than the shock of nearly falling down the stairs, and Clara shrieked as she jumped away from the man.

She straightened her skirts as she turned to face down the man, but her words of rebuke died as she realized it wasn't her brother or cousin.

It was the man from the park.

EIGHT

"**E**xactly how many clocks has my cousin managed to break?" Miss Woodbury's eyes widened in surprise censure.

"I, uh . . ." Hugh didn't know what to say. While he didn't have a great deal of social visits on his calendar, he'd never had to explain his presence after being personally invited somewhere.

It didn't help that he wasn't entirely certain why he was there either. Despite Mr. Woodbury's claim that Hugh was the first person he'd encountered in London who wasn't afraid of spending time with an aristocrat, coming to such a fine house without a purpose felt more than a little strange. Yes, he was evening out the social numbers if one wanted to balance titled and non-titled, but he'd never heard of that being a host's priority.

After his arrival at precisely 5:59, he'd been shown to the billiard room where Mr. Woodbury and Lord Eversly were already waiting. They'd soon been joined by Lord Northwick, and it was suggested they play a few games and venture to the dining room after the ladies departed for the evening.

Hugh had just completed his turn before excusing himself to visit the retiring room, but all he really needed was a moment by himself to put his own thoughts in order. Now that he'd, quite literally, bumped into

Miss Woodbury, those thoughts were even more scattered than they'd been moments ago.

The young woman's brow was deeply furrowed, and her lips were pulling tightly at the corners. Hugh's concern shifted from himself to her. "I say, are you well? You appear . . ." He cleared his throat, searching for a word that could delicately indicate a woman was looking out of sorts. " . . . Distressed. Might I be of assistance?"

Miss Woodbury's straight spine stiffened, and her nose tilted ever so slightly higher into the air. "I am not a pocket watch, Mr. Lockhart. I do not need you to be ceaselessly coming to my rescue."

Once more, sensible words abandoned Hugh's mind. How did people gain the gumption to simply walk away from conversations they no longer wanted to be in? He'd dearly love to be one of those people at that moment. His uncle, however, had taught him it was the height of rudeness, and years of business experience had trained him to never be the one to abandon a potential opportunity.

So he stayed.

And shifted his weight.

And counted to five.

Still the right words, or even a potential option of words, didn't come.

Fortunately, Miss Woodbury tired of the silence first. "Besides, this is not a threat you can simply snatch out of the sky and crush beneath your boot heel."

The anxiety swirling into a fog through Hugh's mind instantly settled. There was actually a threat of some kind? "If you are in need of help and I can be of any assistance, I am at your service, my la—er, miss."

She sighed. "You might as well call me a lady. It's certainly not the worst thing I'll be forced to endure this Season."

Hugh gave her what he hoped was an encouraging smile. "I've always been under the impression that most ladies enjoyed their first Season in London."

"The ladies of your acquaintance have a different idea of an enjoyable time than I do, it would seem."

He refrained from saying his knowledge of ladies stemmed from brief encounters in the shop, occasional observations at church, and daily glances at the society section of the newspaper.

Miss Woodbury sighed and looked down the stairs. "It would seem most ladies also have a different idea of charity than I do." Her lips pressed into a thin line. "Particularly the Virtuous Ladies Society for the Care of Wounded Soldiers."

In his short but concentrated exposure to this family, he'd learned that the elder Mr. Woodbury held a living in Leicestershire. If his daughter had aided him in tending the parishioners, Hugh could only guess what the suggestions of the Virtuous Ladies had sounded like to her. He stifled the urge to chuckle.

Heat flushed Miss Woodbury's cheeks as she turned back to Hugh. "I beg your pardon. I'm speaking out of turn. Please forgive me."

"You are allowed to have an opinion and to express it in private conversation." Hugh nodded down the stairs, toward where he assumed the virtuous ladies were gathered. "They do good work, you know. Well, I don't know about them in particular, but groups such as those. It takes money to buy food and other necessities."

Her frown deepened, forcing Hugh to fight the urge to squirm. "I . . . that is, your father's church. I assume it had collections for the poor?"

"Of course." Miss Woodbury's chin lifted, a feat Hugh would have thought impossible a moment earlier. "I am not unaware of the fact that money is required for the movement of goods, even those that are necessary for sustaining life, but I am personally more accustomed to a deeper involvement that does not seem to be acceptable in polite society."

Hugh pictured some of the areas around his uncle's church where people would go when they needed basic care. He couldn't hold back the wince at the idea of Miss Woodbury and her pristine, fashionable, clean skirts waltzing along the same paths. "Frankly, there are some parts of London that wouldn't be safe for someone of your—"

She narrowed her gaze at him, but he continued, albeit with a different wording than originally intended. "Someone who appeared to be of the more gently reared portion of society."

"Are you telling me there is no one in need of care, attention, and good news that does not live at the docks or wherever it is so very dangerous for me to wander?"

Hugh sighed. "You know that isn't the case. There will be people in ball rooms tonight that are only there because they can't afford food any other way."

"I can hardly go around asking the party guests if that canape is the first thing they've eaten all day."

Why, oh why hadn't Hugh simply said *pardon me* and continued walking? The other gentlemen likely thought him struck with a stomach malady by now.

In the interest of extracting himself from this conversation, Hugh tried to offer a modicum of reassurance. "There are, obviously, groups in London that are more involved in the lives of those they are helping. Then there are the groups that provide the means for such involvement. Both are important."

"Where might I find one of these involved groups?"

"I really should get back." He took a step toward the billiard room.

She followed. "Do you know where they meet? Can you introduce me?"

"Wouldn't it be better to wait until you're married? Then you can find something close to your home and socially appropriate."

Her hands turned into tight fists, and for a moment Hugh genuinely worried for the safety of his chin. Then those tiny fists found their way onto her hips. "You would have me rot away my time in London being utterly useless to both God and man?"

There wasn't a good answer to such a question, but Hugh opened his mouth to try. He didn't get a chance.

"I can't spend all my waking hours in search of a husband, you know. I'll go mad. The Season has barely begun and I'm already halfway 'round the bend." Desperation was evident in her voice, face, and even her posture.

Hugh sighed. "It's not proper for me to take you about and introduce you, but I could maybe put in a word. Tell someone to be looking for you."

She took a step closer to him until the edge of her skirt brushed the toe of his boot. "Where would I find this person?"

"There's a church—"

"I can go to a church."

"It's not in Mayfair."

"I know how to walk."

"It's barely even in London."

"I can take Ambrose's carriage."

"It's not as populated as this area."

"I can take a footman."

"You'd have to go near the dock—"

"For goodness' sake, are you going to tell me where to go or not?"

He'd rather not, but as so often seemed the case when this woman was involved, Hugh didn't appear to have a reasonable option. He sighed. "Have you other dresses to wear? Some that are . . . plainer?"

"What's wrong with my dress? It's far plainer that some of the ones my aunt wanted to purchase."

Hugh sighed. "The people near St. Anne's Limehouse don't want to be considered some wealthy lady's pity project."

Miss Woodbury frowned. "Limehouse?"

Hugh looked from her to the billiard room door a scant few feet away. Had anyone poked a head out looking for him yet? As odd as the invitation had been, he didn't want to ruin this social encounter. Aside from the fact that he couldn't remember the last time he'd actually received a personal invitation and not simply joined a community gathering when he needed company, he had no way of knowing how deep the viscount's pockets were. His name had been connected to an investment or two in the past.

"Right, then." He shifted his weight in the direction of the billiard room. "I'll just . . . go."

"Wait!" Miss Woodbury reached out a hand to grasp at his sleeve. "Who do I ask for?"

Hugh shook his head. "If you show up, she'll find you." He'd send a messenger over first thing in the morning to warn his cousin, but even if Miss Woodbury somehow arrived before his missive, Eleanor would find her. She had a knack for sniffing out a do-gooder.

Before she could come up with another question to ask him, Hugh strode down the corridor. He cast a glance over his shoulder before opening the door to the billiard room.

She had yet to move, but her gaze had shifted to the ceiling and her lips were moving rapidly. Was she praying? If so, the smile would indicate it was one of thanksgiving. Hugh had never been the answer to someone's prayer before, and he really wasn't certain he wanted to start with a fresh-faced, naïve woman from the country.

Much better to focus on creating a business that would allow him to sustain himself, his family, and some of those charitable groups Miss Woodbury wanted to get her hands on.

Back in the billiard room, Hugh managed to push Miss Woodbury and her concerns out of his mind. He needed all his wits about him to traverse his own God-given opportunity.

"There you are, Lockhart." Lord Eversly extended Hugh's cue toward him. "It's your go, though we've put you and Marmaduke in a rather precarious position."

Hugh took the cue and analyzed the table before making his next shot.

Play continued, and the conversation was easy and surprisingly amiable given the mix of men in the room. Hugh refused to laugh at some of the more risqué jokes Lord Eversly and Lord Northwick bandied about, but as Mr. Woodbury wasn't laughing at them either, no one seemed to notice his occasional silence.

The game finished in favor of the aristocrats, and the balls were reset for another game. Lord Northwick leaned over the table and lined up his cue stick. "Lockhart, I hear you're in trade over on Piccadilly."

"Yes. I work with clocks, watches, and chronometers." Hugh swallowed hard, insides shaking enough to make him thankful they'd yet to eat dinner. "Currently I work with Mr. Johns, but I'll have my own shop in the future."

"Interesting." Lord Northwick completed his shot and stood, leaning one hip on the billiard table. "My father has some interest in a shipping company. He met with some of the captains last week, and they were talking about chronometers."

"I don't doubt it. They've no way to reset their clocks when at sea, so a reliable chronometer makes all the difference in keeping accurate logbooks and maintaining daily and shipping schedules."

Lord Northwick nodded. "And you make those?"

"Repair them, mostly, but I've ideas on how to improve the device."

"The Royal Observatory is holding a contest." Mr. Woodbury winked at Hugh before setting up his next shot.

"Are you entering your design?" Lord Eversly asked.

"I'm afraid I haven't the funds or workspace to make the necessary prototype." He could spend his entire savings to make it happen, but he couldn't quite bring himself to gamble everything on a single chance.

"If you had those, would you win?" Lord Northwick crossed his arms and leaned back against a large leather armchair as he considered Hugh. "Could you make something that would truly improve on what captains currently have?"

A steady confidence blanketed some of the vibrating anticipation in Hugh's gut. It couldn't be this easy, could it? Shouldn't God be making him sacrifice something or sweat blood to gain this chance? "Yes. I've some ideas on how to improve upon Harrison's design, thereby allowing captains to more accurately chart their position."

He swallowed hard and committed to the claim that would sell his position. "Greater chart accuracy will allow for the creation of faster trade routes and more precise military navigation plans."

In the silence that followed his statement—the longest he'd made in this group's presence all evening—Hugh found himself unable to breathe. Every part of him, including the air in his lungs, was waiting for the aristocrats' reactions.

Lord Northwick slapped a hand on the edge of the billiard table. "I'm in." He spread his arms out wide as he grinned. "If this works, Father will have to stop chiding me about not paying attention to our financial affairs."

Lord Eversly laughed. "Have you any idea how this will affect your financial affairs?"

One of Lord Northwick's arms gestured toward Hugh. "Didn't you hear him? Faster trade routes." He shrugged, then leaned down to line up his next shot. "Father and Uncle constantly discuss how to trim shipping costs and keep things moving through the warehouses before they spoil or rot. If a new chronometer helps, then I contributed."

"And all without putting down your cricket bat," Mr. Woodbury said.

"Can't have you getting one past me again." Lord Northwick slapped Mr. Woodbury on the shoulder. "I don't suppose you've any interest in switching to the Marylebone Club? I'd rather play with you than against you."

Hugh had to brace his hands against the baize and rail to keep them from shaking as he took his next shot. That any balls connected with each other was pure luck, because he could barely see the table in front of him.

To enter this contest and gain the attention of the Astronomer Royal would change everything. If his chronometer won in the trials—and he was confident that it would—it would garner enough demand from captains, shipping companies, and the British Navy that he could easily go into business for himself. Not even Mr. Johns would be able to keep him in the back room anymore.

His hands itched to grab a pencil and revisit his preliminary sketches, but a verbal indication of interest wasn't actual funds in his pocket.

Besides, as Mr. Woodbury scored the winning point and let out a whoop of celebration, Hugh had to admit he was having an enjoyable time.

The idea that he might be able to make friends, even if only behind closed doors, with such men was a novel idea. The two aristocrats were far above Hugh's station and would likely never acknowledge him in a wider social setting, but Hugh hadn't ever managed to find true camaraderie among the other tradesmen either.

Whether it was his awkward position with Mr. Johns or his upbringing in the church under his uncle, he didn't know. It could even be the fact that he wanted to change his entire industry, not just create a simple business within it. The why didn't matter as much as the reality, though.

As the evening rolled on from billiards to dinner to cards, the conversation would regularly return to a potential investment in Hugh's ideas. By the time he was accepting his jacket from the butler, funds had been promised and workspace secured.

Why had God decided to bless Hugh in such a huge way now? Hugh would likely never know, but that wasn't going to stop him from accepting it and making the most of it. He breathed in the cool night air and began the long walk back to his rooms. As he passed beneath a streetlamp, he looked at his pocket watch. Three minutes past midnight. His someday had officially arrived.

Today was the first day of the rest of his life.

NINE

C lara knew well the stillness of an empty church. She'd grown up relishing the hallowed peace of the quiet echoes of whispered prayers and unspoken hopes that hung in the air long after parishioners departed. She'd walked by the pews, praying and soaking in the surge of anticipation for the lives God would change when the people once more filled the space.

Still, she was unprepared for the almost frightfully humbling awe that filled her as she arrived at St. Anne's Limehouse. The servants had balked at the idea of bringing her here until Clara had threatened to sneak off by herself and hire a hack. She'd refused to bring her maid as she didn't want to appear too high in the instep, but a driver and a footman were currently waiting outside the church.

She wouldn't admit it to anyone, but she'd been thankful for the footman's presence as she'd watched the neighborhood change outside the carriage window.

At first, they'd passed through enough farmland and pasture to make her feel like she was back in the country. But the view from the actual church was nothing like the one from her father's little parish. Large, blocky buildings could be seen beyond the rows of modest-looking terrace homes that framed two sides of the churchyard.

From the steps, she could see the tops of the masts in the nearby dock, their barren limbs poking into the sky like the broken remains of a fallen down barn. Above it all was the same sooty haze that covered so much of London. It was a desolate appearance and the warnings from the Virtuous Ladies slid in a steady stream through the back of Clara's mind.

She walked through the front porch, marveling at the large, curving staircase she could see through doors on either side of the space. The double doors into the nave were open, and her gaze lifted to the columns of the galley and drifted down the clear glass windows as she wandered down the church aisle.

As Clara approached the middle of the church, a woman emerged from a door in the south corner. Her steps were brisk without appearing rushed and her arms were wrapped around a wooden box. A wide smile appeared on her face as her gaze met Clara's.

"Welcome to St. Anne's Limehouse." She came to a stop several paces away from Clara. Her gaze discreetly dropped to glance over Clara's ensemble. "What brings you out this way? Are you new to the area? I thought I had met all our parishioners."

Heat burned the tips of Clara's ears as she, too, glanced down at her skirts. Despite Mr. Lockhart's suggestion that she wear something plainer, she'd donned her best afternoon dress along with the brand-new bonnet that had been delivered just that morning. If she'd done so while considering the chance that Mr. Lockhart might be here when she arrived, then at least she was the only one aware of it. Pride goeth before a fall, indeed.

Since her toilette couldn't be altered now, she plastered a matching smile on her face and pushed on. "No, I'm currently living in Marylebone. I was, er, sent here."

"I see. Of course." She turned to set the wooden box in her arms on the wall of a nearby pew box. "I am Miss Eleanor Porter, and you are most welcome here." She reached both of her hands out to clasp Clara's nerveless fingers. "It is our honor to be a part of God's graciousness."

Clara wanted to frown at Miss Porter's odd wording, but the awareness of her surroundings restrained her.

The young woman didn't seem concerned by Clara's lack of response. "Let's step away from this echo chamber, shall we? The benches under the galleries are quite comfortable and you'll be able to get off your feet. Do you need refreshment? Water? Tea? I have a few cakes leftover from last night." She grinned, one side of her mouth curving a little more than the other. "Father tried to hide them, but I know where they are."

Should Clara answer Miss Porter's flood of questions or ask one of the dozens floating through her own head? Numbly, Clara allowed herself to be led to the side of the nave. She'd greeted many a person in church, but never in such a way.

Finally, she settled on asking the most easily grasped portion of the speech. "Father?"

Miss Porter gave a light laugh. "Forgive me. I assumed you'd have been told when you were sent to me. My father is the rector of St. Anne's parish."

It was the answer Clara had expected and yet somehow, she was still surprised. "Yes, I simply . . . wanted to verify."

"I understand. We take discretion very seriously." They sat on a bench, Miss Porter angled so that her knees brushed against Clara's skirts. "Are you certain I can't provide you with anything?"

"No." Clara stopped to swallow as much to clear her head as to clear her throat. "I had tea before coming."

"Wonderful." Miss Porter's eyes were kind as she once more clasped one of Clara's hands in both of hers. "Now, we'll be as delicate as possible for this conversation, but there are some things I'll need to know."

This time Clara could not prevent the frown from forming. She knew she dressed like a woman from the upper classes, but did Miss

Porter think such ladies possessed a constitution so fragile that the mere thought of the less fortunate would give her a case of the vapors?

Clara pressed her lips into an expression she hoped looked more like a smile than a frown. "Truly, there's no need for delicacy."

Miss Porter's surprise at Clara's statement was evident only in the three rapid blinks she gave before responding. "In that case, perhaps you could tell me how long we have until you need to be out of London?"

It was Clara's turn to be surprised, and she doubted she'd done as good of a job at hiding it. What had Mr. Lockhart told this woman? "I'm not certain what you've been told about my situation. While I'd certainly rather not be in the city, I have certain commitments I need to . . . accomplish before I can depart. That is why I am here. I was told you could provide a . . ." It was probably best not to call a woman's life work a distraction, even though Clara had a feeling that was honestly what it would be for her. "You can provide what I need while I remain in London."

"So you have support at home, then? That's wonderful."

When Clara's frown deepened, Miss Porter pressed one hand to her throat. "You don't? Well, we can move you into the vicarage and make you as comfortable as possible until you are ready to leave." Miss Porter gave Clara's hand a squeeze. "It likely won't be the comfort you're accustomed to, but we'll help in any way we can until it's time to remove you to the country."

"I don't . . ." Clara was so befuddled she couldn't form a sentence. "Why would I need to leave home?" She wanted to devote her life to God's work and use, but she'd been doing it from beneath her parents' roof all her life. She was in a Church of England and not a Catholic establishment, wasn't she? She wasn't here trying to become a nun.

The clack and creak of the main door opening drew both women's attention toward the portal that led out to the three porches making up the front of the church.

Clara was merely curious while Miss Porter's startled expression appeared almost alarmed. She pushed to her feet, speaking to Clara in a hushed whisper. "You may hide in one of the box pews, if you wish. I shall see to whoever has arrived."

Hide in one of the box pews? Clara was hardly ashamed to be inside a church. Her cousin's carriage was boldly parked outside, after all. The footman had hopes that the crest on the side would prevent anyone from bothering her.

"Oh!" Miss Porter's voice drifted into through the open nave doors. "Hugh, it's you."

"Of course it's me. I always come twice a week to wind the clock."

Clara knew that voice. She stood and followed in Miss Porter's footsteps, a new curiosity pushing out her earlier confusion. Mr. Lockhart came here twice a week? Knew he'd be coming today, in fact? He'd sent her here on her own without a proper introduction. Tradesman or not, he should have known such behavior was unbecoming of a gentleman. She stepped into the antechamber to let him know as such.

Miss Porter was attempting to push Mr. Lockhart toward one of the staircases. When she saw Clara, her eyes went wide, and she began shoving harder.

Mr. Lockhart was indeed moving in the encouraged direction, but at a far slower pace than Miss Porter would obviously prefer. The look he gave the exasperated woman was one Clara knew well. She'd seen it on Marmaduke's face more than once when she was pestering him.

Clara's light giggle interrupted the scuffle and drew Mr. Lockhart's attention to her. He turned, nearly sending Miss Porter to the floor, and gave Clara a small bow. "Miss Woodbury. I see you took my suggestion."

Miss Porter stepped between Clara and Mr. Lockhart. "Your suggestion? You were the one who sent her here?"

Mr. Lockhart nodded. "Of course. She wanted to make an active change to her situation, and you were the only person I knew who could do so."

"I can't really change the situation, but . . ." Miss Porter cast a furtive glance at Clara. "You aren't . . . That is, you didn't . . ." Until that moment, the woman, though she appeared no more than twenty years old, had been displaying a markedly older maturity, stamped her foot in frustration. "How did you even know about it, anyway?"

Mr. Lockhart frowned. "Know what? That you aid the less fortunate? This is a church, Eleanor. If you aren't doing such work, I'll have to have a long discussion with Uncle Patrick."

"Not every church treats such situations kindly, Hugh." She took a step closer to him and attempted to whisper, but the stone walls brought her voice directly to Clara. "How are you even privy to the knowledge of her delicate condition?"

"What?" Mr. Lockhart exclaimed at the same time that Clara gasped out, "I beg your pardon."

Miss Porter looked from one to the other, a tinge of pink slashing across her cheeks and growing into two huge dollops of red. "I, um, that is . . ." She fully turned to face Clara. "You aren't here seeking assistance?"

"Well, no," Clara said, still a little breathless. "I came to see if I could be of assistance."

"Oh, dear."

A dull throb formed in the middle of Clara's forehead as she took a step closer to Miss Porter. "Do you mean to tell me this church runs a charity for, well . . ." Unsure how to state it properly, she simply grabbed the side of her best afternoon dress and spread the expensive skirt out. "For people like this?"

"Money doesn't solve all the world's problems, you know." Miss Porter tried to give a little laugh, but it was high pitched and tinged on hysteria. Then she whirled once more toward Mr. Lockhart.

"I had to beg for weeks and weeks to be a part of the Committee. If I lose that position because of this blunder, I'm blaming you."

Mr. Lockhart pointed to himself. "Me? I'm not the one who made assumptions."

"You are the one who sent a lady out to Limehouse without telling me."

"I sent a note." Mr. Lockhart's gaze met Clara's over the top of Miss Porter's head as his lips curved into a tiny smile. "And she isn't a lady." He gave a small shrug. "She gets somewhat churlish if you call her one."

Clara lifted a hand to rub at the growing pain in her skull.

"Not a lady . . ." Miss Porter was once more looking back and forth between Clara and the clockmaker. "What is going on here? I never received a note from you."

"That's because I sent it to Uncle Patrick."

"Father has been gone all day, visiting some of our sick parishioners."

"Oh. Well." Mr. Lockhart held out a hand to indicate Clara. "This is Miss Woodbury. She's the cousin of Viscount Eversly and the daughter of a country vicar. While she's in London for the Season, she was hoping to find somewhere to—" He circled his hand in the air as if the words were floating about, waiting for him to grab them. "To perform a few charitable works."

Clara winced at the potential motives implied by Mr. Lockhart's wording, but she said nothing, as what she truly wanted to do was turn the conversation back to this apparently exclusive charity Miss Porter was now assisting. Even Aunt Elizabeth couldn't protest against Clara helping other women who at least appeared well-to-do.

"This committee," Clara said as she stepped in front of Miss Porter. "Are they accepting new members?"

The flush that had begun to fade surged red again. "Not actively, but when they perceive people have certain attitudes, they occasionally extend an invitation. People in London gossip as often as they breathe.

Finding people inclined to protect rather than vilify is a difficult and painstaking procedure."

Miss Porter clasped her hands together. "Please don't tell anyone I mistook you for having been sent here by them. I'd be in so much trouble with both the ladies and my father." She swallowed visibly, her eyes growing wide and round. "Some of those ladies are terrifying."

Clara had only been exposed to the aristocracy for a short time, but she'd already seen a few ladies, particularly some of the older, titled ones, that could certainly be intimidating if they chose to be. She'd like to think herself immune to such earthly social power, but she'd rather not test her fortitude.

"Your secret is safe with me." Clara gave Miss Porter what she hoped was an encouraging smile. "Is there, by chance, a way I could help this charity?"

While she'd never given a thought to a charity designed to aid the wealthy—and even now she struggled to imagine such a thing—it would be an endeavor that even her aunt couldn't find fault with.

"Oh, yes!" Miss Porter's demeanor shifted from concern to excitement at a rate that did nothing to ease the discombobulation in Clara's mind. "Most of the charity is, er, privately funded, but there are other expenses. We at the church have been trying to cover some of them, but it is a stretch. Have you any experience raising funds?"

A sputter of laughter came from Mr. Lockhart. He pressed a hand to his mouth, trying to suppress the sound, but when he glanced at Clara, who was glaring at him with narrowed eyes, he lost the battle and nearly doubled over in laughter.

Miss Porter looked at him with a frown. "I say, you of all people know it takes funds to move forward on any endeavor."

He waved a hand in the air. "It's not that," he choked out, still laughing.

Clara placed her hands on her hips. "Is there nothing in London for a gently born woman to do besides gather money?"

"Well . . ." Miss Porter blinked for a moment. "I'm certain there is, but . . . Well, I don't know of any to point you to right away."

"Have you no poor that need food baskets? Or children that need to be taught to read?"

"Well, yes." Miss Porter frowned and shifted her weight from foot to foot. "Did you want to do the shopping? I confess, I don't see how gathering the items is all that different from gathering the funds, and, well, to be frank we'd need you to peruse less . . . expensive food markets."

Mr. Lockhart's laughter, which had been tapering off, ramped up once more.

"Honestly, Mr. Lockhart." Clara curled her hand into a fist to keep from shaking her finger at the man. "You were the one who told me I could find what I was looking for here, so I don't know why you're laughing. This muddle is at least partially your fault."

He held up the hand that wasn't clasping his box of tools. With his laughter under control but a wide smile still on his face, he said, "You're both free to blame any and all of life's problems on me if it makes you feel better. The other option would be for either of you to actually talk to the other one instead of jumping to conclusions."

He turned to his cousin. "Eleanor, Miss Woodbury would like to be part of the interactions with the people, not the raising of the funds."

"But we need funds."

"I know. But don't you also need hands?"

"Well, yes." Miss Porter bit her lip in thought and then broke into a wide smile. "Have you time to do both?"

Clara opened her mouth to say she wanted only to be with the people, but conviction grabbed her tongue. *But we need funds.* That was so similar to what Mr. Lockhart had said when he spoke of the Virtuous Ladies Society for the Care of Wounded Soldiers.

She lifted her chin and folded her hands primly in front of her as another hope bloomed in her chest. If she could find a group of ton ladies that viewed charity as a more practical endeavor like Clara did, they could help her better navigate the Season. She might even find a friend or two.

"I'm certain I could find room in my schedule, particularly during the afternoons. Perhaps I could meet with this charity you can't speak of and discuss how best to offer my services."

As soon as the words left her mouth, she felt a pang of guilt. One shouldn't have ulterior motives when doing the Lord's work. Perhaps she should just go back to her aunt's drawing room and sip tea.

"There's only so much more we can do without collecting more money." Miss Porter bit her lip and clasped her hands together so tightly the knuckles turned white.

"I've not much experience." Clara tried to look confidant despite her confession. "But I could ask my aunt."

"She can't know what it's for. This work requires absolute discretion."

Considering Clara didn't even know what the funds would be for, keeping it from her aunt wouldn't be a problem. "If we can't discuss the, er, charity, how do they sell subscriptions?"

Mr. Lockhart groaned. "Must you make everything complicated, Eleanor? There has to be something Miss Woodbury can do that does not require such secrecy."

"Well, yes, but . . . Everyone can help with those. It requires a certain attitude to help with this."

That Miss Porter thought Clara could assist in a way most other people could not was all her mind needed to shove aside that niggling idea of guilt. "I would love to help."

Clara and Mr. Lockhart both watched Miss Porter with expectation, but she offered no additional information.

Finally, Mr. Lockhart threw his free hand into the air with a frustrated groan. "There must be someone who is currently arranging the funds for this mysterious group."

"Of course there is." Miss Porter rolled her eyes toward the ceiling before looking at Mr. Lockhart.

"Then introduce Miss Woodbury to that person. You want one-time donations instead of subscriptions, correct?"

"Well, yes, um, there are a series of private, er, subscriptions currently funding the bulk of the endeavor, so onetime gifts are useful." Miss Porter fidgeted and avoided meeting anyone's gaze.

"Then she can organize an event." Mr. Lockhart waved a hand toward Clara as he shook his head. "Now, if you'll pardon me, there's a clock that a lot of people depend upon that needs winding." After a nodding bow to each of the women, he turned and moved up the stairs.

While Mr. Lockhart made everything sound simple, Clara couldn't help but think there were more difficult aspects he was either missing or deliberately avoiding. If it were truly that easy, every foundling hospital and orphan asylum in London would be doing it. She'd seen charity functions listed in the paper, but not very many.

"Hmph. He always thinks the solution is a simple business problem." Miss Porter crossed her arms.

"What is he wrong about?"

She sighed. "Nothing, I suppose. And everything. Things never work in real life like they do on paper. People have a way of changing things when you add them to the mix."

The sound of a door followed by footsteps drifted from the nave. "Eleanor? Did you change out the candles?"

"Oh!" Miss Porter jumped in surprise, then spun around in a circle. "Where did I leave them?" She frowned for a moment. "On the box pew. Pardon me for a moment, Miss Woodbury."

Miss Porter strode quickly back into the nave, leaving Clara to mull things over on her own.

She wanted to help this charity, as much out of curiosity as a desire to be useful. The idea of possibly being welcomed into a secret society of ministry-minded ladies was also appealing.

Her aunt was certain to approve, especially if the person Miss Porter introduced Clara to was of any consequence, but the idea of sitting through more meetings like she had yesterday made her eyes cross.

There had to be another way to do it.

Her gaze drifted up the winding staircase and its graceful wooden railing, dotted every so often with a simple knob of wood to break the smooth line.

Before she could talk herself out of it, she started up the staircase he'd recently climbed. Perhaps if Mr. Lockhart thought it was so much easier than she was making it out to be, he should be the one to help her do it.

TEN

Hugh carefully connected the winding arm to the mechanism of the church's turret clock. His lips curved as he recalled the conversation from moments earlier. There would be weeks, if not months, of teasing Eleanor over the misunderstanding, and he intended to enjoy them all.

Miss Woodbury probably deserved a bit of sympathy, though. Despite his best efforts to not learn anything about her story, he knew enough to know that she wasn't having the best time in London. Their encounters had been intriguing—even more reason to stay as detached as possible—and she'd seem to come out of them all a little worse for wear.

Hopefully Eleanor could change that.

"Gracious, but it is dusty up here."

Hugh's body twisted as his attention snapped to the opening at the top of the narrow stairs leading to the clock chamber. His tools clattered to the floor as he pushed to his feet to face the woman he'd just been thinking about. Sunlight slanted in through the slatted walls, highlighting her face and form in glowing stripes of light.

"Miss Woodbury." He resisted the urge to wipe his hands on his trouser legs. Given the way he'd just been kneeling, his clothing wasn't that much cleaner than his hands, and he wouldn't be touching this woman anyway.

She took a step closer, leaning toward the open door behind him to get a better look at the mechanism that kept the clock running smoothly and precisely. "What are you doing up here?"

Hugh turned to look at the exposed gears as well. "Winding the clock."

She blinked at him. "You mean like one does for a pocket watch?"

"Essentially." He gave a small shrug. "Less often, of course. The turret has longer weights and a much larger spring and, I say, what are you doing up here?"

"Following you."

The simplicity of her straightforward answer caught him off guard, just as her brother and cousin had done the day before. Did this bald and bold way of talking run in the family then? It would take some getting used to.

He cleared his throat. "I suppose that is the obvious answer. What is less obvious is why?"

Following him wasn't exactly simple. There were awkward doors built into the curved walls, steep stairs, and, as she'd mentioned, a lack of cleanliness that should have scared off a well-dressed woman.

"I've come to enlist your assistance." She said it in the same matter-of-fact tone in which she'd admitted to following him, as if the answer should have been more than obvious.

It was not. "Assistance? Have you a broken clock? Do you need your pocket watch wound and reset?"

A small frown pulled her face together. "Reset, perhaps, but I am diligent to wind it twice a day."

Hugh hadn't actually expected her to have such a watch. He tended to notice such things on a person, and he couldn't recall seeing her wear one at any of their encounters.

Even now he couldn't stop his gaze from roaming over her person, looking for a fob or a clip or even a thin chain that could hold a lady's watch. There were nothing but smooth lines and graceful tucks anywhere he looked.

Clearing his throat, he turned back to the job of winding the turret clock. He couldn't let any woman, even one as interesting as Miss Woodbury, distract him from his purpose. Both his immediate one of keeping the clock working correctly for all the neighbors and sailors that depended upon it and the greater one of opening his own shop.

Miss Woodbury was of another mind, though. "I would like to propose a collaboration with you."

He stopped winding once more and looked up at her. "Collaboration."

She gave a single, emphatic nod, her gaze locking confidently with his. Though he didn't want to be, he was the first to look away. "Collaboration on what?"

"Miss Porter has suggested I might be most helpful if I were to plan a fundraiser."

Fortunately, only the gears could see the grin that stretched across his face. He had told her that collecting money was a valuable part of helping the less fortunate. "I'm hardly of the social class you'll want to attract." He glanced at her but kept his face turned to hide his smile. "Perhaps you should see if your aunt has any thoughts."

"My aunt would refuse to consider anything out of the ordinary, and if I'm to do this, I want it to be novel."

He stood and crossed his arms over his chest as he considered her. "Why?"

"Because novelty draws attention." She curled her left hand into a ball before extending the fingers one by one to count off her points of logic. "Attention can be turned into knowledge. Knowledge can become support. And support can become true moral change."

She dropped her hands primly to her sides. "I refuse to believe my time and efforts are worth nothing but money. If I'm to raise funds for a noble cause, then I will do what I can to make those who open their pockets better people as well."

Hugh tried to untwist her words in his mind and the effort brought a frown to his face. He didn't entirely understand her intentions, but he had to admire her conviction. "What is it you want from me?"

"An idea. My aunt's friends will open their reticules for anything that provides them entertainment, and nothing relieves boredom like something new and shiny."

Hugh shook his head as he gave the crank a few final turns before beginning the process of disconnecting the winding arm. His tone was dry as he said, "Your respect for the aristocracy is overwhelming."

"I have done nothing since I arrived in London but shop and drink tea and gossip." She shuddered and looked through the slats at the buildings surrounding the church. "This is the most comfortable I've been since I arrived in Town."

"Only one who has never been in want of it can find money so despicable."

"I don't find money despicable." She sighed. "I find it despicable when one has no other purpose in life but to gain more of it."

On the surface, there should have been nothing wrong with her statement. He, too, believed life should have a greater purpose than the gaining of coin. Yet something about her attitude didn't sit well with him. Was it because he was in business? Because he spent many evenings hunched over a ledger book? Because every expenditure, including those of a more charitable nature, included a consideration of his hopes to open his own shop?

None of those conditions made him a bad person. He loved the Lord and did his best to better the lives of the people he encountered. Yes, there was a financial aspect to his main objective in life, but that would be true of anyone who was responsible for the care of a household, even a simple household of one. Wasn't that acceptable as long as he didn't step on anyone in his path to greater gains?

A very small part of him could not definitively agree with that statement. That minor unrest somehow got control of his mouth because he heard himself discussing her fundraising problem, further embedding him in her situation. "Eleanor won't let you gather funds directly."

Miss Woodbury frowned. "I know. Do you know what it's for?"

Eleanor had always been discreet about her work. Comments here and there, and particularly those from a few moments earlier, gave him a vague idea of who she was helping, but it had never been confirmed. Even if he knew, though, he wouldn't be the one to share her secrets.

Hugh cleared his throat. "She does a lot of good things and helps a lot of people. Some of the situations are . . . delicate."

"What do you suggest, then?"

"Pick another charity?"

"That would leave your cousin without assistance."

"Not if you raise funds for both."

She waited, eyebrows raised. Hugh shifted his feet and then knelt to pack up his tools.

Miss Woodbury sighed. "If you are going to be this tedious about offering every small bit of assistance, I'll find someone else to work with."

Hugh glanced her way, unsure how he felt about her threat, but knowing that her following through on it would be the best for both of them.

She sighed. "Yes, I know that is an empty threat. I don't know anyone else to recruit. Still, I need you to participate with a little more enthusiasm, if you please."

Hugh couldn't help but grin. "Apologies. I'm accustomed to being around people who would rather I speak as little as possible."

She lifted an expectant brow. "As we have just established, I know very few people here in London. If I cannot name a person who would aid me more enthusiastically than you, I certainly am not aware of another charity I could recruit for this project."

Hugh stepped to the slatted window and looked through the sliver of space to see the land on the other side of the river. "Over there, in Greenwich, there's a home for the orphans of sailors lost at sea. Whether in battle or other disaster, these children are left without support when the ocean takes their fathers. As they aren't in London proper, they are frequently overlooked as a potential place to aid."

Her mouth turned down slightly at the corners. "I suppose that would work," she said slowly, dragging the words out to three times their normal length.

"What's wrong with it?" Hugh packed the winding arm back into his box of tools.

She sighed. "It's just that those children, well, it's a sad consequence of the world we live in."

"And that isn't enough to illicit your sympathy?"

"Of course it is, but . . ." She shifted her weight as her words trailed off. Then she crossed her arms and lifted her chin. "The issue is that no one did anything wrong there, did they?"

"I . . . What?" Hugh shook his head. His mind struggled to follow her logic, but he didn't care for any of the destinations his mind ended at. "Are you saying that because there isn't some moral high ground you can espouse, you don't want to help them?"

Her frown curled into a grimace. "When you put it like that, it makes me sound shallow and manipulative."

If the cap fit, she should wear it. He was somewhat disappointed to learn she was just like everyone else he encountered in Aristocratic London, wanting to find a way to feel better than everyone else.

It was just as well. Hugh didn't need to spend what little free time he had thinking about Miss Woodbury. He should be glad that his thoughts were now free to focus on the improvements he wanted to make to chronometers.

Still, Hugh wanted to encourage her to aid the seamen's children. It was one he thought about often when he was up in this tower. "If it helps, recall that Eleanor's charity is quite the opposite."

Miss Woodbury crossed her arms. "Seeing as she won't see her way to allowing me to assist with that one, I'm not certain I find that helpful."

"What's more important?" Hugh picked up his toolbox. "That sinners find grace or that you are the one to show it to them?"

Her mouth dropped open and then snapped shut as her gaze narrowed on him. "You seem determined to twist my words into ill intentions I do not mean."

"Perhaps." He turned to grin at her. "Or perhaps I simply point out the parts you don't want to admit."

He wanted to leave her there, to jog down the steps from the clock room in triumph at getting the last word, but his aunt and uncle had drilled manners into him from the moment he'd stepped into their home. His body simply wouldn't let him be rude to a woman.

Finally, Miss Woodbury sighed and preceded him down the stairs. They went down, then up, then through another room, before descending the wide steps to where Eleanor was waiting for them at the bottom.

"Oh!" Her worried face broke into a smile upon seeing Miss Woodbury. "You are still here."

"Yes." Miss Woodbury got to the bottom of the stairs and fixed her skirts with a little extra fuss than was necessary. "Mr. Lockhart has suggested we utilize two charities and a bit of clever wording. We can discuss one, but split the money among them both."

"What a fabulous idea." Eleanor clasped her hands together and turned wide blue eyes Hugh's way. "I knew you would be the perfect partner in this endeavor."

Hugh shook his head. "I've no idea what use I can be beyond the initial idea."

"Er, yes." Miss Woodbury stepped closer to Eleanor. "To be perfectly honest, I have the same trepidations about myself. I was hoping to render aid more . . . directly. I'm afraid I know little of holding events."

"Oh." Eleanor bit her lips. "I can find something for you, I'm certain. There are always hands needed to fill the soup bowls and mend the donated rags."

Had Miss Woodbury been a clock, Hugh would have been able to hear the gears clinking against each other as she thought. He could almost guess her dilemma. Feeding and clothing the poor were things she'd come here intending to do, but they weren't as appealing as whatever secret Eleanor was hiding.

"I suppose," Miss Woodbury said slowly, though this time her delay seemed to be more thoughtful and less disappointed. "That it would behoove me to add some additional skills to my own charitable methods." She cut a swift glance in Hugh's direction. "Raising funds is essential for the work to continue after all."

Hugh ducked his head to hide his laughter. At least something he'd said seemed to make sense to her, even if only when it provided some sort of gain.

Eleanor matched his grin with an impish one of her own. "Wonderful."

Hugh shook his head slightly. His cousin was incredibly adept at getting people to do whatever she wanted them to do. Over the years, though, Hugh had never been able to determine for certain if she did it on purpose or not.

If the way she was looking at him like a bug she intended to scoop into a cup was anything to go by, at least some of it was intentional.

"No," he said, knowing that if he didn't get his refusal out first, he might not have a chance.

"You don't even know what I was going to ask."

Against his better judgment, he gave her a nod. "And what was that?"

"If you would assist Miss Woodbury."

Hugh's head shake became more emphatic. "As I informed Miss Woodbury upstairs and the both of you mere moments ago, I've no knowledge of such things."

"Neither have I." Miss Woodbury was clearly happy to see someone putting him on the defensive.

"A willing heart and available hands are all God requires, cousin. Do you doubt His ability to use you in this way?" Eleanor blinked at him, a picture of perfect innocence.

Hugh rubbed a hand along the back of his neck and gave a shrug. He might as well save them all some time and give in now. "I'll do it if you tell me what use I can be. I spend my days with balance plates and pendulums."

Miss Woodbury considered him, head tilted to the side. "Is time not what we all find most precious, though? We are all craving more time. Whether it be the need to find a match before the end of the season or the wish to have one more day with a beloved late parent. Perhaps there is something in that idea we can use to make people more desirous of supporting our event."

Eleanor hooked her arm with Miss Woodbury's and Hugh found himself confronted with a wall of mischievous women.

"God would not have you confine your efforts to a mere carriage clock, cousin." Eleanor grinned and looked toward the bell tower above their heads. "You are capable of such magnificence as the tuning of a cathedral's chimes."

"Indeed," Miss Woodbury added. "Life has richer rewards to offer than the solitary labors you undertake. Though you may seem to make time stand still, it marches on anyway."

Hugh looked from one woman to the other. Conversations such as this were common with Eleanor, but he had a feeling Miss Woodbury was just trying to retaliate for his comments upstairs. "You two did meet just a few hours ago, did you not?"

Eleanor laughed. "Just more proof that time is not the Almighty."

"I am well aware of that." Hugh moved toward the door before they could rope him into anything else. "I listened to the same sermons growing up that you did. Just because I don't spend my days in these hallowed halls doesn't mean I didn't learn it."

This time he allowed himself to have the final say and left the church before Eleanor could try to wind her words around him again.

He circled the church and moved toward the rectory in the back. Whenever Hugh came to tend the clock, he stayed to eat with Uncle William. In the winter months, when the sun would be gone early in the afternoon, he would often stay the night. As the days grew longer with the approaching summer, he would usually return home to use those last bits of light to work on a project in the shop.

He glanced back at the church before stepping inside to greet his aunt. Would Eleanor invite Miss Woodbury to eat with them? If so, would Miss Woodbury accept? He'd noticed the viscount's carriage at the edge of the yard, but more than one servant had whiled the day away waiting for their passenger to need their services again.

The real question was, did he want her to be invited to dine with them?

Not wanting to answer that, even to himself, he stepped through the door and focused his attention on his family.

ELEVEN

What had seemed like such an excellent idea in the dusty room of a clock tower across London felt more than a little ridiculous as she entered her cousin's upscale home. There were no cobwebs or rough-hewn planks of wood here, only gilded frames and pristine tables.

What made her think she could change anything about this world? Her good intentions were nothing but a fool's errand.

"You're home." Aunt Elizabeth strode through the drawing room doorway, arms extended and a deep groove between her eyebrows. She grabbed Clara in a fierce hug that flattened every ruffle on both their bodices.

Finally, she stepped back and took a deep breath. "When Ambrose told me he'd lent you the carriage without ensuring a proper chaperon, I was so worried."

Her tone dropped to a whisper and her eyes darted about the front hall as if searching for someone who might have followed her in from the street to lurk in a corner and listen. "Did anyone see you?"

Clara frowned. "I went to a church, Aunt. What does it matter if anyone saw me?"

Aunt Elizabeth blinked. "You went to church?"

"Yes."

"But it's Tuesday."

"People are in need of assistance on Tuesday as much as they are on Sunday."

"But what did you need?"

The memory of Miss Porter's misunderstanding brought a hint of heat to Clara's cheeks. Hopefully, they weren't turning pink enough for anyone to notice. "I was there to offer assistance, not obtain it."

"Oh." She blinked as she appeared to consider the idea. "I suppose that is suitable. Was there a group meeting? Did you see it in the paper? I'm certain Ambrose would be willing to purchase you a subscription for any group you wished to join while you are here."

Seemingly freed of all previous concerns, Aunt Elizabeth ushered Clara into the drawing room where a tea service was set out on a low table. "Which church was it, my dear? I've heard of no one meeting at St. Marylebone." She clasped her hands in her lap. "Did you go to St. George's in Hanover? That could certainly be beneficial."

"Ah, no. I didn't go to St. George's." Clara sat on the edge of the settee and arranged her skirts as her aunt poured the tea. "I went to St. Anne's." She cleared her throat. "Limehouse."

Her aunt's arm jerked, and tea poured directly onto the tray. Cups clattered against each other as she all but dropped the pot onto the tray before fanning herself with a serviette.

Clara frowned, truly concerned about the state of her aunt's composure. The woman's face had lost all color.

Mother swept into the drawing room. "Oh, Clara, you're back. How was your after—Oh." She came to an abrupt halt, gaze roaming over the mess of the tea tray.

"She went to Limehouse," Aunt Elizabeth whispered.

"She did?" Mother turned a questioning look at Clara. "Whatever for?"

"I heard a church there was doing some charity work I might possibly be able to participate in." Clara set about finishing the fixing of the tea, since Aunt Elizabeth was clearly too distraught to continue.

Mother's smile was closer to what Clara was accustomed to seeing. It wasn't the calculated half smile she'd worn as they went out in London, but the loving, indulgent smile she often wore in their country home. "I see."

"Well, I don't," Aunt Elizabeth muttered. "She could have been seen."

Mother cast a glance toward the ceiling. "Anyone who saw her in Limehouse would also be in Limehouse. That means they aren't likely to appear in a ballroom and if they do, they aren't going to admit where they were."

Clara hid a grin behind her teacup. This was the mother she knew and loved.

"Honestly, Elizabeth, it's better that she go help over there if she's determined to get her hands dirty." Mother took her own sip of tea. "What is it they want you to do?"

This was the difficult part. Clara sighed. "They've requested my assistance gathering funds for now."

Mother's lips twitched and pressed together while Aunt Elizabeth emitted a gasp of delight.

"But that's a wonderful thing to do for charity." Aunt Elizabeth clasped her hands together. "Are you going to hold a fete? Organize a special sermon? The Season is starting up, so a ball might not be in high demand, but if the cause and the hostess are right, it could work. What group is it?"

"Well, the, um, church sponsors several things that could make use of the money, but primarily this would be for the Royal Naval Asylum who cares for the orphans of sailors lost at sea." The duplicity of the statement made Clara uncomfortable, and she squirmed a little in her seat. That she didn't even know the name of the second charity eased her conscious some.

"I have no doubt we could get my ladies on board with such a project. It's so closely connected to wounded soldiers. After all, it is the obligation of our social standing to support those who pay the price for the ultimate bravery in battle."

They were good words, but Clara still winced. It was Ambrose's social standing and position that had kept him from being one of those brave soldiers. As the heir of a titled man in already declining health without a spare in sight, no one had wanted to risk his life.

Not that she wanted Ambrose to risk his life on the battlefield. She had prayed day and night when Marmaduke had been considering making such a choice. She'd alternated between praying for his safety and pleading for God to keep him securely in England.

Now that most regiments had returned home and men were struggling to find work, she was even more thankful that God had led him to a different livelihood than the militia. Otherwise, he'd be at risk of being one of the soldiers Aunt Elizabeth's friends said they wanted to help.

"Some of the ladies are most passionate." Mother frowned into her teacup. "Would they truly be willing to adjust their focus?"

Aunt Elizabeth set her cup aside with a sigh. "Miriam, have you truly forgotten so much as you rot away in the country?"

Clara stiffened and her cup clanked harshly against the saucer as she almost sent another wave of tea flooding down onto the tray.

Aunt Elizabeth didn't seem to notice. Instead, she took the serviette she'd been fanning herself with and held it as one would a delicate, lace-trimmed handkerchief while she dabbed at eyes suddenly sheened with suspicious tears.

"What greater wound is there than death? Our poor soldiers, wounded beyond redemption in this life, their final thoughts likely a plea for God to see to the care of the little ones they shall never see again. We owe those men, ladies, to offer their children a guiding hand, to usher them into the brighter future their fathers boldly fought for. We cannot give those men back their lives, but we can join this noble venture and help them live on in their children."

Even Clara was moved by her aunt's impassioned speech. Perhaps she'd been wrong about the older woman all along. She obviously cared deeply for her cause and—

"You see?" Aunt Elizabeth's tears were immediately gone as a wide smile split her face. "'Tis a simple matter to move a soft heart from one goal to the other."

Forgetting propriety, Clara sagged back against the settee. She had no doubt that the Virtuous Ladies Society for the Care of Wounded Soldiers would be willing to be the Virtuous Ladies Society for the Care of Orphans of Lost Sailors for a time, but she would never look at her aunt the same way again.

What else was an act put on for the sake of propriety and personal goals? Did she truly want to be helping Clara this year? Was her desire to procure a good match for her niece covering some other glorified mission?

The questions plagued her as she spent time on her embroidery, as she dressed for the evening, as she sat for her hair to be curled and pinned, and even as she stood waiting in the hall for her aunt and mother to join her.

In the quiet of the large room, her thoughts finally settled, blanketed by the pragmatism that had driven most of her life. The truth was, it simply didn't matter what was motivating her aunt. It wasn't as if Clara was giving a lot of consideration to Aunt Elizabeth.

She was here because, regardless of her desire for it to be otherwise, Clara needed to marry. If she was thinking of anyone else's wishes on the matter, it was her mother, who would prefer Clara go about attaining the match in a fashion that resembled her own first Season.

No, her aunt's ambitions weren't as important as the fact that Clara had selected a man that fit all her criteria, determined a timeline that would get her out of London at an acceptable speed, and found a reasonable project to occupy her mind in the meantime.

With her thoughts and objectives settled, Clara sat quietly in the carriage, allowing her aunt and mother to chatter on about dresses and people and what entertainment the evening might provide. There was nothing for her to do until they arrived at the ball and she could seek out her intended match.

They had not yet formed a strong enough connection for Clara to expect him to be looking for her, so she would need to find him. Unfortunately, being of average height meant she couldn't see past the people in her immediate vicinity. She considered asking after him, but that would be more likely to make her the object of gossip than the object of suitors' affections.

Hopefully, soon they would have been seen together enough that well-meaning gossips would volunteer his whereabouts as soon as she entered a venue.

Until then, Clara was on her own. She stepped to the right, intending to circle the room and look for his artful blond waves, but her aunt's hand on her arm stopped her progress.

The hand slid around until her aunt's elbow was linked with Clara's. "This way, my dear."

Rounding the rooms to the left would suit her just as well, so Clara tripped along after the older woman. They entered the ballroom and Aunt Elizabeth continued moving, a certain destination obviously in mind.

Clara's gaze slid to the dancers already twirling about the middle of the floor. It was still relatively early in the evening and already there were so many people here. Were there even this many people in her entire little village?

If her aunt hadn't been holding her arm, Clara might have fled for the door. She'd heard of the crushes in London, but never quite expected this.

"How am I to find anyone here?" Clara whispered into her aunt's ear.

"You are not here to find. You are here to be found." Aunt Elizabeth smiled around the quiet words, nodding at people they passed. "The gentlemen will be approaching you, not the other way around, which is why we must position you to advantage."

As Clara had already selected the perfect potential partner, she would prefer all her time and energy go into solidifying the match. That was a naïve notion, though. She might be from a small village in the country, but her mother had the social niceties of a baron's daughter and Clara had been taught them as well.

If only they weren't so frustratingly inefficient.

"Do you know if Mr. Pitt is here?"

Aunt Elizabeth frowned. "Likely. He usually is." She paused and looked Clara in the eye. "We can do better, you know."

By whose standards? Clara had no wish to be in London, to be constantly considering who could help her advance socially or benefit her husband financially, to never know who was being genuine and who was fishing for gossip. "Better is a matter of opinion."

The only response her aunt gave was a low, grumbling grunt. Her frown was soon replaced with the perfect smile as she struck up a conversation with a few other chaperons.

A nudge here and a poke there, and Clara soon found herself removed from the conversation and all but presented to the ballroom. She watched the dancers go by, trying to keep a smile in place as she exchanged brief nods with the other ladies waiting to be asked to join the frolicking ranks.

The dance drew to a close, and the ladies straightened their spines and skirts. Conversations filled with quiet laughter and encouraging murmurs sprang up, but the words were nonsense, a mere excuse to positions their bodies and their fans to advantage.

Gentlemen returned dancers to their chaperons before setting out to select someone new.

Clara's brows drew together. How did they make their selections? The prettiest ones, obviously, were barely released to their mothers before their hand was reclaimed, but what other criteria were being used? If she could find the commonality, then she could get herself asked as well.

There wasn't one she could find, though. Some were plain, some wore enough jewels to all but glitter in the candlelight. Some were smiling and simpering, while others stood tall and proud.

It was obvious if Clara wanted to peruse the entire ballroom and determine Mr. Pitt's presence, she would have to do so by dancing, but there didn't seem to be any rhyme or reason to getting oneself on the dance floor.

"Do stop frowning." Aunt Elizabeth pinched Clara's side. "Mr. Thompson is coming this way."

Clara smoothed her features and turned to the man she'd met at her last event. He asked her to dance, and she accepted because she'd attended enough country dances to know that one refusal left a girl relegated to the side of the room for the entire evening.

The dance was pleasant enough. She did, indeed, see Mr. Pitt dancing with another young woman, and Mr. Thompson was easy enough to converse with, even if most of the conversation revolved around the horse he intended to bet on when he next went to Ascot.

When she'd mentioned that those funds might be better spent elsewhere or perhaps donated to a good cause, Mr. Thompson and only grinned and said, "Think of how much more I can give them after I win, though."

As the night wore on, Clara found that she was not the most in-demand lady at the ball, but she rarely spent two consecutive sets at her aunt's side. Finally, when she'd begun to consider doing something as desperate or apparently scandalous as walking through the ballroom on her own, the man she'd came to see stopped in front of her.

Her smile was wide as she placed her hand in his and allowed herself to be led to the dance floor.

"I've never known Lady Eversly to sponsor anyone for the season," Mr. Pitt said as they joined the lines. "You must be a special young lady, indeed."

A light flush burned the back of Clara's neck as she smiled at the compliment. "She is my aunt."

He tilted his head. "You are the viscount's cousin?"

"Yes."

They stepped away from each other to execute the moves of the dance and Clara took a moment to even her breathing and try to remember all her aunt's lessons. This was the man she wanted to attract, after all, and if he was in London, he would expect certain behaviors, even if he considered them frivolous as a future clergyman.

"This is my first time in London," she said when they could speak again. "Do you come here often?"

"'Tis my primary residence of late," he said with a grin. "What young man wants to be anywhere other than Town, after all."

"Oh? You find the city, er, exhilarating?" Concern nibbled at the edge of her confidence.

"I find the city full of opportunity."

Once again, the dance pulled them apart, and Clara took a calming breath. How could she doubt the man? Of course London was where he wanted to be while unencumbered by family or his own congregation. The city was full of people who needed to know the good news God offered.

The conversation continued in bits and pieces as they danced the set. It was, perhaps, a little predictable and inane, but it was the first time they'd spent any length of time together. Superficial small talk was to be expected.

As they changed to the second dance of the set, she began to worry that such simple conversation wasn't going to be enough to secure his attention.

What else could she do, though?

As they stood at the end of the line, awaiting their turn to engage with the dance again, she took a chance at a deeper conversation. "Have you given thought to the future?"

He chuckled. "As a third son, Miss Woodbury, I assure you that I am always aware of the future."

"Why does that matter?"

"Birth and society haven't set my path as firmly as my elder brothers. My future is something I must invent."

"I feel the same, which is why I agreed to come to London."

The lift of his eyebrow indicated Clara's words might have been a little too bold and honest for such a short acquaintance. The tightness of embarrassment hit the back of her throat as she dropped her gaze.

Fortunately, the dance required they step back into the formation and their conversation returned to polite chatter.

As he escorted her off the dance floor, though, he tipped his head toward her. "Miss Woodbury, might I be so bold as to inquire about which days this week you shall be receiving visitors?"

Years of maintaining her composure kept Clara from clapping her hands in glee. God truly was going before her. "We intend to be at home tomorrow."

He bowed over her hand before relinquishing it to Aunt Elizabeth. "Until tomorrow, then."

Clara nodded back. "Until tomorrow."

"What is happening tomorrow?" Aunt Elizabeth asked as Mr. Pitt walked away.

"I believe Mr. Pitt intends to come for a visit."

The curls draping over Clara's ear danced in the breeze of the hefty sigh her aunt emitted. "If you are truly set on him, then I suppose that is a good thing." She shook her head. "You are too much like your mother. She, too, was determined to throw away any chance for advancement."

Too pleased with her latest accomplishment to be irritated, Clara grinned in return. "That depends on what direction one is trying to go."

The remainder of the evening was frightfully dull. Part of her hoped Mr. Pitt would ask her to dance again, but such partiality so early in their connection would have been suspicious. Even Clara would wonder at such speed. It wasn't as if he could have picked her name out of a book of potential brides.

Besides, she had a project now. It would be much easier to be patient and stop praying for God to move as expeditiously as she'd originally asked.

More time in London also gave her more time with Ambrose. She hadn't realized until moving into his London home quite how much of a reprobate he had become over the past few years. He'd always been something of a scoundrel, but since arriving in London she'd seen him do nothing that wasn't for his own enjoyment, whether proper or not.

All in all, the evening had been successful, and she went to bed counting her blessings.

She woke early the next morning, a little tired, but still in a good mood. Her body refused to adjust to Town hours, and she continued to rise well before the rest of the house's occupants.

Most mornings she would stroll through the ground floor, sipping on a mug of tea as she looked out different windows and watched London awaken in the early morning light.

The last thing she expected to find as she meandered into a small, private drawing room that she'd yet to explore was Mr. Lockhart.

TWELVE

Hugh curled his hand around the delicate spring he'd just removed from the chronometer on the table. The sharp edge bit into his palm, but that wasn't enough to pull his attention from the doorway.

Daylight was just visible through the window behind him, but it would be several hours before the sun trailed through the window enough to properly light his worktable. The lantern he'd placed on the corner sent out a circle of light that seemed to accentuate his unexpected visitor.

Miss Woodbury stood just inside the room, dressed in a pink morning gown, hands wrapped around a sturdy white mug the servants had probably shuddered to provide for her. Steam curled from the mug and caught the steady flicker of light. He followed it up until he met her wide eyes.

The surprised *O* her mouth had dropped into almost made him laugh, but he kept his wits about him as he set the spring and his tool aside and rose to his feet. He gave her a sharp bow of his head. "Good morning, Miss Woodbury."

"What are you doing here?"

His gaze dropped to the table strewn with parts and tools. "Working?"

"Do you not have a shop for that?" One hand smoothed down the edges of her wrap. "And reasonable hours?"

"Seeing as the shop isn't mine, and this work isn't for the shop, no, I don't have another place to do this." He shrugged. "And I also have to do it on my own time."

The obvious discombobulation of his companion made him want to continue to play out the conversation, but he had a limited amount of time to work before reporting for his paying job. That made it necessary to volunteer the information she sought and get back to work.

"Your cousin offered this room as a workspace since it gets a great deal of evening light. He and his friend are sponsoring my entry for consideration in Greenwich."

She blinked a few times. "It isn't evening."

"That's why I have a lamp." He couldn't stop the grin that pulled at his lips. "But I plan to return this evening. I'm afraid I woke this morning with an idea I didn't want to lose, so I came by to test it and add it to my notes."

Not to mention a portion of his evening visit was likely to be taken up by a game of billiards and dinner. It was a strange situation, but his friendship seemed to be part of the exchange for funding, and Hugh had found he was more than amiable to the cost.

Miss Woodbury looked from him to the table and back again before slowly taking a deep drink from her mug.

He expected her to utter a quiet goodbye and beat a hasty retreat, and he found the idea unsettling. Despite the amount of work he needed to do in a very short amount of time, he wanted her to stay.

Company wasn't a normal part of his work environment, but he'd found that talking to her made his mind consider alternative ideas. And he simply liked doing it.

So he tried to keep her there, even as he picked up a pair of delicate tweezers. "Was your evening enjoyable?"

"I suppose." She frowned as she drank from her mug and wandered over to the window. "It was productive, which is likely the best I can hope for."

"Why wouldn't you hope for enjoyment?"

She tossed him a dry look over her shoulder. "I am in London."

"Most of the world considers London a center of culture and entertainment."

"Which is precisely the problem." She shook her head. "While I am certain God places those who are stout of heart in the middle of the mire to cleanse those embedded in it, I find my inclinations are to be more removed from such worldly considerations."

Hugh coughed and gave his head a brisk shake to loosen the scrambled thoughts her overserious words inspired. "Worldly considerations?"

"As a businessman, I wouldn't expect you to understand, but there is little good and honorable and pure in London for me to focus on."

Hugh used the tweezers to affix the spring to a thin hook, then set the tweezers aside to give Miss Woodbury his full attention. At the moment, she was far more fascinating than his new chronometer. "Why would you confine God in such a way?"

Her frown turned from the window to him. "I am not confining God, and it is a horrible idea for you to suggest. God is all-powerful and capable."

"Is He?" Hugh made himself look thoughtful. "Even capable of putting something good, honorable, and pure in the coal darkened streets of London?"

She sighed and narrowed her eyes at him. "I see what you are doing."

That's because she was an intelligent woman. "I should hope so." Hugh grinned. "Otherwise, I would have to seriously question my abilities at communication."

Her attention dropped to the gears and springs strewn across the worktable. "Why do you make clocks?"

"I make clocks because Mr. Johns pays me to." He looked across the table and a deep sense of purpose settled into his middle. "I make chronometers because the world is large and the only thing every place and person on this earth has in common is that they move forward through time to the next moment."

"There is a difference between chronometers and clocks then?"

He nodded trying to restrain his words to something simple that wouldn't have her fainting in boredom. "You carry a pocket watch, do you not?"

"Yes." She frowned. "It is not on me now, of course, but I have taken to carrying one here in London."

"You didn't carry one before?"

"No." She lowered herself thoughtfully onto the edge of a settee that had been pushed against the far wall. "Which is, I think, evidence of the goodness of the countryside."

"You find knowing the time of day a source of evil?"

"I find the limitations placed on me by such adherence to time a distraction from allowing God to mark my path."

He'd never heard anything so strange in his life. Yes, at this moment, she consumed every corner of his mind, burying all thoughts of springs and counterweights. Her views of time were even more important than his desire to educate people on how much more reliable chronometers had to be than a regular clock.

He stepped back from his worktable but didn't cross the room to sit next to her. It wouldn't do for this interlude to appear cozy, should someone else find them here. Best for him to stay standing and the table to stay between them. She might feel comfortably free in this house, but he was well aware that his ability to continue to work and design here relied on the goodwill of her cousin.

The viscount was quite affable for an aristocrat, but he wouldn't take kindly to Hugh doing anything that would call Miss Woodbury's honor into question.

In fact, Hugh should make his excuses and leave the woman to her own space in her own home, but he was too fascinated to do so.

In Hugh's eyes, time was a captivating gift, a way to connect people. It didn't matter how wealthy someone was or how disreputable. Five o'clock was five o'clock for everyone.

"You find knowing dinner will be served at half past five to be limiting God's direction?"

Her nose scrunched up. "It sounds ridiculous when you put it like that, but if you'd ever spent time in the house of a vicar you would know that, yes, it is in a way. I don't know the number of times Cook had to keep food warm or make up a cold plate because Father's duties required his presence in the evening."

Uncle Patrick's house was much the same way, so while Hugh could recognize the truth in her words, he knew such cases were the exception rather than the rule.

"Is it also limiting for a church service to start at a particular time?"

She pointed a finger at him, and the side of her lip twitched. "You are deliberately twisting my meaning, sir, in an attempt to knock me sideways, but I shall not be slain in such a manner. I am aware that time must be observed when multiple people, particularly members of a community, are attempting to align their days or weeks at a certain point."

"Then what makes it a problem in the city? That is all people are doing here."

"There's simply so much of it." She set her mug on the floor and stood to pace from the settee to the door and back again. Three steps, turn, three steps, turn. It was an incredibly short walk that almost made her appear to be doing some strange sort of dance.

He fought the wide grin the picture inspired.

Suddenly she stopped and faced him, hands on her hips. "It is one thing for someone to know that dinner is taking place at half of six or that the Sunday service commences at ten in the morning. It is quite another to have one's entire day blocked off in predetermined divisions. To do so is to tell God how you will spend your day instead of allowing Him to direct it."

"You make no plans for tomorrow?"

"Ye know not what shall be on the morrow."

"But you are here in London, attempting to make a marriage match. What is that if not planning for the future?"

She sighed. "That would not be my first choice."

Hugh chuckled. "And yet."

"My need for a husband, and the provision such a relationship brings, is simply an indication of the fallen world we live in."

"So is that dress you are wearing."

Heat crawled up his neck at the implication of his statement and a matching flush appeared on her cheeks. For a moment they both stared at each other. He didn't know what she was thinking, but he was giving serious consideration to what it would be like to hold her in a dance or walk along the street with her arm tucked in his.

They were all but alone in this quiet house, and he was suddenly very aware of that fact.

He cleared his throat and busied himself setting the table to rights. "What I mean is there are many aspects of this world that exist because of man's imperfections. Knowledge of time is simply one of those. Why do you consider it worse than the others?"

She retrieved her mug but remained standing by the door. "Have you seen Ambrose's diary?"

"Er, I confess I have not."

"It is full of meetings. Some of them are with himself so he can go over ledger books or answer correspondence. Even his leisure time is predetermined."

That seemed a normal way of living to Hugh. Many of his customers lived life in such a way, which was why their clocks and watches were so important. "What is wrong with that? It seems normal to me."

"I suppose it is normal if one lives life consumed with business or politics."

"I'm to gather from the tone of your voice that you think little of such endeavors."

"They do seem to swallow the whole of London."

"It is a city. One can hardly grow a crop of wheat along Pall Mall or keep chickens in Grosvenor Square. There are still sheep in Hyde Park, but they are the concern of a select few."

"That is my point, exactly." She indicated his worktable again. "The more people concern themselves with things they make instead of caring for and developing that which God placed under our domain, the further we get from his holiness." She ran a finger over the edge of a gilded frame on the wall. "And then we become consumed with gaining more of it."

An immediate rebuttal formed in his mind, but he clamped his lips shut to keep it to himself. The intensity of her words belied a significant conviction, and that deserved his honest contemplation.

After several moments of consideration, he concluded she was wrong. Mostly.

"You've a kitchen garden at the rectory, I presume?"

She frowned in confusion. "Of course."

"Do you use a rock to prepare the soil?"

Her frown deepened. "Of course not." Her chin lifted a notch and her gaze slid away from his. "It is normally prepared and planted by someone else, but I've worked our garden enough to know what a hoe and a rake are."

"And how long have such tools been used in gardens?"

Wide eyes turned back to him. "How would I know?"

He shrugged. "I haven't the faintest as I don't know the answer either. What I do know is that Cain didn't have them."

"Are you referring to Cain in the Bible?"

"The very one."

"Of course he didn't have one. He's"—she waved her arms about—"one of the first people to walk the earth."

"Yet someone, somewhere invented such tools. Someone invented the needle you use to make stitches and the stove your cook uses to make toast. Do you consider visiting the ladies or your parish a noble, God-honoring pursuit?"

"While I believe you are trying to trick me with this question, the answer is obviously yes. It is important to know what is going on in the parish and for the people to know they are cared about."

"The pot that holds your tea and the carriage that takes you to the village are all things that changed how people spent their day and where they gave their attention. And yet, you have no problem seeing how God can use these items."

"What is your point?"

"My point is that maybe it isn't a lack of good and honorable things in the city, but a determination not to see them for yourself."

She stood and narrowed her gaze. "That is quite the stretch, Mr. Lockhart. One has only to consider the many areas of Town where I am not allowed to venture, or how very delicate my reputation seems to be while I am here, to know there is far more darkness lurking here than in the country."

"Is it more darkness or simply different risks?" He'd been to the country to deliver large clocks, and he'd heard the customers discuss their days away from the city. He had yet to see evidence that people who collected their own eggs instead of purchasing them from the market were all that more holy.

"Speaking of risks, the hour grows late, and I should not be dallying alone in this room with you."

He couldn't refute that statement. The gentlemanly thing to do would be to leave her alone in the room and make his way home, but he wasn't particularly keen to leave her with his work when she seemed to despise it.

Lord Eversly has assured him the staff would be instructed to leave this room untouched and the thin collection of dust on the edge of the table indicated he had followed through.

Miss Woodbury's presence this morning meant she had not been given the same instruction. She might not give his work the same respect.

Yet, he considered himself a gentleman and the right thing to do was still the right thing to do. This was more her home than his. "I will—"

"I bid you good day." She clasped her mug to her chest, stuck her nose in the air, and strode from the room.

Hugh stood for several minutes, feeling oddly like he'd been put in his place instead of having the last word in their near argument.

Finally, he picked up another spring and turned it in the light of the lantern.

When he'd taken his apprenticeship, Uncle Patrick had made Hugh memorize Colossians 3:23 and recite it every morning. He still rolled the verse around in his mind when he woke each day.

And whatsoever ye do, do it heartily, as to the Lord, and not unto men.

Never before had he stopped to ask himself if the burning desire to make a better chronometer was a fitting interpretation of the verse. His entire life felt far more unstable than it had half an hour ago.

And he had Miss Woodbury to blame.

THIRTEEN

Mr. Pitt indeed came to visit Clara. He was, in fact, the only man to
come visiting. They took tea and discussed the previous night's
ball. Aunt Elizabeth carried as much of much of the conversation as
Clara. Possibly even more.

Clara had not anticipated how awkward it would be to try to have a
discussion or get to know a man with her aunt and mother in attendance.
She couldn't say anything without examining the sentence in her mind
first to make sure the two chaperons would approve.

It had to have been even worse for Mr. Pitt. No wonder he didn't seem
inclined to speak of anything of consequence. The situation must feel
like something of an inquisition.

Had society always been like this? No, it couldn't have. There were
certainly cases of parental involvement in Biblical marriage accounts, but
that was different than today's brief visit.

Mr. Lockhart's words from that morning drifted into her head, reminding her that people and societies grew and developed and changed
over time. She pushed the words away. Yes, the world changed, but God
did not, so the idea of accepting new technologies and conveniences did
not change the consistency of character a person should possess.

Her confidence in that stance was more than a little shaky, though.

She considered the idea off and on throughout the day, as she drank
cup after cup of tea, and visited with her aunt's friends that stopped

by for a chat but were secretly wanting to know if Clara's Season had managed a successful start.

As the only other man to come calling was an older gentleman who seemed more interested in Clara's widowed aunt than Clara, she would guess that most of London would consider her entry to society as less than a splash.

Mr. Pitt had come by, though, so in Clara's mind she was well on her way to success.

At least, she wanted to see things that way. The words of a trades-man had her second-guessing that way of thinking, though.

Even as she prepared for that night's gathering, the early morning conversation played through her mind. Was it London that was the problem, or was it her?

Exactly whose fault was it that she felt out of place in this city? Then again, it was possible no one was to blame because her discom-fort wasn't a fault. It was merely a preference of lifestyle.

But if that were the case, it meant she was wrong about the dark-ness and depravity of London, and she simply couldn't accept that based on her recent observations.

The swirl of thought was enough to leave her quite out of sorts. Her heart thumped hard enough in her chest that drawing a full breath was difficult as she walked beside her aunt into another ball.

Candles flickered everywhere until there was nary a shadow to be found in the grand ballroom. No one would be escaping to dark alcoves tonight, it would seem. Not that she had plans of doing so, but she'd heard the whispers in the retiring room and the plainly spoken speculation in her aunt's drawing room.

She took a deep breath and stepped further into the room. This new trepidation was silly. Her situation was the same today as it had been yesterday before she talked to Mr. Lockhart.

Because she didn't want to be a burden to her parents, she needed a husband.

Because she loved her mother, he needed to be somewhat socially acceptable.

Because she wanted to be like her father, he needed to have a heart for the people around him.

Because she wanted to truly know the people who surrounded her, he needed to want a fairly quiet life in the country.

Daunting though such a task might seem, she was confident that she'd found the perfect candidate, so it didn't matter what Mr. Lockhart thought of her view of the world.

Except . . .

She sighed. Choosing a man was one thing. Getting him to choose her back was another. Yes, Mr. Pitt had come to visit today, but she had to admit he hadn't looked to prolong his stay beyond the point of politeness.

He lived primarily in London, which meant he understood the expectations of the Season. If she wanted to garner more than a passing curiosity from him, she needed to show that she knew how to socialize.

Fortunately, God had provided Clara with an expert.

"Where would you like me to go, Aunt?"

"You've finally seen the light, have you?" Aunt Elizabeth gave an approving nod, the feather in her hair bobbing in merry agreement. "We'll place ourselves near that end of the room. It doesn't appear to be where the top-tier debutantes are gathering, but, well, you'll be able to make some friends between dances. That looks good. No man wants an unliked bride."

Clara refrained from frowning, but only by sheer force of will.

As they approached the area, Clara searched the faces of the well-dressed ladies and the handful of gentlemen engaged in conversation. She didn't know any of them.

Aunt Elizabeth made the introductions, beaming at the entire group. She then stepped aside to strike up a conversation with two other nearby matrons.

Though it was difficult, Clara maintained her smile as the group indulged in the common idle chatter new acquaintances relied upon. Even though it was necessary, she found the situation tedious. It was so much easier when everyone already knew each other and people were willing to discuss their true feelings and problems.

That wasn't the way of London, though, and Clara was determined to make a show of giving the city a try so that Mr. Lockhart couldn't accuse her otherwise when she declared the area unacceptable.

"I believe I saw you last week? At a dinner Mrs. Benneton hosted?" Miss Harlington smiled, her lips the same shade as her pale pink gown. The expression didn't feel all that welcoming, despite the curved lips. Perhaps it was the flatness of her eyes.

Clara returned the smile, hoping hers looked more natural than Miss Harlington's. "Yes. I was there. It was my first London outing, actually."

"Oh?" Her eyebrows lifted as she looked Clara up and down. "This is your first time in London?"

"Where are you from?" Another girl, whose name Clara had already forgotten, asked.

"Eldham."

"I've never heard of it. Is it quaint?"

"Oh, it's lovely. There's a glorious field outside of town. It's surrounded by trees, but you get the most glorious views and the breeze comes through there in the summer." Clara's smile felt far more natural as she spoke of home.

Miss Harlington's still looked rather wooden. "I myself find the summer breezes do very inconvenient things to my bonnet strings."

"Oh yes," the other girl said. "I spend half my life redressing my hair when staying in the country."

"Such a shame you've had to wait so long to experience London. You must be, what, three and twenty?"

It was now Clara's smile that was forced. Clearly Miss Harlington was not in the mood to make new friends. "Not quite yet. I am but two and twenty."

"If you truly want to experience a relaxing summer, you should travel to Bath," Mr. Payne said.

"Oh, yes." Miss Harlington clasped her hands together as she rolled into an account of the healing waters and fashionable assemblies. "It was very restorative." She fluttered her fan and her eyelashes.

Clara's stomach fluttered in disgust.

Still, she smiled and nodded in all the right places until the string quartet in the corner began to play. The men each selected a lady and departed for the dance floor, leaving Clara, the girl without a name, and another young lady with a particularly pinched expression standing in a cluster on the edge of the floor.

Perhaps Clara could make headway now that the group was smaller. "Have you been to the theater this year? I hope to attend soon." It was the one city indulgence she'd been looking forward to in London.

The girl with the pinched face managed to pucker her expression even more. "Do you find life so unappealing that you must pretend to live someone else's for an evening?"

Clara's mouth dropped open a little as the girl beside her sidled away, chirping, "Oh, my, I believe my mama is beckoning me."

It would now be unspeakably rude for Clara to beg a need for punch or some other excuse. She would have to remain in this unhappy girl's company.

"The frivolity is rather cloying, is it not?"

Clara made an indeterminate noise that might or might not have been agreement. At least she could find comfort in knowing that despite her lack of success—and she had to admit her attempt at conversation had fallen flat—she wasn't the most unsociable person in the room.

This wasn't what people thought of her, was it?

Just as the couples were squaring off to begin the dance, a gangly fellow approached her end of the ballroom. She didn't know him, had never been properly introduced, but she'd agree to dance with him anyway if it got her away from this conversation.

But he didn't ask Clara.

He asked the pinched-face girl.

What she wouldn't give for the closest alcove to be just a little bit darker right then. She set her teeth and resolved to learn more from the evening.

There'd be another chance tomorrow.

Hugh had spent most of his life knowing exactly who he was. Whether it was as a dutiful son, an obligatory apprentice, or an overworked shop clerk, his role in life had always been obvious. Thanks to his uncle, he'd grown up knowing that role wasn't who he was as a person, but even a child of God had a place he belonged in the world.

Now, though, Hugh didn't even know which door he was meant to enter the house through. He'd come in through the front door the day he'd come for dinner, but now that he was essentially working here, it felt necessary to enter through the kitchens.

His time in the house, though, was hardly spent like a servant's would be. It was almost like he was renting a room but without the exchange of money. He worked on his own projects and was occasionally pulled into conversation with the master of the house. Such activity would imply he was more of a guest than an employee.

And yet . . .

Hugh slid his hands along the brim of his hat as he climbed the stairs to the ground floor of the house. Today he'd opted for the kitchen door, but it had been an uncomfortable entrance for all involved.

There were so many confusing elements to his current position that it was best to just stumble along as best he could and hope it all worked out.

At the top of the stairs, he turned to head toward the drawing room he'd been directed to but almost ran headfirst into Mr. Woodbury.

"Goodness, my man." Mr. Woodbury chuckled and steadied himself with a hand on Hugh's shoulder. "Didn't know you were there. I was just with Ambrose, though, and I don't recall Hodges announcing you."

"I, ah, came in through the kitchens."

He frowned. "Why would you do that?"

"Because that's what people of a certain rank do." Perhaps the athletic man wasn't as bright as Hugh had originally given him credit for.

Mr. Woodbury grinned and pointed the deck of cards in his hand toward Hugh. "That's the beautiful thing about a home. Guest is a most honored rank."

"But I'm not a guest."

"Did the lord of the manor ask you to be here?"

Hugh could see where this was going, but there was no stopping it now. He sighed. "Yes."

"Do you have any specific tasks to do while you're here?"

Technically speaking, he did have a specific task to do, but it wasn't being watched over by Lord Eversly. "Not as such."

Mr. Woodbury nodded in recognition of Hugh's decision to not deliberately misunderstand the question. "Are you being paid to be here?"

With a lift of his eyebrows, Hugh said, "After a fashion."

Mr. Woodbury shook his head. "No. I was there for the agreement. Your bills are being paid, not you."

It was a fine point of distinction, but Hugh had to acknowledge it was true. A single dip of his chin was the only admission he was willing to give.

"See? You are a guest." Mr. Woodbury stepped to the side. "Hodges, are you there?"

The distinguished older man stepped into the front hall. Hugh leaned to the left, trying to see which room the man had materialized from. Had he been listening in? Probably. Lurking was the best way to know everything that was going on in the house, after all.

"You called, sir?" The butler inclined his head toward Mr. Woodbury and then Hugh.

"Mr. Lockhart here"—Mr. Woodbury clapped a hand on Hugh's shoulder—"is to be allowed entrance to the house through the front door when he comes and goes. It'll probably be odd hours of the day, but he's got free access to that back drawing room."

The butler's gaze slid briefly to Hugh before returning to Mr. Woodbury. "I have already been instructed as such by his lordship, sir."

Mr. Woodbury gave Hugh a slight shove as he lifted his hand. "You see? Guest. Just walk up and knock."

Hugh knew better than to argue with the butler who wasn't about to argue with the man in charge of the house. If Lord Eversly wanted Hugh to use the front door, he would use the front door.

Even if the idea made him feel even more out of place than before.

Hugh gave the butler a respectful nod. "I shall endeavor not to arrive at too inconvenient an hour, Hodges."

"Now that we've settled that, come up to Ambrose's study." Mr. Woodbury waved the deck of cards in the air. "He's making me play Speculation."

Hugh should make an excuse. He had limited time and light with which to work, but it had been so long since he'd done something just because it sounded fun.

Besides, keeping his investor happy with him could only be a good thing.

Hugh waved a hand toward the stairs. "Lead on."

"Excellent."

The card game didn't last long, and they quickly ended up back in the billiard room. Hugh kept one eye on the clock and another on the light coming through the window. Fun or not, rare or not, he still needed to spend time in his work room if he wanted to finish his chronometer.

He leaned over the table, sent the trio of balls bouncing around the bumpers, and scored enough points to call it a win.

"Good game, Hugh. May I call you Hugh?" Lord Eversly took a drink from the tumbler of scotch that had been ever present all evening.

Either he was taking the smallest sips known to man or he was adept at secretly refilling his glass. Not knowing which it was only bothered Hugh because it was impossible to know how genuine his apparent friendship was.

"I would be honored for you to use my name." Hugh slid the cue into the rack.

"Excellent." Lord Eversly gestured toward Hugh with the hand still holding the glass of amber liquid. "In private, you may call me Ambrose."

"Even though that's not his name." Mr. Woodbury stored his own cue as he laughed.

Ambrose frowned. "It is so my name." He shifted his weight. "It just isn't my first name." The viscount sighed and added, "My first name is Richard, but my father's name was Richard as well, so growing up everyone called me by my second name, Ambrose. My full name is Richard Ambrose Whitney, Viscount Eversly." He winced. "Mother always said it was because I was enough trouble for three little boys."

"As she would have saddled you with the moniker before you'd had a chance to misbehave, that would seem to be a self-fulfilling prophecy," Hugh muttered before he could stop himself.

There was a beat of silence and then both men started to laugh.

"You're all right, Hugh Lockhart." Ambrose nodded.

The discussion rolled on for a few more minutes until the viscount began discussing his plans to go out for the evening. At that point, Hugh removed himself before they could try to rope him along on that misadventure.

In the quiet of his small drawing room, he took a few minutes to consider how quickly life could change. Things he'd never allowed himself to want, never allowed himself to think of as lacking in his life, were coming his way.

Without his permission, his gaze slid to the seat by the door where Miss Woodbury had sat that morning.

He shook his head and gave his attention to the chronometer. It wouldn't do to be greedy. His life had the potential to be better than he'd dared to dream. He wouldn't risk that by thinking he could reach for the moon.

FOURTEEN

C lara wasn't able to make any marked progress at the musicale Aunt Elizabeth took her to nor at the card party her mother suggested. No matter what she did, it seemed like she couldn't find a place amongst the other attendees.

She could only hope that she'd do better at the casual, impromptu gathering in Hyde Park. Several young men had decided to race rowboats up and down the Serpentine and most of the ton had showed up to watch.

Despite her best intentions, though, Clara found herself tucked into the middle of a group of matrons and spinsters, people she would normally be happy to converse with but not the people she was supposed to be associating with.

Aunt Elizabeth was trying not to frown in her direction and even Mother was avoiding eye contact. On a positive note, Mr. Pitt's mother was among the ladies chatting about the boats sliding down the lake. Forming a relationship with her would have to help her cause.

"'Tis a particularly fine day to watch the boats." Clara tried to keep her smile wide enough to appear genuine, but not so large as to seem maniacal. "After yesterday, I feared it would be too hot."

"How true." Lady Blitzmoor's smile was barely polite, not an encouraging sign when Clara was hoping to become her daughter-in-law. "We are fortunate the rain came through to cool things down."

"Such a rarity in England," another woman said with barely contained laughter.

Even though Clara had said nothing about rain, she felt the heat in her ears and fluttered her fan faster, hoping to avoid a full blush.

"How refreshing it is to have a young perspective added to our conversation. It is far too easy to forget the innocence of youth."

Lady Blitzmoor's words seemed kind, but even Clara recognized the underlying insult. She could hardly offer a rebuttal, though. Not only because she wanted this woman to like her, but because her aunt had informed her that one could not address the unspoken. It simply wasn't done.

Of course, if Clara said it, then it was no longer unspoken, but that seemed to break the rules as well.

Why did London have to be as much a dance of words as it was of bodies? Her mind had been forced to perform far more complicated maneuverings than her feet so far.

"Please pardon me," she murmured, "I see someone with whom I must speak."

She slipped away, attempting to look like she was moving with purpose when, in truth, she couldn't see any other person or group in which to insert herself. The shores of the Serpentine had become a labyrinth of silk and snobbery.

Before she could find someone to connect herself to, Aunt Elizabeth appeared at her side, hooking their elbows together and slowing Clara to a meandering stroll.

"My dear niece, a word of counsel."

"Of course, Aunt Elizabeth."

"I am delighted that you have finally chosen to take this opportunity of a London Season seriously."

Clara held her breath, certain that this seemingly complimentary statement was soon to be followed by one of censure. That seemed to be the way of London, after all.

Aunt Elizabeth did not disappoint. "However, you must find a way to portray a more amiable version of yourself."

"Amiable?" Clara had never been accused of being anything less than gracious.

"Yes. I'm certain your mannerisms do you well in the country, but I'm afraid your mother hasn't quite prepared you for the refinement of society."

Clara bristled at the less than veiled insult to her parentage.

However, her aunt wasn't finished. She gave a light laugh. "Not that I blame her. Considering how long she herself has been away from refined company, what she was able to manage with you and even your brother is admirable."

Clara blinked. Was that a compliment to her mother, an insult to Clara, or a judgmental dismissal of them both?

"Now, what you need to do," Aunt Elizabeth said with a pat of Clara's arm, "is learn how to balance."

"Balance?" Wasn't that what she'd been doing? She'd been withholding her displeasure and desire for deeper conversation to put forth comments about the weather and England and the lace trim of Miss Warren's new gown.

"Yes." Her aunt smiled and nodded at someone as they passed. "You need to be the very image of sincerity without appearing to be nosing into anyone's private affairs, make the other person feel esteemed without falling into false flattery, and display your wit and intellect without taking over any conversation."

Oh. Was that all? With such simple instructions, how could Clara ever falter?

"Oh, and most importantly." Aunt Elizabeth drew them to a stop near the edge of the gathered aristocracy. She turned to face Clara with a very serious expression. "You must choose your company more wisely."

"I beg your pardon?"

"If you speak with the spinsters, people will assume you to be one despite your tender years." She winced. "In truth, if this weren't your first season, it would be easy to assume you'd chosen to join their ranks already."

Clara's mouth dropped open as she tried to respond, but the truth was the spinsters and matrons were the only group that didn't disperse within moments of her arrival. Everyone else found a reason to leave her side, usually on the arm of a gentleman, as that was everyone's goal.

"I'm afraid, Aunt, that the other debutantes do not stay still long enough for a conversation."

"Exactly." She beamed at Clara like a teacher whose pupil had finally learned proper addition. "That is why you must be friendlier. You have only a moment to establish yourself as the one to be chosen."

Was that what she was meant to be doing?

"Now." Aunt Elizabeth brushed at a curl which slid right back into the same location against Clara's cheek. "Go dazzle them, will you? It is my reputation on the line as much as yours."

Clara rather thought her situation was a little more tenuous than her aunt's, but she didn't argue the point.

Instead, she walked with her aunt back into the heart of the crowd. Eventually she saw one of the marriage-minded ladies that had been somewhat more friendly than the others, and she slipped away from her aunt to greet the young woman who was standing with another lady Clara had met but not talked with much.

"Miss Cavendish, that rose in your hair is simply divine. Is it from your garden?"

"No." Miss Cavendish leaned forward with a conspiratorial grin, eyes darting from Clara to the third woman in their group. "I snipped it from a bouquet Lord Bancroft sent."

The other woman, whose name Clara had finally remembered was Lady Mary, gasped and lifted a gloved hand to cover her answering smile. "How scandalous."

Clara tried not to frown. This was scandalous? Was there a secret language to flowers that she didn't understand?

Lady Mary continued, "What will your other suitors think?"

Miss Cavendish shrugged. "Should they ask, I will imply it is from our garden, but Lord Bancroft will know differently."

"Are you hoping he'll make an offer?" Clara asked.

"Of course." Miss Cavendish looked at Clara as if she had lost her head. "The man is in line for an earldom."

"But . . ." Clara was fairly certain she'd seen Lord Bancroft with Ambrose on multiple occasions. If he was taking part in some of the same activities as her cousin, he was hardly a desirable husband. "Are you certain of his character?"

"His character is that he will one day be an earl," Lady Mary said.

"You'll have to forgive her," Miss Cavendish said in a kind voice. "This is Miss Woodbury's first season, and she is from a tiny village in Leicestershire." She turned to Clara. "Who is the highest-ranking personage in your parish?"

Clara swallowed. "The Earl of Gimbleton has an estate in the district but he is rarely, if ever in residence. Baron Winslow maintains his estate there, though."

"You see?" Miss Canvendish waved her hand as if Clara were an exhibit in a museum. "We must make allowances."

Lady Mary came around until she flanked Clara's other side. "I see." She hooked arms with Clara much as Aunt Elizabeth had done moments earlier. "Stick with us, Miss Woodbury. We shall teach you all you need to know."

For the rest of the afternoon, she followed the two other young women, restraining her contributions to various conversations to smiles, nods, and murmurs of "Do tell" and "Please, continue."

While she didn't get abandoned and her aunt seemed more than pleased with her afternoon's progress, Clara was nothing but frustrated. How was she to be friendly and amiable if she was nothing but a walking doll? How could she gain Mr. Pitt's attention if he never heard anything from her but murmurs and sighs?

Once, she tried to copy Miss Canvendish's method of conversation, but it quickly fell flat, and she returned to her smiles and nods. Perhaps it simply wasn't possible for one raised as she was, outside of high society, to truly mingle with the upper crust.

After arriving home, she was slow and thoughtful as she handed over her gloves and parasol. Her aunt and mother retreated to the drawing room for tea, but Clara wasn't quite ready to join them for a dissection of the afternoon and Clara's performance.

A knock at the door behind her startled her out of her thoughts.

The butler admitted Mr. Lockhart and Clara's eyes widened. When had he started coming in the front door?

"Good afternoon, Mr. Lockhart." The butler took the man's hat and coat as if he were a daily visitor.

"Hugh!" Ambrose came down the stairs, greeting the tradesman with a smile. "You shall not best me today. I'm feeling quite nimble in my fingers today."

"The challenge shall be a pleasure." Mr. Lockhart smiled in return. "How did you find the new chocolate shop this morning?"

Ambrose placed a hand to his chest. "Ever so much better than my old one. My club doesn't even make a hot beverage as well."

Hugh chuckled. "Nice to know the best is available to us normal folk as well."

"Perhaps, but I'm going to sneak you into White's one day so you can feel an appropriate level of jealousy."

"If you insist." Mr. Lockhart didn't seem to feel strongly one way or the other about getting into the exclusive club. He noticed Clara standing to the side of the hall and gave her a brief bow. "Miss Woodbury."

Ambrose greeted her briefly then waved Mr. Lockhart toward the stairs. "Come, come. Lord Northwick is already upstairs and is trying to convince Duke to take me as a partner today. He thinks having you on his side will even the odds."

"But you are feeling nimble."

"Indeed I am. Which is why, now that I think about it, I should have you on my team to ensure my ego survives the afternoon."

The two men chuckled as they disappeared in the direction of the billiard room.

Clara watched with solemn determination. Apparently, it wasn't simply her status. There was a way for a lower-born personage to befriend those of higher rank.

She just needed to learn how.

She was still muddling over the problem when she came downstairs for dinner. After spending the day outside, she was more than happy to agree to her aunt's suggestion that they take an evening to rest at home.

If the suggestion was prompted by Clara's continued inability to attain enough attention to inspire a home visit, well, she still welcomed the respite.

Seeing Ambrose outside the dining room was even more welcome. Was he, too, spending a quiet evening at home? Was he possibly seeing the merits of a more settled life?

"Good evening, cousin." Clara gave him a warm smile. "What an honor to have you dining with us this evening."

"It is you who are dining with me," he said with a pointed look. "I frequently eat at home before going out in the evenings."

Clara blinked. So much for a more settled life. "Oh."

"My frequent haunts aren't much known for their exceptional food, I'm afraid." He offered his arm to escort her into the dining room.

Clara accepted the offer, her mind whirling over possible responses. All the half-formed sentences departed as she took in the other people already in the room.

Marmaduke was to be expected, of course, since he was in London. How much longer could he stay? Surely, he would soon need to return to the team that paid him for his cricket skills.

Aunt Elizabeth and Mother were also unsurprising inhabitants.

Mr. Lockhart, however, was something of a shock.

The settings had been placed so the six diners would be clustered around the end of the twenty-person table. Mother and Aunt Elizabeth sat to either side of Ambrose's place at the head of the table. Duke was seated beside Aunt Elizabeth and next to Mother was Mr. Lockhart.

He stood as Clara stepped fully into the room.

"Nice of you to join us, Clara." Aunt Elizabeth frowned.

Clara looked to the clock in the corner. "I thought you said dinner was at seven."

"Honestly, Miriam, have you not taught her to gather in the drawing room at least a quarter hour before the expected dinner time?"

Mother looked at her sister with a wide-eyed innocence that was obviously tinged with irritation. "Honestly, Elizabeth, no. I did not teach my children to observe formal manners when dining casually with family at home."

Aunt Elizabeth sniffed. "'Tis best to always behave in a way that creates proper habits."

"Alternatively, one could teach intentional discernment."

Clara started to say that, had she known they had a guest this evening, she would have come down early. But when she glanced Mr. Lockhart's direction, she received a small grin and a wink. The exchange reminded her that Aunt Elizabeth did not view Mr. Lockhart as a man of consequence. Why then did she seem to find his presence perfectly acceptable?

Clara took her seat beside Marmaduke and Ambrose slid into his chair, breaking the direct connection between the older sisters.

"What is happening?" Clara leaned close to Marmaduke in order to speak discretely.

Her brother grinned until the corners of his eyes crinkled. "We're having dinner. Fish, I believe."

Clara wrinkled her nose. She'd never particularly cared for fish. "Why is Mr. Lockhart here?"

"Because people of all classes tend to eat, dear sister."

Why was the man being deliberately obtuse?

The servants came in, placing the dishes on the table and all conversation stopped until the room was once again family only. Well, family and Mr. Lockhart.

"Really, Ambrose," Aunt Elizabeth said as she filled her plate with small selections of food. "You must attend at least a few gatherings with us this year. It is high time to include more proper company in your life."

Clara's gaze went straight to Mr. Lockhart. The comment was obviously aimed at him. Otherwise, such an admonishment would never have been given in front of a non-family member, no matter how inconsequential his station.

Duke considered his aunt. "And here I thought you were happy I'd come to London so that I could be a positive influence on him." He looked around the rest of the table. "Turns out I'm not proper."

Aunt Elizabeth sighed. "You are always welcome here, Duke."

"I do believe his lordship is foisting you off on me," Mr. Lockhart said. "If you've another friend to occupy your time, it frees Lord Eversly up to pursue more refined connections." Mr. Lockhart looked directly at Duke, not allowing anyone else to catch his eye. "Why else would I be here?"

Why else indeed? Except it had been Ambrose that greeted him warmly in the front hall this afternoon.

"How true." Marmaduke nodded toward his cousin. "With Mr. Lockhart here to amuse me in my spare time, you will not have to spend your evenings seeing to my company. You can accompany your mother to the ball tomorrow, after all."

All of Aunt Elizabeth's consternation fell away. "Oh, truly? You will attend with us?"

Ambrose glared at Duke, who lifted a serviette to hide his silent laughter. "Of course. Marmaduke was the only thing holding me back, obviously."

"Well, then." Aunt Elizabeth glanced at Mr. Lockhart and gave a little nod. "It's good that is sorted."

Clara placed her fork on her plate and all but gaped at the clockmaker.

"Clara, I would like to ask you a question. What do you think of the Season thus far?" Marmaduke turned to her with a wide, overly innocent smile.

At the end of the table, Ambrose covered his laugh with a cough followed by an enormous bite of asparagus.

The look Clara gave her brother should have sent him slithering under the table, but it didn't. How dare he bring their game to the dinner table here in front of Aunt Elizabeth and Mr. Lockhart?

Still, rules were rules. She gritted her teeth and took a moment to put together her answer. "London is quite a change from Eldham. I'm meeting people the likes of which I'd have never encountered in Leicestershire."

Both of those statements were true, and she sent Marmaduke an inquiring look to see if he would accept her answer.

He appeared deeply in thought. "While that is true"—he allowed the word to drag on until even Mother was frowning at the rudeness of it—"that doesn't tell me your opinions or feelings on the matter."

"What an insightful observation, Duke." Aunt Elizabeth beamed at Clara. "I've been so focused on our objective, I've forgotten to allow you to tell me how much fun you're having."

Clara was going to sneak into her brother's room and smother him with a pillow. Not enough to actually hurt him. Just long enough to make him wonder if she would.

She cleared her throat. "There have been so many new experiences since coming to London." Truth. "I'm sure that my best hopes for the future are swirling through these ballrooms." Partial truth. "I'm ever so glad we made the trip." Utter lie.

And Marmaduke knew it.

"Ambrose, would you mind passing the asparagus? I believe Clara would like to eat five more pieces of it."

Her stomach turned.

"Truly?" Mother's eyes were wide as she watched the plate of disgusting spears move down the table. "I didn't think you cared for the dish."

"Oh, it's taken quite the command of her palate." Marmaduke grinned while he slid a pillar of grossness onto Clara's plate. She'd already choked down two out of politeness.

Five was a rather harsh command for fibbing the answer on a single question, though. "I'm not certain my appetite can attain five more. Perhaps two would be sufficient."

"Why have two when you could have three?" Marmaduke looked to Ambrose. "Don't you think?"

Ambrose nodded. "Three is an excellent addition to her plate."

At least three was better than five. Clara forced a tight grin. "I agree."

Mother was still looking confused, obviously aware that something more than the obvious was occurring at the dinner table. Many years ago, the cousins had discovered that their parents, at least Clara and Duke's, had a tendency to turn their game into an opportunity for moral lecture and pious activity. As much as Clara enjoyed visiting the poor and reading to children, having to clean the cobwebs out from under the pews felt more like a punishment than a command.

They'd made the rule that her parents weren't to be made aware the game was still continuing.

Mr. Lockhart spoke up. "I think a little extra asparagus sounds ideal."

The bowl circled back around the table.

"Have you found anywhere in London that serves such exemplary asparagus?" Ambrose leaned toward Mr. Lockhart.

"As a man on my own, I confess I've eaten at many establishments, but have never had as fine a serving of this vegetable elsewhere." He gave a nod of his head. "Your choice of chef is to be commended, Lady Eversly."

Aunt Elizabeth smiled at the compliment, even though it had come from someone she deemed as inconsequential as the clockmaker.

As Clara forced herself to chew the asparagus, she paid close attention to the way Mr. Lockhart seemed to ease in and out of the conversation, until by the end even Aunt Elizabeth didn't seem to mind his presence.

By the time Clara polished off the last bite of pudding, she had come to a conclusion. Everything with this mysterious man was not quite what it seemed to be.

FIFTEEN

"**A**re you a gentleman?"

Hugh paused in the middle of filing down a balancing plate. He knew the voice and turned to look at the woman in the doorway with more than a little trepidation. Their previous encounter had filled his thoughts more than he would have liked over the past several days.

Miss Woodbury didn't look angry, exactly, but there was an intensity about her that made him proceed carefully. "I beg your pardon?"

"My brother's esteem isn't all that exceptional as he tends to like everyone, but Ambrose? I didn't think he truly considered anyone a friend aside from Marmaduke, and here he is inviting you to family dinners and giving you permission to call him by his first name."

"It's his second name, actually." The moment the words left his mouth, he knew they were the wrong thing to say, but there was no taking them back. Besides, what would be the proper response? Was she disparaging his character? Questioning her brother's discretion? Challenging her cousin's judgment?

She blinked and narrowed her gaze. "You know what I mean."

That was a rather bold assumption. "Actually, I don't."

She turned a full circle in the doorway before stepping fully into the room. "Are you a gentleman?"

He coughed. "My lady, I deeply apologize if I've given you cause to question my behavior." He'd done his level best to avoid her since their conversation a few days ago. How could he have done anything untoward if she hadn't seen him?

She blew out an annoyed breath. "Not that sort of gentleman."

"Of course." This conversation had gone from confusing to downright bizarre, and he was now far too fascinated to cut it short. Slowly he set his tool and part on the table and crossed his arms over his chest. "If I may ask, what sort of gentleman are you inquiring about?"

"A proper one."

He merely lifted his eyebrows at her.

She began to pace, her hands fluttering as if she could pull the words from the air around her. "An official one. Someone who can put esquire after their name and such."

Hugh would rather move the conversation back to the bizarre instead of the uncomfortable weight it now held. He cleared his throat. "If you are asking my placement in society, I'm afraid I am solidly below you on the ladder. I am a man in trade, though not the owner of my own business. I am the son of a candlemaker and the nephew of clergyman. Even my highest aspirations would not have me stepping far from that sphere."

Never in his life had Hugh considered himself inadequate or lacking. He'd been born into a certain social position, but that was merely circumstances and had nothing to do with his worth or importance as a man. Yes, he'd done everything he could to make the most of his situation, but he didn't begrudge the men such as Ambrose who had been born into a different one. It took all sorts to make society function, after all.

"Then how did you do it?"

At least the conversation had rolled back around to confusing. "Do what?"

"Become friends with a viscount."

Were they friends? What did that even mean? "I'm not certain what—"

"I have been in London for two weeks." She started pacing again. "In that time, according to my aunt and even my mother, I've managed to ostracize half of London because I'm not being amiable enough."

Hugh lifted a hand to his mouth to cover the grin that formed. No, amiable was not the word he would use to describe Miss Woodbury. Fascinating, intriguing, and even somewhat captivating, yes, but not amiable. She was far too opinionated for that.

She propped her hands on her hips and glared at him. "You're laughing at me."

"I'm not—" He had to stop as laughter indeed slid from his mouth when he attempted to speak. After clearing his throat, he tried once more. "I'm laughing, yes, but not at you. More at the idea that you would want to be considered amiable. It just doesn't seem a priority for you."

Her face fell from determined to devastated as her body dropped into a chair. "You find me disagreeable? I thought—"

"One moment. How did we move from *not amiable* to *disagreeable*? That's quite the jump."

"Not according to my aunt."

In Hugh's opinion, her aunt was not the best judge of character. The woman was as shallow as a puddle and a caricature of a typical aristocratic lady. He winced at his own judgmental thoughts. He was likely being unfair, but the things he'd heard the woman say to her nephew and her son were definitely the words of a woman who was very aware that she'd climbed up in society and didn't want to be reminded that she'd ever lived elsewhere.

He could only imagine what sorts of things she was saying to her niece.

"Do you wish to be amiable?"

She frowned. "I wish to be considered at least somewhat affable, I suppose. I haven't exactly been making friends here, you know."

"Eleanor liked you." She'd liked this woman an awful lot if the note she'd sent round reminding him he'd promised to assist in Miss Woodbury's project was anything to go by.

As if she expected Hugh to renege on his commitment just because the situation was awkward.

He had, of course, hoped the entire thing would go away if he ignored it, but he didn't like that Eleanor had assumed he would do such.

Miss Woodbury didn't respond to his statement, but her face clearly said she was aware that Eleanor was not the sort of person she needed to impress while in London.

Of course, she also wasn't aiming to gain the respect of a man such as himself. So what was she doing seeking him out? Her first visit was an accident, but tonight's was obviously intentional.

"Right." Hugh cleared his throat, desperately combing his mind for the right words to say. There was something desperate about Miss Woodbury that made him want to help her. Something her brother had said nudged his memory and he frowned. "I didn't think you wanted a match from the upper crust."

"I don't." She crossed her arms. "That doesn't mean I don't want to be invited."

Hugh laughed. Miss Woodbury sprang from her chair. "I've never had to deal with this before. In the country, I was invited everywhere. I went to simple birthday celebrations with tea and cakes, and I attended several of Lady Witherton's assemblies and parties. No one there has ever told me I was less than amiable or called me aloof."

"And here?"

"Here even Mother said I need to consider my actions more carefully."

As a man who constantly thought about the impact of his choices, he couldn't imagine a person not thinking through their actions. Surely it wasn't that Miss Woodbury was acting without intention. "Why does she think that?"

"She says it's because I'm not in the country anymore." The wistfulness of her words had Hugh bracing himself to have a crying female on his hands soon.

"She isn't wrong. London is not the country."

"My current location is not of my doing." She stuck her nose in the air. "I never asked to come to London."

"Then why do you care if London suits you?" Hugh busied himself with reorganizing the parts he was keeping in a small tray. He had a feeling that this conversation would end if she thought herself an imposition to his work.

Keeping himself busy also kept it from getting awkward.

Hopefully.

"I care," she said slowly, as if Hugh's need for an explanation was his fault, "because I am a woman."

"Such a condition hardly makes you lacking in discernment or circumspection."

Her response was a narrowed glare.

Hugh bit his lip to keep from laughing. "Honestly, Miss Woodbury, if this life is not what you want, it shouldn't matter if it doesn't suit you."

"I meant that I need to marry."

A pang of unease speared his stomach at her pronouncement of the obvious, and the sensation surprised him a little. Marriage was the natural order of things. It was practically a necessity for women, particularly those born above a certain station. The idea of her marrying someone should not make him want to cut this conversation off immediately. "Are there no men in the country?"

"I'm afraid there aren't many unwed men of consequence in the district. Certainly none that my mother would happily see me wed to."

"You would change the course of your entire life to please her?" If that was the case, Hugh had nothing to offer. His father had expected Hugh to go into candles, to follow his father's footsteps. The lure of clock mechanisms was too much for Hugh to ignore, though.

"I believe it is possible to appease us both. Aunt Elizabeth is more exacting, but her disapproval will have little bearing on my choices." Miss Woodbury smoothed her skirts and gave a decisive nod. "This is why I have settled on Mr. Pitt as an option."

Hugh tried not to laugh again but once more failed. "It is usually the man who decides if he wants to be a suitor."

"If you truly think that, then you are not as understanding of women as you claim to be."

"I never claimed to understand them at all."

"Are you going to tell me your secrets or not?"

Hugh was going to be walking back through the conversation in his mind for days trying to find where he kept losing the direction. "Please recall I never claimed to understand women when I tell you that I have no idea to what you are referring."

"You have made connections above your station. I need to do the same. Mr. Pitt is at least a little bit interested, but he shall stop calling on me if I ostracize everyone in London."

Hugh had never moved in society. He had a small group of friends that he met with on occasion, and he enjoyed talking with people at his uncle's church. Still, he liked to think that he had a decent rapport with the aristocrats and gentry he'd worked with over the years. Was that at all the same as Miss Woodbury's situation? It was the best he had to give her.

"I find an easy smile and a quiet tongue make most of them happy."

She frowned. "I'm not certain I can do that."

"Me neither."

Her frown slid into a look of consternation. Probably trying to ascertain whether or not Hugh was making fun of her. He wasn't, but he didn't think meekly following along was a skill Miss Woodbury possessed.

Finally, she sighed. "Is that what you do with Marmaduke and Ambrose? Smile and nod?"

"Ah, well, no."

"Then what do you do?"

"I simply . . . be myself?"

It was the only advice he had. To be honest, he still wasn't sure he could say how he'd become connected to the viscount and his cousin, and at first, he'd tried to avoid it. Somehow, he'd ended up their friend anyway.

"You are naturally amiable, then?"

Hugh shifted more things in the basket, heat flushing the back of his neck. "I like to think so, I suppose. I haven't given it that much thought."

"Hmm." Her mouth flattened and she appeared to be in deep thought. "I suppose I shall have to learn by observation then."

The basket slid across the table and almost fell on the floor as Hugh jerked in surprise. "You . . . you intend to observe me with your brother and cousin?"

What was she going to do? Huddle in the corner of the billiard room? Hide under the table in the study?

"When we were children, the three of us were inseparable. I have, admittedly, spent more time away from them in recent years, but I believe we are still close."

Hugh believed they were as well, given how often her plans for the evening or her progress in London was mentioned during the billiards game.

Still, her presence would change the dynamic, and Hugh wasn't certain he'd still be welcome in the room. Her aunt and mother might have dismissed him at dinner, but those two men were well aware that Miss Woodbury was unmarried and Hugh was an unrelated man.

Miss Woodbury seemed not to consider these things though as she smiled and gave a decisive nod. "Besides, the first of the month is tomorrow."

Hugh frowned. "What has that to do with anything?"

She stood and straightened her shoulders. "I shall become the commander."

SIXTEEN

Hugh was glad that the next day was Saturday. He sent his excuses round to Lord Eversly and spent the evening with his uncle's family. Then, since Sunday was Sunday and he tried not to work on that day if he could help it, he had a reason to stay away again.

Come Monday, though, Hugh was back at Lord Eversly's home. He gave serious consideration to entering through the kitchens again. It was possible he could get to his little drawing room work area without being noticed. Then he couldn't be pulled into a game of cards or billiards or convinced to join anyone for dinner.

Additionally, if he didn't see Miss Woodbury, she couldn't closely inspect his mannerisms, as if he held the key to matrimonial success. His lack of a wife should have been enough to prove this, but apparently it didn't. Hugh didn't particularly think watching him would help, but on the chance that it would, he wanted to avoid it, if at all possible.

Hugh didn't like thinking about the stubborn, vibrant woman obtaining a calculated, loveless marriage. His parents had done so and while they were living a perfectly adequate and seemingly happy life, he couldn't recall either of them ever being very vibrant. Granted, he didn't know if they'd been vibrant before their marriage either, but he did know that everything from when to change the price on a candle (down ten percent every Monday after it had been on the shelf for a month) to when they chose to have him come visit (every other year in the summer when the upper crust of London fled to the countryside) was decided with the same level of practicality.

It worked for his parents. He was pretty sure that one day it would work for him. But he couldn't see it working for Miss Woodbury. As eminently practical as she seemed to be, she also cared far too much to leave everything to cerebral motivations.

Then again, he'd met the woman less than two weeks ago. What did he truly know about her?

Because Ambrose had threatened to pull his funding if Hugh snuck in through the kitchens again, he climbed the steps and lifted the ornate silver knocker.

The butler let him in and took his hat and coat. "Thank you, Hodges."

"Lord Eversly has asked that you be taken straight to the billiard room as Cook has forbidden me from having the tray sent up until you arrive."

It was impossible to detect either censure or approval in Hodges's voice, but Hugh dropped his gaze all the same. Since he'd been coming to the house on the regular, he'd been setting and winding all the clocks, free of charge. It was a simple enough way to thank the household for supporting his work.

From a comment he'd heard after that strange dinner Friday night, it was possible the housekeeper was redirecting the funds normally set aside for such duties to the food budget for the staff. One of the maids had mentioned getting lemon cake just because it was Thursday.

Hugh went up the stairs and turned toward the billiard room.

Marmaduke all but leapt from his chair when Hugh appeared in the doorway. "At last! A man of sense has arrived."

"He is not a man of sense, he is a man of trade," Lord Northwick said. "I am a man of leisure."

"And good taste." Ambrose toasted his friend with the short, cut glass tumbler in his hand.

"But not enough breeding," Marmaduke muttered.

Hugh winced. It was true that when Lord Northwick was in attendance, these games were far more . . . uncomfortable.

"Select your weapon." Duke waved toward the rack of cues.

As Hugh selected a cue, Ambrose set the balls in place on the table, and Lord Northwick tipped his head thoughtfully in Hugh's direction. "Have you another recommendation? Ambrose and I went to that chocolate shop, and it was scrumptious." He laughed. "The proprietor was a bit taken aback by the presence of two lords, but they'll soon get accustomed to that. We told everyone at the club about it."

If aristocrats started frequenting the shop he stopped at for the occasional treat, he hoped they were dropping his name as well. That way he would get a discount when the prices rose to match the pocketbooks of the customers.

The balls had barely clacked together when another voice cut through the general discussion, bringing the commentary on Duke's skills at the billiard table to a complete halt.

"Good evening, gentlemen."

Three male heads swung toward the door, but Hugh hung his with a slight groan. He should have known she would carry through on her threat. This nightly stint in the billiard room was the only time she could observe him interacting with these men, but somehow Hugh hadn't thought she would actually dare to intrude.

"Ah, Miss Woodbury. How honored we are that you've graced us with your presence." Lord Northwick all but tossed his cue toward the window alcove as he crossed the room to bow over her hand.

He came to a halt as Ambrose growled a threat to impale him on a cue stick if Lord Northwick so much as touched her.

The other aristocrat turned back toward the table with a grin. "Have you found your protective instincts?"

"Yes." Ambrose leaned over the table and sent the cue ball rolling. "I'm protecting you from her sharp tongue. You are most definitely not the sort of man she views with benevolence."

"As she is not the sort of woman I—"

"I do believe it is your turn, Marmaduke," Hugh said stiffly. In truth, he didn't know whose turn it was, but anything to keep Lord Northwick from finishing that sentence.

"What are you doing here, Clara?" Ambrose pushed Lord Northwick back toward the table and stood between his cousin and the rest of the room.

"I . . . um . . . That is, I wish to learn billiards."

Hugh almost snorted out a laugh. Obviously, the presence of Lord Northwick had altered the course of her plans. Spending time with her brother and cousin were one thing, but adding an unmarried aristocrat to the mix was another.

Hugh's marital status didn't signify. While the staff had been told to treat him like a guest, they were well aware that he was closer to their status than that of their employer. It was why Hugh wasn't completely afraid for someone to find Miss Woodbury visiting his workroom.

No, the unwilling debutante scared him far more than the gossiping parlor maid.

Not that he was hoping to marry her.

Not that he would mind doing so.

It was just that she wouldn't be a wife that could stand by his side and help him make a solid business for himself.

And he wouldn't be the settled country husband she required.

It was his turn to hit the balls and the force of his shot nearly sent his cue ball launching from the table.

"I shall be happy to teach you, but perhaps now is not the right time." Ambrose looked over his shoulder at the three men taking random shots at the cue ball. Any sense of an actual game had been lost.

"Perhaps I can watch. There's a lot to be learned from observation."

Ambrose sighed. "It isn't proper, Clara."

Her eyebrows arched in accusation, and Hugh almost winced as he guessed what she was going to say next. "Since when did you care about what was proper?" She narrowed her gaze and looked to Marmaduke. "I have a question, brother."

Both of her male relations groaned.

"I don't know what your question is," Marmaduke said with a sigh, "but I know it's going to be one I don't wish to answer." He gave his sister a narrow glare. "Which is not how this is meant to work."

"Desperate times call for desperate measures."

Ambrose snorted out a laugh of disbelief. "You can hardly be desperate to learn billiards."

"And yet, I think I should gain command of the game." Miss Lockhart grinned in triumph.

"They're serving lamb stew at the club tonight," Lord Northwick announced as he slid his cue into the rack and scooped up the jacket draped over the back of a chair. "I believe I shall see what entertainments await there."

With a flurry of nods and murmured goodbyes, the man left. At the door, he sent another speculative glance at Miss Woodbury. Once his footsteps had faded, a tightness eased from around Hugh's chest.

When he allowed his own gaze to land on the woman settling herself into a curved, upholstered chair, the discomfort returned. She was looking right at him with a triumphant grin.

Hugh leaned over and sent the cue ball rolling once more.

Clara should have felt a thrill of triumph over both having the nerve to walk into the billiard room and convincing Ambrose to let her stay. Instead, all she felt was frustration.

The men had played two games of billiards. More than half of their conversation had been about whose turn it was or what the balls had done. It was just like the talk in a ballroom where people could speak of nothing but when they would get to dance and who had already been on the floor with whom.

The only observation she'd been able to make so far was that Mr. Lockhart was a decent shot and both Duke and Ambrose respected him for it.

When the conversation did turn elsewhere, it was normally Marmaduke and Ambrose falling into the same teasing banter they'd enjoyed as children. Mr. Lockhart simply let that flow around him, seemingly content to remain oblivious to any references to shared experiences or mutual acquaintances.

Clara tried to join in the teasing once or twice, and while they seemed to welcome her contributions, the rhythm of the conversation was lost. Had they changed so much? Or had she? Surely it hadn't been that many years ago that they could have spent entire afternoons together and never run out of things to say or games to play.

When it was time for her to leave to get ready for that evening's outing—she didn't even remember where they were supposed to be going—she wasn't feeling any more prepared for her next attempt at fitting in with London society.

Her hair had already been tended, so all that was needed was a change of dress and Clara would be ready. Mother came in while the maid was fastening Clara's buttons.

"Oh, my dear, I'm so sorry, but your aunt has a headache."

Did that mean they were staying in tonight? She could join the men at dinner. Surely the atmosphere would be more social there than it had been in the billiard room. It wouldn't do to look excited about the canceling of plans, though, so Clara tried to focus on the sympathy she felt for her aunt. "I'm sorry she isn't feeling well. Is it very bad?"

"Not so bad that she's taken to bed but enough that she is not leaving her room." Mother glanced around. "I thought I would join her there, and we would have a quiet dinner brought up. Would you like to come as well?"

"If she is seeking a quiet interlude, I fear the two of us might talk too much for her comfort." Clara was all but jumping at the chance to see if the men had already adjourned to the dining room.

"Very well." Mother stepped back to look at the dress. "You look positively divine in that gown, though. Be sure to set it aside to wear another evening."

As if Clara would let such an expenditure go to waste. "I will, Mother."

As soon as the older woman was gone, Clara dismissed her maid and counted to ten. Then she left the room and made her way downstairs.

The men were just sitting at the table when Clara made her entrance. It was a simple matter to request the footman bring another place setting, and she moved to sit beside Marmaduke.

Unfortunately, dinner was just as fruitless as billiards had been. Yes, the conversation lit on a far larger variety of topics and yes, both Duke and Ambrose seemed to find Hugh an amiable and engaging companion, but Clara could not determine what Hugh was doing that made him so.

He asked questions about the other men's activities.

She had asked after her party companions' activities.

He laughed at their terrible jokes.

She had forced amusement when it seemed the rest of the group found something humorous.

He even made a controversial observation or two.

She had striven to never speak with contention at a gathering.

It would seem she should be doing better than Mr. Lockhart, but clearly that wasn't the case. It could be that Ambrose and Duke had far different temperaments than those who were moving in fine society this Season, but it couldn't all be dependent on other people.

Mr. Lockhart had to be doing something.

The only problem was he didn't seem to know what. Occasionally he would catch her eye and give her a sad smile as if he knew he wasn't helping her at all.

As soon as dinner finished, Mr. Lockhart excused himself. After giving Clara and the two gentlemen a brief nod, he left the room.

Clara stared at the remains of the fruit tart that had graced her plate and frowned. Finally, she looked up at her brother and simply asked. "What was it about Mr. Lockhart that made you want to start spending time with him?"

Ambrose choked on the tea he'd just taken a sip of, and Marmaduke laughed.

"Seriously. It isn't as if the two of you regularly seek out tradesmen to fill your social calendars."

"At first, I spent time with him because Duke asked me to." Ambrose shrugged as he dabbed at his mouth with a serviette. "After that, I don't know. He's an enjoyable fellow to be around, despite the lack of common interests. I was surprised, really."

Duke grinned. "I asked because he was the first non-titled man I'd seen in Ambrose's company that didn't fawn over his existence. I needed someone to balance out the aristocracy in the room."

While it was clear both men thought highly of Mr. Lockhart, neither of those answers gave her something to work with. No, she wasn't titled, but she wasn't disconnected enough to be a novelty.

She thanked them and left the room. Instead of walking upstairs, though, she traced the path to Mr. Lockhart's workroom. After a brief knock, she pushed open the unlatched door.

"I rather thought I'd see you." Mr. Lockhart gave her a smile before leaning over the small box on the table that would someday hold his masterpiece.

"But you don't have a way to help me."

"The best I can say is what I've already told you. Be yourself. I don't know how that works or what it looks like, particularly for ladies."

She sighed and dropped into the chair by the door. "I am doomed to failure then."

Instead of leaving, she let the conversation continue. She enjoyed his company. Surely if they weren't talking about anything serious, they could avoid a debate.

It didn't take five minutes for them to disagree, though. This time it was over the best flavor of cake. Mr. Lockhart declared it to be a ginger and cinnamon cake his aunt made around Christmas while Clara was solidly on the side of citrus flavors such as lemon and orange.

Still, when she finally left, having felt she had stayed longer than could be considered polite, there was a smile on her face.

SEVENTEEN

For the next week, Clara sought out Mr. Lockhart on a regular basis. She would tell him how her most recent outing went and attempt to get him to help her discern what she could have done better.

He would always look at her for several moments with a blank expression and then ask her what she had actually wanted to do in that situation.

It was an incredibly frustrating experience as Clara was not looking for encouragement to be herself. She wanted instructions on how to fit in. If being herself could have garnered her a husband her family would approve of, she wouldn't have had to get a new dress for each and every possibility London could provide. She wouldn't have had to sit through hours of lessons from Aunt Elizabeth on proper behavior and social interactions. She wouldn't have received several less than gentle suggestions from her mother on topics that should or should not be brought up while amongst the ton.

Somehow, no matter how deliberate Clara tried to be in the conversation, she and Mr. Lockhart ended up on one of those not-to-be-discussed subjects. Whether or not they agreed, the conversation was always interesting to the point of sending her scrambling when the clock's chime indicated she was supposed to be meeting her mother and aunt soon.

"You truly don't know what you would have done in that situation?" Clara scoffed as she leaned back in her chair by the door to his drawing room.

"No," he said firmly as he slid a gear into place. "I cannot fathom what I would do should I be asked to dance by the most loathsomely boring man on the planet." He sent Clara a glance filled with humor. "It's not a situation I've ever remotely encountered."

"You are of absolutely no help."

"I did tell you that would be the case."

"So you did." She huffed out a breath and crossed her arms. "But I rather thought that was just because you'd never given it a great deal of thought."

"I haven't given it a great deal of thought, and no matter what question you ask, I can't seem to contemplate an answer. I just . . . let people be themselves. It's all they really want."

Annoyed with an answer that seemed so simple yet was truly outrageously complicated, she stayed away from his workroom the next night.

Two days later, a note arrived for Clara shortly after breakfast. It was from Miss Eleanor Porter, requesting her to come by St. Anne's Limehouse at her earliest convenience.

Had she thought of something Clara could actually assist with?

She arrived, anxious to learn if she would be helping with children or putting together baskets for the sick or elderly. Miss Porter, or Eleanor as she insisted Clara refer to her, didn't take her to a workroom, though, or in fact any area within the church. No, the younger woman pulled Clara around the building toward a simple, clean house across the street.

"Where are we going?" Clara looked around, confused and a little nervous. Ambrose's driver was on the other side of the church and couldn't see her leaving.

"To have tea." Eleanor smiled widely.

"Tea?"

"Yes." They entered a cozy kitchen where a tea service was already set out on a square wooden table. Eleanor waved Clara into one of the chairs around the table before filling a kettle to place on the black stove in the corner. "How do you take it?"

Nothing much was said until both women were seated at the table, cups of tea in front of them.

"Not that this isn't nice," Clara said slowly, "but this is a long way to come for a cup of tea."

"Oh!" Eleanor grinned. "You aren't here for tea. You're here for information."

"On what?"

"Hugh."

Clara was very glad she was at a table and not balancing her tea in her lap. "I'm not certain I know—"

Eleanor's face clouded with confusion. "But he said you wanted to know how he got along with people."

"Well, yes, I do, but . . ." But what? That was information Clara had asked for. It seemed rather strange that he would request Eleanor's help to answer such a question. "Did he ask you to tell me?"

"Oh, no. He was actually complaining about it when he came for dinner last night. Not about you asking, but more wondering how anyone was meant to understand how and why they behaved in certain ways."

"But you understand him?"

Eleanor shrugged. "Not always the why, but I have noticed the how before. The man manages to fit in wherever he goes."

Envy had Clara tightening her grip on the teacup. "That must be nice."

"I know." She shook her head. "Sadly, though I've observed his methods, I can't seem to replicate them. Maybe you can."

Clara certainly hoped so.

Eleanor selected a biscuit from the plate in the center of the table, but she didn't bite into it. Instead, she examined it as if the answers to life were in the delicate crumbs clinging to the biscuit's surface.

"The short answer is that he allows other people to talk first. Once they've established the mood and the topic, he participates to the level he desires."

Clara frowned. "I don't understand."

"As near as I can tell, when he lets the other person, or people as is usually the case, set the tone, they are happy with the conversation. If he can match the tone and add to the topic, he does. Otherwise, he stays quiet." She shrugged her shoulders. "It's remarkably effective."

Clara applied this explanation to the conversations she'd seen Hugh participate in. The observation fit them all well. Somehow, he managed to allow everyone else to be in charge of the interaction while being true to who he was.

Eleanor wasn't finished observing people, though. "I think for you, they would also need to be people you can help." She gave Clara a wink. "You're clearly a helper. Hugh has no problem being silent around an absolute stranger, but you need people with commonality so you can make their life better."

Clara wasn't certain she liked being so accurately summed up, but the explanation was helpful.

"Tell me more about how he does this while still being himself."

Then Clara settled in, ready to learn.

All of Eleanor's rules were still swimming through Clara's head as she took a deep breath and stepped into the front hall of one of London's grand townhouses that evening. She could do this. She could look for the people she might connect with. She could be friendly without compromising her principles. She could nod and smile while her aunt and mother gave directions and then carry them out in her own way.

That last conviction sent her heart climbing up her throat where it pounded until she could feel it beating in her teeth.

Could she truly redefine things on her own terms in a way that didn't disrespect the woman who had raised her? Then again, wasn't that exactly what her mother had done? She'd found love and made a life that didn't fit with her family's goals, and she'd done so without losing contact or relationship with her parents and sibling.

"There's a fine group near that window," Aunt Elizabeth whispered. "If you position yourself correctly, you can claim yourself a seat when they sit down to cards."

The group by the window was, indeed, fine. They were also people Clara had tried to converse with before and failed. None of those ladies wanted to talk to her for the length of time it took to procure a dance partner, much less for the duration of a game of cards. None of the gentlemen were ones that had caught her eye either.

"I'm going to . . ." She looked around, desperate for something—anything—she could claim as a reason to step away from her aunt's side and her well-intended suggestions. "See who's in this room first."

Her statement was weak, but as she was already walking away when she said it, her aunt couldn't stop her.

Slowly, she moved through the rooms. Card tables were set up in two drawing rooms and several trays of food were set out for the wandering guests. For a while it looked as if she wouldn't find what she was looking for, but there, in the second drawing room, three young ladies stood in the corner.

Unlike most of the other people in the house, they weren't watching the other guests. They were happily having their own conversation. It was such a refreshing change that she was drawn across the room to them before she could make the conscious decision to.

"Good evening," she said gently.

They all turned her way with wide smiles.

"Oh, I know who you are. You're Lady Eversly's niece." A young lady in a pale blue gown pressed a palm to her chest. "I'm Lady Emily. This is Miss Lenmore and Miss Dravern."

The other two girls gave Clara a nod.

Everything in Clara wanted to start asking how they were enjoying their season and if they lived in London year-round, but she reminded herself that she couldn't know if something worked unless she tried it.

So she said nothing.

The ladies immediately fell back into their earlier topic of conversation which had apparently been how best to paint a sky with watercolors.

Clara wasn't much of an artist, but she did love nature. Could that connect?

She soon found herself agreeing with the idea that accurately portraying the beauty of nature was a very difficult skill. None of the women proclaimed to possess such a skill, but the desire to do so was admirable as well.

When Miss Dravern suggested they sit down to a game of cards, Clara readily agreed. An entire hour passed before she realized she'd spent the entire time talking with this small cluster of ladies.

And she'd had fun.

As they rose from the table, an elegant older lady was standing near their table, smiling at the group.

Lady Emily greeted the woman and introduced her to the other three as Lady Grableton.

"I believe I know your aunt," Lady Grableton said to Clara. "Lady Eversly, isn't it?"

"Yes, milady."

"How are you finding London?"

Clara started giving the same answer she gave everyone, which included gratitude over the opportunity, a confession that the city was a tad overwhelming, and an observation that people in London were far different from those in Eldham. All of those elements were true, but she knew she was phrasing them in a way that didn't completely communicate her views and opinions of those observations.

Lady Grableton, however, somehow knew how to press behind the words. Soon Clara was telling her about trying to hold on to her purpose and supporting a local charity while she was here. Lady Grableton asked more questions that had Clara coming perilously close to telling the woman the whole truth.

When she realized that, she snapped her mouth shut and fought back a horrified blush.

"Oh, don't worry, dear." The lady placed a gloved hand on Clara's shoulder. "Your secrets are safe with me. I simply adore seeing young people truly enjoy themselves at these parties and had to meet you." She paused and gave Clara a searching look. "I am intrigued by this project you've taken on. A good cause is worth supporting, but a vital cause, well, that could be worth risking your reputation over."

"I . . . I agree."

Lady Grableton gave a short, brief nod. "Good. I hope God blesses the rest of your evening."

Though they parted ways after that, Clara seemed to see the woman everywhere for the rest of the evening. She was always in the corner or near the door, talking and smiling.

And watching.

Clara met her gaze on more than one occasion because she turned to find the woman looking at Clara. Every time the lady would give Clara an encouraging smile and a nod.

The confidence created by the exchanges meant that by the time Clara was in a conversation with Mr. Pitt, it was difficult to hold back saying something that would encourage him to progress the relationship.

She played an entire game of whist with him, managing to remain demure and on topic. After the game, he offered to take her on a turn about the room. Walking with the man with their arms hooked together, she lost the battle against the urge to make this interaction count.

"Do you know what I've yet to do in London?" she asked, still debating within herself about whether or not this was a good idea.

"What is that?"

"Ride in an open-air conveyance." She gave him what she hoped was a smile that simply looked like personal chagrin and not pointed encouragement. "I've ridden in wagons in the country, of course, but everything finer has been an enclosed carriage."

"I have a new phaeton," the man said. "I would love to take you for a ride later this week."

"How gracious of you. That would be lovely." She couldn't resist giving it a little push. "I must confess I've been hoping you would offer such."

"Then we shall both be fortunate enough to achieve our goals tomorrow."

The rest of the evening was equally smooth.

Clara smiled as she climbed in the carriage. One simple lesson and her entire London experience just might be saved.

Hugh jumped back so quickly he nearly fell onto his backside when he entered his workroom and was immediately greeted by a waiting Miss Woodbury. He clutched his shirt as if he could calm his pounding heart and supported himself with a hand on the door frame as he took in the wide-eyed young lady.

"Oh, my, are you all right?" Miss Woodbury took a step forward, arm outstretched as if she intended to offer assistance, but she stopped and lowered her arm while still two steps away.

"Yes, I'm . . ." Hugh took a deep breath and straightened his stance. "What are you doing here?"

"Waiting on you."

"So I see." He stepped further into the room, keeping as much space between them as the small room allowed, and moved to stand behind his worktable. He set his bag on the surface and took another stabilizing breath. Now that the table was between them and she had a clear route of departure, he felt better about the situation.

He cleared his throat and busied himself with unpacking the bag of tools he was taking back and forth to work. "And why were you waiting on me?"

"Because I need to talk to you."

He waited but nothing more was forthcoming. Finally, he said, "Are we to discuss the weather? Perhaps take another stab at dissecting my interpersonal skills?"

She frowned. "Why would we discuss the weather?"

"I haven't the slightest idea," he said with a chuckle.

"We need to discuss the charity event."

He frowned. He'd rather hoped she had either become too busy with other social engagements that she'd forgotten her mission or that her aunt's friends had been providing enough help that he could bow out without guilt.

It would seem neither was happening.

"I don't know anything about planning a society event. I can't even explain to you how I keep getting invited to dinner." Though the turn of events was having a very beneficial effect on his ability to save up funds.

She waved a dismissive hand in the air. "The event won't matter if I can't determine how to fund both of the charities. What if someone asks to follow up to ensure that the collected money is donated? If I say it's for the Royal Asylum and only a portion of the money goes to those orphans, it will look bad."

"So don't say it's going to the Royal Asylum."

She began to pace the small room. "But I can't just say give me money, either. People won't do it." She sighed. "Besides I already mentioned the orphans to my aunt."

Hugh set his files aside and leaned on the table, giving the problem his full consideration. She was correct. People wanted to know where the money was going, and no one would appear very noble if it was discovered they were lying about where the money went.

"What if we said it was going to children but didn't specify who?"

"If I want the help of my aunt's friends it will need to include the survivors of the sailors."

Hugh nodded. He hadn't particularly liked his idea either.

Miss Woodbury propped her fists on her hips. "You were the one with this idea to begin with."

"That doesn't mean I have the answer."

"Why not? How were you expecting it to work when you made the suggestion?"

He looked at her, a smile growing on his lips but at least he was able to keep from laughing. "You always know the details when you toss an idea out into the world? It was an idea. Not a solution."

"An idea without realistic possibility just leaves everyone fluttering in the wind."

"I didn't say I wouldn't come up with an option. Just that I didn't have one yet. I'll think about it."

He gave his attention back to his tools and parts and began setting up for his evening's work.

Miss Woodbury didn't leave.

"Don't you have plans this evening?"

"Yes." She looked out the door and waved an arm toward the depths of the house. "I don't remember where, though. Only that this is the appropriate level of dress."

Hugh couldn't stop himself from looking her ensemble up and down. It was pale blue and fairly simple as far evening dresses went. It fit her very well.

He cleared his throat. "Have a good time."

"I shall try, I suppose." She grinned. "Tomorrow will be fabulous, though."

He shouldn't ask. He told himself not to ask. It wouldn't do anyone any good if he asked. "What's happening tomorrow?"

"I am being taken for a ride." She bounced on her toes. "In an open-air conveyance."

The bitter stab of . . . regret? Envy? Some other emotion he couldn't quite name? bit through him. He didn't have time to take a woman riding in the middle of the week. Nor did he own a conveyance, open-air or otherwise, with which to do said ride.

Not that he wanted to be the one taking Miss Woodbury for a ride. Nor did he crave to be the one who she was so excited to see that she bounced on her toes.

"I hope you have a good time." The words tasted like a lie.

"Oh, I will. I selected the man from a book."

Hugh blinked but managed to keep himself from asking a follow-up question.

She looked from Hugh to the door. "I suppose I should go. But you'll think about the description for the fundraiser, won't you?"

Hugh nodded. "I'll ponder some ideas while I'm working."

"Wonderful. Then we will discuss it tomorrow. I shall stop in before we go to the theater. Ambrose is actually going with us."

"I'll have plenty of time to work, then." He should be happy he didn't have to divide his evening between billiards and his work, but part of him was less than excited. He'd have to feed himself as well.

She took her leave and Hugh got to work. He did spend some of his time thinking about how to word the donation request.

He spent a great deal more wondering if the man taking her for a ride tomorrow was aware of how pretty she looked in light blue.

EIGHTEEN

The note confirming Mr. Pitt's intention to take Clara out for a ride was written in fine, elegant script. The lines were neat and well-spaced without a splotch of stray ink or a smeared letter.

Clara smiled at the note in approval before inspecting her reflection with a critical eye.

She would have Mr. Pitt's attentions for a solid hour today, and she needed to make it matter. His change from barely to definitely interested had to be a sign that God meant this man for her.

Still, Clara wouldn't fool herself into thinking the matter was settled. She needed to put effort into strengthening their connection until he was ready to make a declaration of intent.

This was progress, though, and she thanked God for it. That she'd also been granted success in the eyes of her aunt by gaining the attention of Lady Grableton was an added blessing she hadn't even thought to pray for.

Of course, that lofty attention would likely make her aunt think they should aim much higher than Mr. Pitt, but Clara had already started entertaining the connection and even Aunt Elizabeth wouldn't be rude enough to stop it now.

With a last brush of her skirts, Clara departed her room and went to the drawing room to await his arrival.

Once she was seated on the settee, there was nothing to occupy her hands or her mind. She should have brought a book or some embroidery with her. Her thoughts were her only current company, and they were making her more nervous than she already was.

"What are you doing?"

Clara's head snapped up. Aunt Elizabeth stood in the door to the drawing room, face twisted into a look of surprised horror.

"Preparing for my ride with Mr. Pitt," Clara said slowly. "His note said he would be here at half past four."

"Precisely." Aunt Elizabeth waved her hands wildly, indicating Clara should follow her from the room. "He'll be here any moment."

"That's why I'm waiting here." Clara stood slowly, a frown marring the perfect picture her maid has worked so hard to achieve.

Once Clara was in reach, Aunt Elizabeth slid her arm around Clara's and hurried her out of the room. "You can't be waiting on the man."

"Whyever not?"

"Because then he'll know you're interested."

Clara rather thought her bold confession at the party the other night had already given him that idea, but her aunt didn't need to know about that. She cleared her throat. "I am interested, Aunt Elizabeth. Why wouldn't I indicate so?"

"Because a man without curiosity is dull."

"I . . . what?" Clara could do nothing but gape at the older woman as they crossed the front hall to move deeper into the house.

Aunt Elizabeth patted Clara comfortingly on the arm. "A man needs to be curious enough about you to put in a little bit of pursuit. If he is without curiosity, he will most likely be too dimwitted to sufficiently provide for you. It probably indicates he is dull as well, but one can work around that."

Clara tried to follow her aunt's logic but got nowhere. "He's taking me for a ride in order to get to know me. Is that not a show of curiosity?"

"It is a show of good manners, and, at best, a modicum of sense."
Aunt Elizabeth sniffed. "You are residing in the home of a viscount.
A man would be a fool not to attempt to gain entrance and possible
audience."

Clara stumbled to a stop. "Are you saying Mr. Pitt is calling upon me
in an effort to get to Ambrose?"

"I'm rather surprised more men haven't attempted to use this av-
enue."

Clara's mouth gaped open in shock.

"It's Ambrose's fault, really. If he would attend more events with us
more people would be reminded that you have a titled connection that
would be worth marrying into."

"Aunt Elizabeth!"

The older woman carried on as if Clara had not just expressed her
very justifiable outrage. "I suppose that is in Mr. Pitt's favor, that he has
dared what no one else has yet, but that's no reason to toss away proper
behavior."

"Wouldn't proper behavior be waiting for him in the drawing room?"

"Hardly, my dear. It's proper to leave the man waiting for ten minutes. No more than fifteen and no less than five."

"But why?"

"So you can make a proper entrance, of course. You want him to sit
and think on you, to create in his mind an idea of the outing you are
soon to venture on. Then, when you appear in the door, you will be as
if his very imaginings have come to life. You will be, in a way, the lady of
his dreams."

"What if I don't match the lady he imagines?" There had been more
than one expectation of ladies that Clara had not managed to live up to
since arriving in London. "It would be better for him to spend the time
getting to know who I actually am."

"Only if you intend to scare him off."

"Aunt Elizabeth!" Clara ripped her arm away and stood, staring at her aunt in the middle of the dining room where she'd been led.

Aunt Elizabeth waved her hand in the air. "That isn't an aspersion on you, directly, my dear. It's best for any woman if a man becomes infatuated with some imaginary version first."

"But what about when he finds you are not his perfect creation?"

"It is your job to make sure he never does. Once you are married, there will be plenty of time to be yourself when he is not about."

"I do not think—"

The butler appeared in the door, giving no indication that he found it odd for them to be in the dining room when there was no meal being served for several hours. "Mr. Pitt is in the drawing room, my lady."

"Excellent." Aunt Elizabeth pushed Clara into a chair and pointed at a clock in the corner. "Five minutes, at least, Clara. Then you can make your way to the drawing room."

And then she was gone. Leaving Clara staring at the door in shock.

If this was what was required for a young lady to have a successful Season, Clara was even more convinced that a London lifestyle and a society marriage weren't for her. Such machinations could not allow a person to fully embrace their God-given mission.

With a glance at the clock that had barely budged, she stuck her nose in the air and strode from the dining room. Sitting about in an empty room for five minutes while the man she had chosen to marry waited to see her in another room didn't make the least bit of sense to her, and she refused to participate in such silliness.

As she entered the hall, movement on the stairs distracted her from her intentions to cross straight to the drawing room. Mother was descending and Clara waited until the woman was standing in front of her wearing a wide smile.

"I thought you would be waiting in the drawing room. I'd intended to be down here with you, but I was somewhat delayed in my preparations."

"I was in the drawing room," Clara said softly, "but Aunt Elizabeth took me to the dining room with instructions to make Mr. Pitt wait."

Mother frowned. "Oh?" She bit her lip. "Perhaps we should delay our arrival, then."

"Why?"

"Your aunt is far more aware of the intricacies of London manners than I am. I confess my single Season was a long time ago and obviously not successful in the idea of marriage."

"How fortunate for me," Clara muttered, "or I would not be standing here now."

Her mother sighed and shook her head. "Perhaps we should return to the dining room?"

"Seeing as I have no intention of building a life in London, I do not see why I should attempt to establish a relationship that follows London's manners, particularly when they make no sense."

"But Mr. Pitt will expect it."

"If Mr. Pitt is the man of sense I think him to be, he will appreciate my promptness." She winced. "Or my minimal lateness as the case may be now."

Clara took a deep breath and forced a bright smile. "Besides, this conversation has likely delayed me the requisite five minute minimum so I may present myself now even according to Aunt Elizabeth's strange rules."

Mother sighed and placed a heavy hand on Clara's shoulder. "She only wants the best for you."

"What is best is a matter of opinion. I have intentional and valid reasonings for selecting Mr. Pitt, but she is disregarding those and is determined to direct me toward other candidates."

Mother winced. "She wants you to have options, dear."

"But none of her options meet my criteria. It's as if she didn't listen to my preferences at all."

Mother twisted her hands together. "Aunt Elizabeth has not had the chance to see a different side of life as you and I have. I'm afraid she is only aware of one way for a woman to ensure her future."

It was all well and good for Mother to believe Aunt Elizabeth cared only for Clara's future wellbeing, but Clara herself wasn't as convinced. As she was well on her way to ensuring a future that would satisfy everyone concerned, though, there was no reason for her to ruin her mother's opinion of her sister.

"I'm certain you are correct," she said with only a minimal twinge at the lie. With a smile and a nod, she stepped toward the drawing room. "I shouldn't keep Mr. Pitt waiting any longer."

After taking a moment to smooth her skirts and repair her composure, Clara stepped into the drawing room. Mr. Pitt scrambled to his feet, obviously having expected her to leave him waiting for a while yet.

Which meant he'd been in London long enough to know the peculiar habits women like Aunt Elizabeth had created.

It did not mean her aunt had been correct.

Clara gave the man a wide, welcoming smile and he smiled in return before taking her hand and placing a light kiss in the air above the knuckle.

"Miss Woodbury, you are a delight that would have been worth waiting an hour for."

What was this obsession people in London seemed to have with not being on time? It seemed exceptionally rude.

And wouldn't Mr. Lockhart laugh to know she was thinking such a thing?

She curled her hand into a fist until the nails bit into her palm. There was absolutely no reason for the tradesman to be entering her mind just now.

Returning her attention to Mr. Pitt, she gave him a slight curtsy. "How fortunate we need not delay our time together, then."

"Indeed. My phaeton is out front. Shall we go for a ride?"

"I would be delighted."

Clara's mind swirled with the reminders from her aunt and mother as well as the lessons from Mr. Lockhart and Eleanor. The occasionally conflicting ideas had her so distracted, she floated through the climb into the carriage without much attention. She needed to do better.

It was imperative that Mr. Pitt enjoy her company. While she would prefer he do so while she was acting entirely as herself, this Season had taught her that certain expectations had to be met before most people were ready to get to know an individual.

Despite how Aunt Elizabeth seemed to think a connection to a viscount was a powerful thing, in Clara's experience, being the daughter of a country vicar was easier. Back home, people were inclined to accept her company and even seek it out. There were always invitations and opportunities.

In the billiard room and at dinner, Mr. Lockhart had allowed Ambrose and Duke to start the conversation. Joining an established topic had also worked at the party. Hoping for similar success, Clara sat primly while Mr. Pitt settled into his seat and took control of the horses.

They rolled down the street and around the corner and still, he didn't speak.

Was there a different rule when only two people were present? Was there some expectation when a lady was present that Aunt Elizabeth hadn't warned her about? Ambrose certainly didn't wait for Clara to set the topic, but it might be rude for a suitor to address her first.

The silence was dragging on far too long, broken only by the clinking of the harness buckles and the wheels clattering over the cobblestone. Clara jumped into the first topic of conversation she could think of. "The weather is lovely today. The air seems especially clear after yesterday's rain."

Mr. Pitt nodded, giving her a warm glance. "It is God smiling on our outing, no doubt."

Of course he would recognize God's hand in the weather. Mr. Pitt was going to be a man of the cloth, after all. "What a wonderful idea." Clara turned her body slightly, so she could more easily give her attention to Mr. Pitt. "I have often thought particularly fine days were like a smile or hug from the Lord. Of course, there is beauty in the rain as well. Crops cannot grow with nothing but sunshine."

"Er, yes. Of course." Mr. Pitt turned onto a path through a large park. "I noticed Lady Grableton speaking to you last night. I wasn't aware you had met."

"We met just last night. She expressed an interest in my charity endeavors." Clara still couldn't believe last night had gone as well as it had. Today was going excellently as well. If everything came together this smoothly for her charity project, life in London would be as perfect as possible.

"It is a rare woman who takes such an interest during her debut season."

A burst of pleasure sent a tinge of heat to her cheeks. "I believe our service is due to God no matter where we are in life."

"Er, yes. Of course."

The conversation lapsed as they greeted another couple going in the opposite direction on the carriage road.

When they began to talk again, the topics fell into the polite and perfunctory ones she'd endured far too often since arriving in London. Wasn't the point of a ride such as this to go beyond such superficial subjects? They would hardly have a more private moment to get to know one another.

She found herself paying more attention to the way the steady click clack of hooves marked the even spacing of the trees than Mr. Pitt's observations of the other horses and carriages.

Such disconnection would not further her goal.

"I was particularly moved by Sunday's sermon at St. Marylebone. Is that where you attend as well?" It was a somewhat abrupt change of conversational direction, but Clara had to do something.

"No. I live in St. George's parish." He gave a solemn nod. "The services there have been more enlightening of late as well."

"Oh?" Clara's heart beat a little faster. Finally, there were getting somewhere.

"Indeed." Mr. Pitt greeted another couple, then turned a conspiratorial grin Clara's way. "Take that couple, for instance."

"Miss Jenkins and Mr. Grammery?"

"Yes. He was seen sitting in her family's box this past Sunday."

"Oh?" How else was Clara to respond to that?

Mr. Pitt nodded. "I would imagine an announcement is soon to be forthcoming. If not, she might as well return to the country for the Season as everyone will wonder why whenever they see her."

"Oh." She had certainly sat through enough drawing room teatimes and charity meetings to realize people in London did not have the same view of gossip that those in her country parish tended to have.

Not that the ladies back home would hesitate to share someone else's particularly interesting or scandalous business, but they did it in hushed tones and with a haste that indicated they knew what they were doing was questionable and wanted to move on as fast as possible.

In London, it seemed a matter of pride. Entire conversations revolved around news and the ensuing speculation. Entire papers were published to share the on-dits.

That had to be why Mr. Pitt felt comfortable with this gleeful tittle-tattle. He was, after all, currently a man of London. He was also a man of God, though, so she waited for him to bring the topic back around to more spiritual matters.

He didn't.

He did, however, have something to share about the next couple they passed. And the next.

Finally, they entered a stretch where there was not an oncoming stream of gossip inspiration. Clara used the opportunity to jump in. Without a third party about, she could not truly utilize the rules of Mr. Lockhart's interactions so she would revert to her normal directness.

"I have heard you are in line for a living?"

"Yes. As a third son it is the best my family can do for me. I am pleased, though, that the current rector appears in good health. I have many years to remain in London before being confined to the country and its daily duties."

"You are not anxious to take up the work, then?"

He laughed. "As the daughter of a vicar, I'm sure you are aware of all the tasks aside from preparing sermons and overseeing services that fall upon the shoulders of a country clergyman."

"I am indeed."

He nodded. "I would like to delay those distractions for a while so that I may focus on other, more pleasurable endeavors."

The unease that had been growing in Clara settled. How fortunate that she had looked in a book and discovered a man that found such enjoyment in the studying of God's Word and the contemplation of its application that he treasured the time he had before other more practical duties would infringe upon his study.

"You shall need a partner that will shoulder some of those duties, then, and allow you ample time for study and reflection."

"Indeed." He gave her a long, deep look. "A wife that will relieve the more burdensome aspects of clergy life would be an asset. Perhaps even allow me to be away from the parish for a time on occasion."

"Indeed. My father would occasionally travel to speak at other parishes when they were between clergy or simply in need of temporary assistance. Mother and I would oversee many of his ongoing duties during those times."

"I'm sure you did so excellently."

"I considered it a blessing even if the work was difficult."

It had been an honor and where she had learned to truly appreciate her ability to help those in her parish. How fine it was to know Mr. Pitt was of a similar mind.

Once more, Mr. Pitt gave her a smile. "That is good to know, indeed."

Clara smiled as well, confident that they'd made progress toward an understanding. Yes, indeed, God must be smiling on her plans.

NINETEEN

H ugh had given up trying to sleep at the first hint of lightning in the sky. He'd dressed and taken the long walk to Eversly House, hoping that the hour wouldn't be too obscenely early by the time he arrived there.

Now he was testing the length of certain springs to see which provided the tension he desired and occasionally stopping to eat a bite from the meat pie the cook had sent up with a pot of tea.

The last thing he expected was company.

"Oh good, you're here. I wasn't sure how often you came by in the mornings."

Hugh swallowed the half-chewed bite of pie and fought not to cough as he chugged a cup of tepid tea to get the bite to clear his throat. Once it was safe, he addressed Miss Woodbury. "What are you doing here?"

"I happen to live here." Her grin was impish as she toasted him with her mug of tea. "But in the interest of time, I'll tell you that I was hoping you'd be here and that you'd have come up with an idea of how to manage the multiple charities without saying there are multiple charities. The Virtuous Ladies are meeting today."

Hugh nodded and took another drink of tea, just to be safe. He hadn't given the wording of the event invitation a great deal of thought, mostly because he hadn't given this charity project a great deal of thought. It was surprising, given how often his thoughts seemed to turn to Miss Woodbury.

"How was your ride yesterday?" He didn't really want to know, but he needed to buy himself some time to come up with something, so he didn't have to admit he hadn't given her request any consideration.

"Productive, I think." She lowered herself to her customary chair and wrapped both hands around her steaming mug. "We think the same about a lot of things."

Hugh's finger slipped and a spring went skittering across the table. He didn't know much about Mr. Pitt, but he'd done work for the Earl of Blitzmoor, and he hadn't thought it an environment that would raise a very pious individual.

"That's, uh, good then." He tried to subtly use a ball hammer to scoop the spring back toward himself.

"Yes." She seemed to think for a minute and slowly her expression slid into a frown. "He does tend to gossip a little much for a man who will one day be a vicar, though."

If that was the man's worst habit, she could certainly choose a worse fellow to marry.

He wanted to use the little hammer to pound the delicate spring flat.

"Is he coming to visit again?"

"I don't know." Her frown eased into an expression of desperate hope. "I hope so. I truly think we would suit nicely."

That should be enough for him. But still he found himself asking, "Why?"

"I'm certain you are not interested in the many reasons I believe we'd suit." She sighed and gave him an indulgent smile. "But if concern for my welfare is behind the question, I assure you that he has an allowance for now that seems to keep him provided for and is lined up for a living. My wellbeing would be set with him."

"Is that what you've decided to focus on, then? Your provision for the future?"

"No, I haven't quite moved myself entirely over to your camp of ledgers and balances, but I assumed that would be the portion you were most interested in."

Hugh allowed himself to shift his full attention in her direction. The words felt like something of an accusation, but her expression didn't seem antagonistic, so he let it go.

Even if part of him wanted to know how well he would fit the desired qualities she wasn't mentioning.

Provision in life couldn't be ignored and Hugh couldn't really offer her anything better than Mr. Pitt. Couldn't offer her anything at all, really. Not that it mattered, because she didn't want anything from him.

Except help with her charity function.

He cleared his throat and hooked gears and springs together in a haphazard fashion that he'd spend an hour undoing that evening. "You should use the name of the church. Say you are partnering with the children's support ministries of St. Anne's Limehouse to provide aid for the Royal Asylum."

She followed his change of subject easily enough to confirm that she hadn't been debating Hugh's merits as anything more than a partner in purpose or possibly something of a friend. "Doesn't that still say the funds are going to the orphans?"

Hugh shook his head. "No. You're partnering with the ministries of St. Anne's." He shrugged. "It's a gray area, but then, so is the charity."

"Do you know what it is, then?"

"Not exactly, but I've put together enough to know that children are involved."

"That helps, then. We can just refer to the beneficiaries as children, not orphans." Her nose wrinkled. "It still feels less than honest."

"It depends on your definition of honest."

She frowned.

Hugh grinned.

And until their tea grew cold and the household awoke around them, they nitpicked over the definition of honesty.

By the time Hugh departed the house, he'd adjusted his stance slightly from being comfortable with truth in specific, technical definitions of words, but wasn't in full agreement with Clara's idea that honesty required a person to ensure the hearer's complete understanding. Some things just weren't anyone else's business to know.

Clara entered the drawing room, feeling fully equipped to take control of all the different areas of her life. Things were going well with Mr. Pitt, the lessons she'd learned from Eleanor seemed to be making a difference, and Mr. Lockhart had provided her a plan to accomplish her fundraising goal. She was ready to make herself heard in the meeting of the Virtuous Ladies Society.

As the women gathered and the tea was poured, she kept her head up and her smile on. She listened to the conversation around her and tried to add to it instead of changing the subject. Her strategy wasn't quite as easy as it had been at the card party since she couldn't select the people she joined, but she was determined to make it work.

She forced herself to do nothing but listen as she drank half a cup of tea. Mrs. Hargrove despaired of her son ever settling down. Lady Elliot couldn't believe that waistlines were going higher yet again. Mrs. Leonard anticipated a large turnout for the ball she was holding next week, but worried some of the higher-ranking invitees wouldn't come.

None of these were conversations that interested Clara in the least. Mrs. Hargrove's son was in the enviable position of choosing to wait to settle down, and Clara couldn't imagine encouraging his mother to infringe upon that choice. She rather thought that if the ladies wouldn't spend a fortune every year to purchase new gowns that looked like those in the fashion plates, the waistlines would be more likely to stay put. As for Mrs. Draven's ball, well, Clara was of the mind that a party should be for having fun with one's friends and community, not establishing social position.

Yet these were her options.

Perhaps it was time to simply skirt along the truth.

With Mr. Lockhart's views of honesty in mind, she took one more sip of tea and smiled at Mrs. Hargrove. "It must be difficult to have someone else's preferences interrupt the plans you had for yourself."

The other woman preened under Clara's comment. "That is it precisely. Without a wedding to plan or grandchildren to prepare for, I hardly know what to do with myself."

Clara patted the other woman's hand. "Fortunately, you have the Virtuous Ladies Society to give your days a little purpose."

"So true, so true." Mrs. Hargrove leaned in and whispered to Clara. "I must confess I was a little worried about you when you first arrived in London, but your aunt assured us it was merely a nervous constitution brought on by the unfamiliarity of London." She gave a decisive nod. "You're doing quite nicely for yourself now."

"I confess I did not know what it would be like in London before I came." She hid her grimace behind her teacup as Mrs. Hargrove gave her a smile and turned to the woman on her other side.

Clara turned as well and spoke to Lady Elliot in sentences that allowed the other woman to be the one truly guiding the conversation. While Clara couldn't quite bring herself to agree that new fashions made one's previously attained clothing unwearable rags, she could agree that it was a shame the style of a dress let everyone know the age of the garment.

Eleanor and Mr. Lockhart really did know what they were about with the idea that people just wanted to be free to be themselves.

Now she just had to see if these new, sympathetic relationships would allow her to put forth ideas about the fundraising event.

Before she could attempt to get Aunt Elizabeth to help steer the ladies onto the topic at hand, the butler appeared in the doorway. "My lady, her ladyship, the Countess of Grableton has requested an audience with the Virtuous Ladies Society members."

A hush fell over the circle of women. Clara swallowed the last of her tea. Grableton? The nice lady Clara had spoken to at the card party?

Aunt Elizabeth found her voice first. "Of course. Please show her in." She rose from her chair, and everyone quickly shifted to allow her space on the settee. A fresh cup was placed in front of the now vacated chair. Every spine in the room straightened and every skirt was smoothed.

Clara followed the example of the ladies around her because she didn't want them to think she didn't fit in with them, but she was far more curious than concerned.

Lady Grableton swept into the room, a gracious smile on her lips for everyone in the group. "Thank you so much for allowing me to interrupt your meeting." She stopped at the chair and pressed a hand to the bottom of her throat. "Is this for me? How gracious."

"We are honored you wished to join us." Aunt Elizabeth set about fixing the woman's tea and slowly the ladies settled back into their seats.

"I confess I am here with a purpose. I talked to Miss Woodbury several evenings ago, and she informed me that you were temporarily expanding your interests." Lady Grableton accepted the teacup but did not drink from it yet.

"Yes." Three women said at once, all apparently wanting to be the next to speak with the countess. Everyone else was too busy giving Clara curious looks, including Mother and Aunt Elizabeth.

Clara cleared her throat. "We are partnering with the children's support ministries of St. Anne's Limehouse to provide aid for the Royal Asylum."

Lady Grableton sent Clara a considering look that almost appeared proud as she gave a slight nod. "The cause is very precious to me, and I would love to request the boon of temporary membership in your society so as to aid in this benefit."

Everyone rushed to assure her that she was more than welcome.

Clara was fascinated by this look into society. As they were both aware of what sort of husband Carla was likely to attract, neither Mother nor Aunt Elizabeth had sought to introduce Clara to higher society gentlemen such as earls or dukes or even viscounts. That meant she had not yet had the opportunity to see how such elevated status changed behavior.

Lady Grableton had seemed a very normal sort to Clara, but it was fascinating to watch two viscountesses, a baroness, and a cluster of other ladies who'd been daughters of loftier titles or had married high-ranking gentlemen, all but preen for the attention of a countess.

It was rather like watching the debutantes try to attract a dancing partner.

"You are here at the perfect time," Aunt Elizabeth said, casting one more inquisitive look Clara's way. "We were opening the discussion to ideas for what our benefit should be."

"One cannot go wrong with a ball." Lady Elliot leaned in to pull the attention of the circle. "It would require no one to set aside their other objectives in order to support our cause."

It was now or never. Clara took a deep breath. "I rather think a ball would be lost in the stack of invitations. There are so many of them, after all. What would make people choose to attend one in which they needed to pay?" When no one immediately berated her opinion, she pushed forward. "I was thinking we invite them to an event at which they gain something for themselves that they would not find elsewhere."

She wanted to press on, to discuss the advertisements she'd seen for special sermons, but even though this was her event that had been brought before the society, she attempted to apply the principle of allowing other people to have guiding input to the proposal as well as to general conversation.

Once other people were in line with the idea of having people purchase tickets that would not only help their cause but help themselves as well, she could make her suggestion. This was London, so the more famous traveling preachers would hardly be a novelty, but it would be different than the other season's events.

After a moment of silence, a murmur grew as people considered her suggestion. They seemed in agreement that a ball might not stand out amongst the other social opportunities as much.

"What about a musicale? I've a large music room with doors that can open into two drawing rooms if you need a hostess." Lady Grableton's voice cut through the noise and Clara knew she'd lost her opportunity. The countess had spoken, and everyone was going to agree. Especially if the countess was willing to host the event.

All was not lost. Perhaps Clara could sway the selection of music towards something that would inspire more holiness in those who listened.

Suggestions were flying about the room with people naming the debutantes that had especially good musical talents as well as the music masters that were known amongst the ton.

Before Clara could determine a suggestion in line with her objectives, Lady Grableton spoke again. "Perhaps a private opera performance? We could persuade Miss Henrietta Thistleton to support our cause, I am certain."

The room was filled with oohs and aahs and gasps of delighted agreement.

Clara had yet to attend the opera, so she didn't know who Miss Thistleton was. That didn't seem to matter, though. This event was no longer hers. And Mr. Lockhart, who was supposedly her partner in this endeavor, certainly wasn't getting a say.

Not that he seemed to particularly want one, but it didn't sit right that he had no hand at all in the benefit.

"A lottery," she blurted out.

All heads turned in her direction.

"We could increase the price of the tickets if they were also for a lottery." Because the funds were getting split between two groups, she wanted to make the total as high as possible.

All attention swung toward Lady Grableton, as if her opinion was the only one that mattered. Clara gritted her teeth. Did everyone simply forget they had a brain when a higher title walked into the room?

Lady Grableton was looking at Clara again, though, with that look of expectation, admiration, and pride that seemed out of place given how little they knew each other. "I think that is a fine idea."

Clara looked to Aunt Elizabeth and there was no doubt in her mind that for possibly the first time since coming to London, her aunt actually approved of her.

Hugh was still setting out his tools for an evening of work when Clara knocked on the open drawing room door.

He looked up with a smile that froze on his face as he took her in. It wasn't the first time she'd come by his workroom. There were many evenings she would come by to say hello or encourage him in his progress. She was already dressed to go out for the evening this time, though, and the picture stole his breath away.

Her hair was pulled up in a pile of loose curls, while other curls framed her face. The dress was cut to show off her figure and the pale green color made her skin almost glow.

It wasn't that different a presentation than hundreds of other young ladies across London would be giving that evening, but Hugh couldn't remember the last time he'd been this close to one of those hundreds. In his world, even at what limited social events it held, the ladies' finer dresses wouldn't be a trimmed satin ballgown.

"Twice in one day. I'm truly honored." He cleared his throat. "You look lovely."

"Thank you." She gave him a smile and a nod before sighing and looking down at the dress. "I do believe this might be my favorite of the gowns Aunt Elizabeth selected." Her smile was almost impish when she looked up. "Perhaps that is why I got ready so quickly this evening."

"And used the spare time to come show it to me?" What was Hugh doing? This was not how he should be talking to his new friends' sister and cousin. This wasn't how he should be talking to a lady at all. He was making a business now.

Pink tinged her cheeks. "Actually, I came to tell you that the plans have been set for the charity event."

He set down the tools and gave her his full attention. "Oh?"

As she told him about that afternoon's society meeting, he only gave half his attention to the plans. The other half was wondering why she didn't seem happier about it.

"What is it you don't like? I confess I'm glad you don't actually need my assistance, though thank you for including a clock." She'd told him they intended to have each ticket include an entry for a large case clock. He knew just the one he could convince Mr. Johns to donate to the cause.

She sighed. "I had a different idea."

"What was it?"

"Last year, Charles Simeon came through our village." She lowered herself to perch on the edge of her normal chair. "We sold tickets to a special sermon he was giving on the importance of mission work. It was our largest collection of funds all year."

Hugh had seen ads for charity sermons and the like over the years, but he'd never been tempted to attend one. "That doesn't seem like a normal event for the London Season."

"Which would have made it stand out." She sighed herself into the chair. "It would have been a light into the darkness of London."

Hugh coughed out a laugh and went back to sorting his tools. "Which do you want more? To help the children or convict the hedonistic society of London of their sins?"

"I see no reason I can't do both."

"Other than the fact that it wouldn't be the hedonistic ones attending your sermon?"

Her shoulders slumped. "I suppose that is true. Ambrose would likely buy a ticket and then fall ill to some mysterious malady that only prevented him from attending that one event."

Hugh had to admit there was some truth to that. "At least he would purchase a ticket. The main purpose is to help the children, after all."

She squirmed in her seat. "Do you think that is enough? The truth is, while everyone keeps saying how good this is of me and even Lady Grableton thanked me particularly for allowing her to be a part of my event, I've done exceptionally little."

Hugh's first thought was that only the underworked would consider an easy success to be problematic, but given the conversations he'd had with Clara so far, he had to think there was more to this problem. "What is truly bothering you?"

She stood to pace. "This was to be my redeeming moment, the one that brought something good from this entire stay in London. If all I do is shake a few hands, that is hardly a righteous endeavor."

Did this woman truly not see how hard she'd been working? "You've spent the past week striving for nothing but the ability to connect with other people. If learning a skill such as that isn't work, I don't know what is."

She frowned. "What do you mean?"

"If you are concerned about God seeing your days as holy enough, you need only ask if everything you do is done with righteous intention with a goal of aligning with the will of God."

Conviction slammed through him as he parroted the words his uncle had told him time and again as he worked through his apprenticeship. There were Sundays where, despite his best intentions, he fell asleep in church. There were nights when he dreamed about gears and springs.

Always, Uncle Patrick would tell him that God honors hard, honest work, and as long as Hugh didn't forget why he was doing what he was doing, he wouldn't lose God along the way.

Ever since he'd begun this new chronometer, though, Hugh wasn't sure he'd been giving the clock shop a full day of hard, honest work. His hand was suddenly too sweaty to hold the fragile gear he'd picked up.

Miss Woodbury continued, unaware of his uncomfortable considerations. "Do you think gaining a husband is a righteous goal?"

He cleared his throat and forced his thoughts to the conversation at hand. "I think making sure your family is cared for and supported is one."

"I suppose." She frowned. "Is that your goal?"

Was it? He'd honestly been working toward his own shop for so long that he couldn't remember if that had been why he'd set out on the path to begin with.

"I . . . yes." As he said the word, he could see a new future. One that, yes, involved a successful clockwork business, but also a family to come home to, a wife and children to support.

It was a far-off dream. His current rooms might could hold a wife who enjoyed the simple life, but a family was out of the question.

She turned her head to stare out the open door, as if considering what she'd be going to do when she walked out of this room. "I think . . ." She let the words trail off as her gaze seemed to blur and her face went slack with deep thought. "I think it would be very easy to lose track of that in London." She blinked and renewed determination covered her features. "I don't want that to happen to me."

Hugh could barely swallow over the lump in his throat. "Me neither."

She glanced at his worktable. "I don't think you are. This chronometer, it's supposed to open doors for you, isn't it? I know you said progress has been slow, but this is a step forward."

It was. If this chronometer was as good as he thought it would be, it could change his life.

Miss Woodbury's smile was brilliant. "Perhaps marriage is my chronometer. It is the step I need to focus on in order to live a more God-honoring life."

Hugh didn't like the sound of it, but he couldn't tell her she was wrong. "It might be."

She rose and held out her skirts as she twirled. "I'd best get to it then. Have a good evening."

And then she was gone.

Hugh looked down at the gears and springs, the spare wooden boxes and the delicate pointed tools. He could, if he tried very hard, remember the giddiness he'd felt the first time he built a clock from scratch. He could almost recall the excitement of his first day as a shop clerk.

He definitely remembered the first custom order he'd created and the way he'd stood in the corner, listening while the owner praised Mr. Johns for several minutes.

What he couldn't find was the last time he'd felt that way. Life had become a series of tasks, of next steps, of ever-moving objectives. Even his visits to his uncle's house were almost forgettably routine.

In this room, though, he felt alive again.

And he could only hope it was because of the steadily progressing device on the table and not the occasional visits from a certain intriguing young woman.

TWENTY

C lara had thought she was grasping an understanding of how London Society worked. She'd been participating in it for a month now and the rules seemed to constantly be adding another level of nuance.

She'd seen how her aunt's title, or rather her cousin's, had kept her from being ostracized. She'd worked to understand how the level of deference given to the countess affected those around her. Not only did they change their behavior toward her, but the countess's seeming acceptance of Clara had altered how they treated her as well.

Nothing had prepared her for the change that would happen when Lady Grableton had her son ask Clara for a dance.

Clara hadn't even had time to look around the ballroom to see if her companions from the card party were available, when the handsome, dark-haired man and his mother had approached and asked for an introduction. Then he'd asked if she would like to join him for the first set of dances.

"Of course she would," Aunt Elizabeth said before Clara could formulate an answer.

She pushed Clara forward, making her stumble a couple of steps.

Lord Wharton bowed his head, took her arm, and led her to the floor.

They didn't speak much through the first steps of the dance, but it wasn't an uncomfortable silence. In actuality, Clara found it a relief.

The dances required people to step away from each other so often that maintaining the line of conversation was often difficult.

As they stood by each other at the end of the line, he turned to her. "Are you enjoying the Season?"

She started to give the bright, expected answer she'd given to numerous people in the past few weeks, but something about the earnestness of his face had her being a little more honest. "I confess it is not quite what I expected it to be." She gave him a smile. "There are a lot of people."

Something in his face shifted as he listened to her answer. He was quiet for a moment and then gave her a nod. "Mother tells me you are raising funds for her charity."

Her charity? Was Lady Grableton involved with the Royal Asylum? Or . . . Clara nearly gasped as she fought to twist her neck about to look for the countess in the crowd. Was she representing the mysterious second group? Clara didn't dare ask, as Lord Wharton might not drop any additional hints if he was aware that she wasn't as well-informed as he might assume.

Clara smiled and tried to breathe deeply enough to calm her racing heart. "I'm not doing much, really. After suggesting the original idea, other people have done most of the planning."

"But you care." He looked around at the rest of the ball's attendees with a pensive look. "That's more than can be said for most people."

They rejoined the dance then, and while they didn't fully fall back into silence, the conversation lapsed into the normal conversation between strangers at a society function.

When the set was complete, he walked her over to the side of the ballroom and bowed over her hand. When he lifted his head, his grin was crooked. "Enjoy the rest of your evening."

The sentiment was one that had been uttered to her multiple times over the past few weeks, but somehow Lord Wharton's seemed to mean something far different from the polite parting of ways.

She'd barely risen from her curtsy when another man was there asking her to dance. She'd met him on two occasions, but they had never exchanged more than a nominal greeting.

Mr. Pitt was waiting for her after that set and whisked her straight back onto the floor.

"I very much enjoyed our ride and would like to take you out again."

A sense of satisfaction rose in Clara as she gave him a demure smile in response. "I would like that."

And she would. Yes, the conversation had been somewhat dull, and they hadn't found much in common, but what was that when compared to a life of mission and purpose?

"Did I see you dancing with Lord Wharton this evening?" He cleared his throat and leaned in to speak softly as they circled another couple. "I was unaware that the two of you were acquainted."

Did the man ever think of anything except who was seen with who and who knew who? "I have recently been working with his mother on a charity benefit."

"How fascinating." He proceeded to ask about the charity, expressing concern for the children and interest in the Virtuous Ladies Society as a whole.

Clara felt a little remorse for thinking harshly of him a few minutes prior. It was a good thing that the man paid attention to people, wasn't it? He could hardly care for their needs and their souls if he didn't know what was happening in their lives.

"We shall be selling tickets to a musicale hosted by Lady Grableton." Clara shared the details, finally feeling a little bit of excitement for the event in the face of Mr. Pitt's obvious enthusiasm.

"I shall be the first in line to purchase a ticket," the man said with a decisive nod. "Are you enjoying working with Lady Grableton? The connection must be going well for her to introduce you to her son."

"I think so." Clara studiously avoided frowning as she tried to think through whether she and Lady Grableton had actually formed anything that could be considered a friendship.

"I am impressed." Mr. Pitt leaned down to ensure his gaze caught with hers. "I did not know you would be able to make such a mark in London in such a short time."

In that moment, Clara decided her aunt was wrong. Mr. Pitt hadn't started visiting Clara because of her connection to Ambrose. He'd been intrigued but was waiting to see if she would be a suitably impactful vicar's wife.

The set ended and Mr. Pitt escorted her from the floor, promising to call during her next at-home day.

Clara didn't have time to bask in this confirmation that her choice was a good one and their relationship was growing in the right direction, because she was escorted right back out again. Throughout the next hour and a half, she was never more than a foot from the dance floor.

There was no standing on the side, making idle conversation with the hope of being chosen. No drinking yet another glass of weak lemonade, trying to look like she'd planned to stay off the dance floor for another set.

Instead, after an eternity of non-stop dancing, she was craving that weak lemonade and a shadowy alcove to drink it in. Finally, she grabbed her mother and claimed a need for the retiring room just to have a break.

The corridor was quiet and cool, a balm to both Clara's mind and body. "Mother, what has happened?"

A large grin stretched across her mother's face as she opened the fan hanging from her wrist to send a brisk breeze toward her daughter. "Lady Grableton happened, my dear. Whatever you did impressed that woman greatly."

"I don't understand."

"Lord Wharton is going to be an earl, Clara. He's young and hand-some and charming and titled. He doesn't have a reputation of debauch-ery or drunkenness. I'd say there isn't a much greater catch roaming the ballrooms this season, though people are saying he hasn't been around much." She closed the fan and hit Clara delicately in the shoulder. "And he stood up first with you."

"That was all it took?"

"That was all it took."

How should she feel about that? How was anyone meant to feel about that? If people's opinions could change on such an arbitrary considera-tion, how was anyone to know anyone else's true feelings or opinions? Fortunately, the only man she was interested in had noticed her long before Lady Grableton had.

Why didn't that truth elicit any sort of happiness within her? A sense of satisfaction, yes, but nothing that one might term excitement. "Moth-er?"

"Yes, dear?"

"What does love feel like?"

Mother almost stumbled as she took her gaze from the corridor in front of them and fixed it on her daughter. She came to a stop, turning Clara so they were standing face to face. "Why do you ask?"

"Because I don't know. You want a love match for me, and while I'm not certain it is something I can wait for or completely see the merit in seeking, I would like to know what it would be like." Clara frowned, giving free rein to the confused expression in the privacy of this conversation. "If I attain what I set out to accomplish, is that what love feels like?"

"Oh, no, my dear." Mother laughed. "Love is not some fulfilled sense of purpose." She sighed as her face turned serious. "Nor is it those giggles one hears from the girls on the side of the dance floor when a handsome man walks by."

Clara waited, hoping Mother had more to say. It was, of course, helpful to know what something was not, but there were far too many more options for Clara to use such deductive reasoning to answer her question.

"Love is . . ." Mother took a deep breath. "I suppose love, at least the type of love between a man and a woman, is life. It is that person that makes your life more . . . complete, more meaningful. When you want to stand by a person's side and have their back at the same time. When being with them makes your day better, and . . . and . . ."

The words trailed off as the older woman's chin started to shake and her breathing broke into small bursts.

"Mother?" Clara rested a hand on her mother's shoulder. "Are you well?"

"I miss your father," Mother whispered. "More than I thought I would. We agreed he couldn't leave the parish for this long, but . . ." She sighed.

The sound of voices coming toward them from the direction of the ballroom had both women pressing into the wall until the trio of ladies had passed.

"You can take the carriage home if you need to," Clara said. "They'll easily make it back here before Aunt Elizabeth is ready to depart."

A single tear crept down Mother's cheek. "I don't want to leave you. This Season is very important."

"I shall hardly notice your absence." Clara gave what she hoped was a wide, reassuring smile. "After I take a moment to breathe here, I'm certain I won't have a moment's respite from the dance floor."

The prospect was more than a little daunting, but she was thankful for it if it gave Mother what she needed.

After a few moments, Mother nodded and agreed that might be the best solution.

They hugged and parted ways. Clara continued to the retiring room on her own. She would wait there until she'd settled her own emotions, then go back to the ballroom with another set of ladies.

Several chairs and settees had been arranged at one end of the room, with a collection of screens set up for privacy on the other. A couple of maids stood talking in the corner, waiting for their services to be needed.

Most of the occupants seemed happy to simply do what was necessary and head back to the ballroom. Clara needed more than that brief respite. Her feet hurt, and in truth, her mind was somewhat foggy. Whether from the dancing or the conversation, it didn't matter.

She found a chair that had been tucked mostly behind the curtain. Clearly some other girl had been through here, needing a moment to herself tonight.

Gratefully, Clara slid into the chair and even fluffed the curtain a bit to hide her skirts. After three slow, deep breaths, she set about doing what she always did—make sense of whatever seemed to be in turmoil.

So far in life, Clara had never seen reason to allow emotion or flimsy intuition to guide her way. Truth and practicality were far more dependable. After tonight, Aunt Elizabeth would have enormous ambitions supported by nothing but a night of masculine curiosity. Lord Wharton had asked her to dance, and the other men had wanted to know why. Aside from Mr. Pitt, most of them had not seen fit to ask her before.

Clara would not let such aspirations get to her head. She'd chosen Mr. Pitt before her temporary popularity, and he was as fine a choice now as he'd been yesterday.

Satisfied her mind was back in order, Clara went to stand and return to the ballroom until a sniffling cry on the other side of the curtain had her quieting once more.

"There, there," one woman said. "No one is in here but us. You're free to cry."

"I, I, I—" *hiccough* "I should have, have known it was too good to be true." The words were interspersed with gasps and sobs from the crying woman.

"You are the one who is too good to be true," a third woman declared. "I wish I'd warned you about him when he first came to visit you."

"Did you know he was a cad?" The first woman sounded surprised.

Clara turned her head to hear everything. It was horribly uncouth to sit here and listen but emerging now would devastate the poor, crying girl. Clara couldn't embarrass another lady like that.

"No, but my brother told me to avoid him if possible and that he's known to pledge more than he should at the tables in the clubs. That should have been enough for me to warn you as well."

"I fear we are not in the same situation," the sad woman said. "This is my only Season. If I do not find someone to marry in the next couple of months, I will be limited to the selection back in the village." She sighed. "My aunt and uncle are being very generous to sponsor me, but we can't afford another year."

Clara knew that situation all too well, and her heart went out to the woman. Especially if the man indulged in the pursuit of vice like Ambrose did. Though she was fairly certain her cousin wasn't gambling away money he didn't have.

"Are you certain you are . . . Are you well?"

"I am well." Another shaky breath broke the last words. "He only kissed me."

The third woman gave a snort of disgust. "And then told you he could not listen to his heart but had to choose the woman his head required."

"Absolute cad."

Clara was inclined to agree with the first woman's decisiveness.

"How did he lure you out there in the first place?"

The lady let out a deep, watery sigh. "He asked if I would like to get a breath of fresh air as my cheeks appeared flushed from all the dancing."

"My brother said he dances with all the women in your situation. To the world he probably looks like the gracious sort, dancing with the would-be wallflowers."

"We should call him out," the first lady said. "Go stand in the middle of the ballroom and let his ungentlemanly ways be known."

"No, I can't!" The desperation in the sad woman's voice stabbed Clara in the gut. "I cannot risk the damage to my reputation.

One of the women sighed. "That must be how he gets away with it."

"You think he's done this to other women?"

"I think he must have. Do you remember who he was seen with last Season? Are any of them still in London."

"Only Mrs. Penwith but she doesn't come out in society much anymore."

The sad girl spoke again. "He was too practiced. He knew what he was doing. He has to have done this before."

"I suppose," the first woman said with resignation, "that we can be glad all he wanted to steal was a kiss."

Again, the woman let out a sound of deep disgust. "Doesn't mean Mr. Pitt shouldn't be thrown into the pits."

The three girls laughed, which was loud enough to cover Clara's gasp. This entire time, she'd been upset on this poor girl's behalf, in solid agreement with everything her friends were saying. And the man in question had been the one she'd thought would make the perfect husband.

How could she have been so wrong about him?

The women departed the room soon after, and Clara waited for her heartbeat to settle into a quiet rhythm before sliding out of her hiding spot. She made her way back to the ballroom, mind spinning with a myriad of thoughts.

She was immediately pulled into the next set of dances. Two partners later, Mr. Pitt was once more waiting to ask her to dance.

"Two dances in one night would certainly be tipping your hand, sir."
The statement was bold, and two hours before, she'd have been overjoyed
at the implication.

Now she didn't know what to think.

He gave her a pleasant smile. "You are right, of course. I wasn't thinking. The time for such declarations is yet to come." He glanced over her
shoulder. "Perhaps we should step out onto the terrace then? Get a little
fresh air? Your cheeks appear a bit flushed from all the dancing."

If Clara's cheeks had indeed been flushed before, she was certain they
weren't now. Those were the words the lady in the retiring room had
claimed Mr. Pitt used to lure her away from her protection.

There were no words in her throat as she looked up at him, nothing in
her mind but a screaming sort of noise as everything she thought she'd
put in order seemed to shake.

She needed to think. She needed to determine what was real.

She needed to get out of there.

Without a word, she took two steps back, then fled to find her aunt.

TWENTY-ONE

E very last remnant of that night's revelry faded away into the darkness of the night as their carriage rolled away from the noise and lights of the ball. By the time it stopped in front of Ambrose's townhome, Clara was wrapped in despair.

The clandestine exchange between the ladies, who had no inkling of Clara's eavesdropping, had to be given proper credence. Words said in private carried more weight than those said to impress in public, after all. If what they'd said about Mr. Pitt was even a little bit accurate, he was not the man of virtue she'd thought him to be.

Righteous life, indeed. Clara crossed her arms over herself and pulled her wrap tighter as she and Aunt Elizabeth exited the carriage and filed up the stairs and into the house. She could feel nothing but pity for his future congregation if they were to be subjected to such a roguish shepherd. And to think she'd envisaged herself as the man's wife.

Mother was waiting in the front hall. The servants took the ladies' wraps and disappeared into the dark house. Aunt Elizabeth gave a rousing tale of Clara's triumph, declaring they were sure to have a drawing room full of gentlemen in a day or two. Clara said nothing.

Eventually, Mother and Aunt Elizabeth started for the stairs, but Clara's feet seemed to be glued to the tiles of the front hall.

"Mother," she said softly, and both of the older women stopped their climb.

She looked at their inquisitive faces, knowing the question she had to ask would let them know her abject failure. Still, she had to know. "Is it common for a man who will one day take his orders to . . . to . . ."

"Indulge in unbecoming pursuits?" Aunt Elizabeth finished Clara's question before sighing. "It isn't unheard of, especially among younger sons of the ton."

Both women retreated back down to the floor of the hall and took a place on either side of Clara. Mother wrapped an arm around her daughter's shoulders while Aunt Elizabeth gently grasped Clara's hand between her own. Sympathy covered her features.

"I'm certain Mr. Pitt will step away from his more frivolous inclinations when the gravity of a living is placed upon his shoulders. The necessity of propriety will demand it, even if the time required for more sacred duties doesn't." She smiled, as if this idea would ease all of Clara's concerns.

They, in fact, did the opposite. The numbness that had been working its way through her since overhearing the conversation in the retiring room fell away as an anger she considered entitled and righteous flooded her chest. Many of England's churches were being led by younger sons and nephews of the aristocracy. Surely they weren't all of the same mind as Mr. Pitt. "A man cannot discard his less savory proclivities like a snake sheds its skin."

Her cousin was proof that such a lifestyle was a deeply ingrained ideology.

"Do not underestimate the transformative power of the heat of obligation." Mother's face grew thoughtful. "Life is a crucible that refines even the basest of metals."

Clara looked to her mother, but the older woman would not meet her daughter's gaze. In her younger years, had mother been more like Aunt Elizabeth? Had she been refined by the fire of being a vicar's wife?

Clara swallowed hard before saying, "Even the hottest refining fire cannot reveal a substance that is not already there."

Mother's arm tightened into a hug as a small smile touched her lips. "I suppose you are correct."

"Only God knows the future." Aunt Elizabeth gave Clara's hand a squeeze and then let go to move back toward the stairs. "We must aspire to build the life we desire and allow time to reveal everything else."

With a gentle sigh, Mother, too, moved toward the stairs. "There is some wisdom to what she says, Clara. We must all move forward in a way that will allow us to attain that which matters most to us. If a living position is what you crave, you must decide what you are willing to give up to attain it."

"As you did?"

"If you think my ultimate desire was to be a vicar's wife, you are mistaken." She paused with her hand on the newel post, an expression of utter peace on her face. "That is the lot I accepted in order to be your father's wife."

Clara blinked. "It wasn't what you wanted?"

"I loved your father, and a life of service was what he wanted." She smiled. "I do not regret what our life has been and the service I have been able to give God is a blessing in itself. But it wasn't my girlhood dream, no."

When Clara didn't say anything, Mother gave another sweet smile and disappeared up the stairs.

Clara waited until the steady swish of her mother's skirts had faded before lowering her gaze to the floor as if the answers would somehow form in the swirls of the marble tiles.

Her maid would be waiting to see to her hair and put her to bed, but Clara couldn't bring herself to go about her evening as if all her plans were still in place. Sleep wouldn't come when she was this unsettled, after all.

Instead, she wandered into the dark drawing room. Without even a lamp to chase the shadows away, the room closed in about her like a cold shell. The isolation matched the feeling of lostness in her bones.

She lowered herself into an armchair, allowing her mind to toss to and fro, hoping the peace of the empty room would seep into her soul somehow.

It didn't. If anything, the stillness gave her senses nothing to latch onto aside from the ticking of the grandfather clock in the corner, which grew more mocking and ominous the longer she listened. It felt like a knife, chipping slowly away at the life she'd thought she'd been creating.

It was almost a relief to hear a commotion in the front hall that gave her something else to contemplate. She walked to the door and saw Hodges opening it for a very disheveled Ambrose.

He tossed his hat, cane, and greatcoat to the butler, and leaned against the wall, humming lightly under his breath as he tugged at his poorly tied cravat.

"You would return home in such a state, knowing I, your aunt, and even your mother are in residence under the same roof?" Clara asked before she could stop herself.

"Seeing as you, my aunt, and my mother should either be dancing away your satin slippers or tucked in your beds, I didn't think the state of a person at two in the morning would matter, no." Ambrose ran a hand through his hair and gave her a sloppy grin. "You didn't mention Duke's delicate sensibilities, I notice. Do you believe I've already irreparably corrupted him?"

Heat flushed Clara's cheeks. "Marmaduke is capable of handling his own concerns."

Ambrose nodded sagely. "But you, my mother, and Aunt Miriam are not. That is good information to know. I shall endeavor to act more the protector for the remainder of the Season."

Clara nearly gave in to the urge to stomp her foot. "That is not what I meant."

"Then say what you mean, dear cousin. You've usually no problem telling me plainly how you feel about my condemned soul."

She narrowed her gaze. "Are you drunk?"

He glanced down at himself as he pulled his cravat from his neck. "I can see where you would make such an assumption, but no, I have not overimbibed." He grinned again. "My pockets are a great deal heavier, though."

"You've been out gambling?" Clara blinked.

"Yes." Ambrose pointed at her. "And before you admonish me for it, consider all the other sins I could have been committing. Save your harshest criticism for the worst of the lot. Otherwise, this Season is going to be exceedingly dull in its lack of variety."

Clara gripped her skirt in tight fists, possibly crushing the delicate fabric beyond repair. How could he be so flippant? "'Tis only that I have a care for your soul."

"And how improper do I have to be for you to consider my soul beyond redemption?" Ambrose strode toward the stairs and began to climb. "Because I assure you, dear cousin, in my twenty-seven years, I've done worse than your restrained imagination is capable of conjuring."

By the time Clara's tongue loosened from the top of her mouth, he had disappeared up the stairs. Numbly, she trailed after him, finally seeking her own room and the fitful sleep she was doomed to endure as her mind tried to settle on all of the night's disappointments.

Her eyes felt gritty when she blinked them awake the next morning. For the first time, she was grateful that she didn't have to make any effort to prepare herself for the day. The dedicated maid her aunt had insisted upon did it all. It was even possible Clara had dozed off for several moments while her hair was being dressed.

The breakfast room was peaceful and calm, filled with the quiet shuf-
fles of servants and the slight clink of cutlery on plates. Aunt Elizabeth
sat at the head of the oval table and waited until Clara was settled with a
plate of her own and a cup of tea before speaking.

"You look quite fine this morning, Clara." She nodded in approval.
"'Tis smart to put on a good turn for the Virtuous Ladies Society meeting today. Lady Grableton should be in attendance again, so we can put
the final details on your charity event."

"Of course, Aunt Elizabeth." Clara curved her lips into a dutiful smile.
She hadn't wanted control of the event in the first place, but now calling
the event "hers" was simply ridiculous. She'd had practically no say in the
event planning and, aside from helping her establish the wording of the
initial idea, Mr. Lockhart had been completely removed.

After breakfast, she took her maid and went for a walk. The fresh air,
or at least the freshest air London was capable of providing, helped to
chase away the melancholy she'd woken with. By the time she ensconced
herself in the drawing room with the Virtuous Ladies, her spirits had
returned to their normal resiliency.

This was still her event, and she would have a say.

Ambrose was still her cousin and despite his belief otherwise, his soul
was not too far gone to save.

Mr. Pitt, well, he was still in line for a living, but that particular issue
might not actually be salvageable. As her mother had said, she had to
decide what was important enough to her that she was willing to sacrifice
a few ideals to get.

"Since we are coming together to support a cause," Clara said, inter-
rupting the gossip to bring attention to the purpose of the meeting. "I
thought it would be nice to bring more inclusion to the attendees. We
are, of course, being entertained by an esteemed singer, but perhaps there
could be participation as well? A group singing perhaps? Maybe some
hymns?"

"I don't think there's any reason to be quaint," one woman said, nose wrinkled into a near frown.

"This is an exclusive musical performance," another woman noted. "Not a fete at the vicarage."

"Peonies are absolutely essential," Mrs. Hargrove declared, stabbing her closed fan into the air to punctuate each word. She then flipped the accessory open and delicately fluttered it toward her face. "They are the embodiment of philanthropic grace."

"True," one lady, whose name Clara could not remember, said slowly. "However, do we want to be constantly reminding everyone that they are in attendance at such an event? Their work is finished after purchasing the ticket to be there. We don't want to make them uncomfortable."

"It wouldn't be a bad thing for the ton to remember there are less fortunate, troubled people among them in London." Lady Grableton's gaze locked onto Clara's as she spoke.

The air backed up into Clara's lungs. She'd wondered if the countess was part of Eleanor's mysterious group, and this all but confirmed it. The question was, had Eleanor's prodding prompted her presence or had Clara's social improvement truly caught the woman's eye?

Lady Grableton looked away from Clara and picked up her teacup. "For some, it will give them a sense of superiority."

"I agree with the countess," Aunt Elizabeth said, because of course she would agree with the woman of highest rank in the room. "It isn't as if we're parading the children through the room."

"No, of course not," Lady Grableton said before smiling into her tea.

Frustration churned through Clara. Frustration at the ladies who dismissed her ideas out of hand because they weren't what was already being done. Frustration at Eleanor for keeping the true benefactors of this event a secret. Frustration at Lady Grableton, who was clearly in on the secret and found the entire business ironically amusing.

Once the internal listing of frustrations had begun, Clara couldn't seem to stop them.

She was perturbed at Marmaduke and his seeming lack of concern that Ambrose was traveling further and further down the road of impropriety. Then, of course, she was also frustrated with Ambrose himself, as he clearly seemed to know the repercussions of his actions and no longer cared.

From there, her mental complaints drifted to her parents, the ones who had insisted she make this trip to London in the first place. She could have made a greater effort to participate in the local social scene. Surely that would have been enough to find her a suitable match.

If she was going to end up compromising eventually anyway, she might as well do it in the comfort of what was familiar.

She sat in silence for the remainder of the meeting, nodding along whenever Aunt Elizabeth seemed to be in agreement as that would cause her less grief later.

Finally, everyone dispersed, and only Clara, her aunt, and her mother remained in the drawing room.

"I do believe everything is falling into place." Aunt Elizabeth patted Clara on her knee. "I'm glad you came around to my vision of the event. Elegant is always the answer when asking people to part with their money."

Mother made a noise that wasn't an agreement or a dissension.

Clara frowned. "The church is frequently the recipient of monies for the less fortunate, and we are not in the habit of couching such requests in elegance."

"Are you not?" Aunt Elizabeth stood and placed the last of the remaining teacups on the tray. Her tone was gentle and matter of fact, without a trace of judgment. "I know it has been a while since I visited your village, but I believe you do have finer boxes for your local gentry to subscribe to?" She paused and looked at her sister. "You haven't gone the way of nothing but free benches like the Baptists, have you?"

Mother cleared her throat. "Er, no. We still have boxes."

Aunt Elizabeth gave a nod. "As you should. People need to feel at home in the church." Considering the matter closed, she pressed a hand to her chest with a sigh. "My, but it has been many a year since I've been this active in a Season." She grinned at Clara. "You're keeping me young, I daresay."

"I do what I can," Clara muttered with a tight smile. "Even in my youth, though, I am feeling the drain."

If her fatigue was more emotional than physical, well, that didn't stop it from being a reality.

Mother stood as well and looked about the room. "I'll let the servants know they can come in and clean up now." She smiled at Clara, but there was sympathy in her eyes. "We are attending a dinner this evening, but the event is small and meant more for your aunt and I. If you are in need of a rest, I'm sure your absence will not be considered a slight."

"Of course." Aunt Elizabeth nodded. "There will be few prospects there, and those that are will likely be all but spoken for. As tired as I am, I have not been spending my evenings dancing." She laughed. "I remember how exciting but exhausting such constant activity could be."

Clara accepted the reprieve, hoping that an evening to herself would set things to rights and clear her mind. Not wanting to risk her peace being disturbed by another argument with Ambrose, she selected a book from the library and requested a light, simple meal be brought to her room.

Less than an hour into her calm evening, though, a restlessness filled her as the frustrations she'd pushed away returned to occupy her mind.

Sighing, she set the book aside and paced around her room. Without thought, she left her planned peaceful confines and strode about the house. When she realized her feet were taking her to the back drawing room, she paused.

She was meant to spend the evening relaxing in her own company. Did she truly want to seek out someone else?

As she considered that the someone else she was seeking out was Mr. Lockhart, a sense of urgency propelled her feet into motion once more.

Later she would question what could possibly be pulling her toward him, but for now she simply held her breath and hoped the closed off room would be occupied for the evening.

If she felt a small thrill at the band of light coming around the nearly closed door, well, no one knew that but her.

TWENTY-TWO

H ugh carefully turned the screw on the casing of the chronometer. Too tight and the box would bind, restricting the accurate movement of the carefully balanced mechanism. Too loose and the interior parts could shift, throwing everything out of alignment.

Satisfied, he sat back and looked at the device. Had he made all the right choices? Only time would tell.

A grin touched his lips and some of the tension eased from his shoulders as he appreciated his own mental joke.

"Don't you get tired of spending your evenings here?"

There was no quelling the snap of pleasure that sliced through him as he looked up and confirmed that his visitor was indeed Clara. He should discourage her visits, but there was something so refreshing about conversing with someone who wanted nothing from him but his thoughts and could provide nothing for him aside from companionship.

Not having to weigh the benefits of maintaining an easy relationship was more of a luxury than he'd have guessed.

He considered her question and gave a one-shouldered shrug. "Not really." And soon he would have less reason to be here. Checking in daily to maintain the device and verify it was keeping accurate time wouldn't require him to spend hours in this room.

He didn't tell her that. "I only have a month until the device has to be turned into Greenwich. Of course, it will be a year until they announce a winner."

Clara's eye widened. "That seems a long time."

"It's the only way to test a chronometer and see how accurate it remains without being adjusted." He grinned and shared his earlier joke with her. "Only time will tell."

She gave him a small smile and shook her head as she came further into the room. "That makes sense." With a deep sigh, she sat in her customary seat near the door. As if her proximity to escape would be enough to assuage anyone's displeasure if they were to find her in the room with him unchaperoned.

He fiddled with the items on his worktable, needlessly arranging and rearranging them. In truth, there was little more he could do tonight. Since she hadn't come by already this evening, he'd assumed they'd gone to an earlier evening event, and he might see Miss Woodbury upon their return. He'd intended to be well away from the house before that could happen. Not only did he badly need a full night of sleep, but he needed to separate himself from the nightly discussions.

They were making him discontent with his life in ways he might never be able to rectify.

Now that she was here, though, he couldn't bring himself to leave.

They couldn't just sit here in silence, though. The obvious topic would be the charity fundraiser he was supposed to be helping her with but had so far done nothing toward.

A man did not deliberately bring up his shortcomings to a beautiful woman, though, even if he did not have romantic intentions toward her.

"Mr. Lockhart," she said softly, "might I ask your opinion on something? As a man?"

Maybe he wanted to discuss the charity after all. Hadn't she wanted a clock for a lottery or something? He swallowed. A gentleman really couldn't deny a request such as hers, not if they were friends. "If you need to ask, I am, of course, at your service."

"Do you have a sister?"

Of the dozens of possibilities that had flooded through his mind, that question wasn't even on the fringes. "I . . . no."

"But you have your cousin Eleanor."

"Yes."

Miss Woodbury frowned. "Do you listen to her?"

Hugh grinned. "She would box my ears if I didn't."

The sigh she emitted was the deflating kind, the sort someone gave when they were on the verge of admitting defeat.

He didn't like hearing it from her.

"What has you so troubled that you stayed in tonight? The servants mentioned the carriage left hours ago."

"I didn't want to come to London, you know." She twisted her fingers together in her lap. "But since I had no choice in the matter, I tried to make the best of the situation. There are always possibilities, even in the most dismal of circumstances."

There weren't many young ladies in England that would find a fully sponsored Season in London a dismal circumstance, but he wisely kept that observation to himself.

"By the time we arrived, I had dreams of what I would do here."

That sounded like a far more normal circumstance. Even Eleanor occasionally dreamed of what she would do with a London Season, even though she'd never have one that included aristocratic balls and theater boxes.

When she fell silent, Hugh prompted, "I assume that things are not progressing according to plan, then?"

"No." Her voice was small. "They are not."

Every time they'd spoken, Hugh had stayed firmly in position behind his worktable. The distance now seemed almost rude when the woman appeared to be near tears. He crossed the room and took the chair that had been pushed up against the wall behind the door.

"What has you troubled, Miss Woodbury?"

Her face scrunched up into a frown as she rose to her feet. "My apologies. I should not be imposing on you in this manner."

Hugh's eyebrows lifted as he stood as well, careful to keep a proper distance between them. "If I'd felt your conversation was an imposition, I'd have put an end to it the first time you visited me."

She crossed her arms as if all that was holding her together was sheer force of will.

"I shan't stop you if you choose to go, but you may depend upon my discretion if you need to speak freely, Miss Woodbury."

Her nose scrunched again, and Hugh almost laughed. "It's the Miss Woodbury, isn't it?"

She sighed. "Yes. I'm afraid I haven't had a confidant that wasn't my family or a friend from childhood. All of them call me Clara."

"Have I your permission then? You, of course, may refer to me as Hugh if you wish."

She nodded. "I think that will help."

"Shall we try again, then?" He gestured toward the chairs, and they both lowered themselves to the seats.

"What has you troubled, Clara?" The intimacy of her given name in his mouth nearly drove him to his feet once more. Perhaps, since it was just the two of them, he would simply not call her anything. Yes, that would be safer.

"While I didn't particularly want to come to London, I knew the marriage was a necessity. I can hardly live on my family's generosity forever." She took a deep breath. "After I got here, I made a plan. You inspired it, actually."

"Me?"

"Yes. You." Whatever Hugh had been expecting to follow that revelation, he could never have been prepared for the flood of words that followed.

Once Clara started talking, there was simply no stopping her as the thought process behind selecting Mr. Pitt was detailed, along with her growing concerns over Ambrose's depraved habits and her failure to do more for Eleanor's cause than provide a plausible front for her true mission.

"Nothing is going the way it should." Clara clenched her fists together in her lap.

Hugh took a deep breath and sent a silent prayer for wisdom heavenward. Was this what it would have been like if he'd had a sister? Not that he felt all that brotherly toward Clara, but maybe if he'd grown up with an understanding of what happened when a woman let loose all her problems, he would know better what to say.

Since he didn't have experience to lean on, he was just going to have to tread carefully and follow his instincts. "How do you know it isn't?"

She blinked at him. "Weren't you listening? This wasn't the plan."

"I know, but you aren't the one in control."

"That's exactly what I'm saying. Everything is running away from me like a frightened horse."

So the *put your trust in God* angle wasn't going to work tonight. What was Eleanor always telling him to do? Try a little empathy? "You feel powerless."

"Yes." Clara slumped into the chair. "No matter how badly I want to drive life in a certain direction, my efforts are insignificant." Her voice roughened as if tears were imminent. "I want to return to the village where I matter."

Against his better judgment, Hugh reached across the space and took her hand, bumping the door a few more inches closed in the process. "You matter here. Your intentions are noble, and your motivations are good. Regardless of the outcome, you can only ever control your own actions."

Her hand squeezed his as her head dropped back against the chair. She stared at the ceiling as if the answers to life could be found in the floating dust. "Why wouldn't noble and good actions have the desired reaction?"

"I didn't say your actions were good. I said your intentions were."

Her head snapped up and she narrowed her gaze at him. "What do you mean?"

How should he put this? He cast his eyes around the room, desperate for inspiration. His eyes lit on the worktable and the scattering of clock components on the surface. "Have you ever wound a clock?"

Her hand let go of his so she could cross her arms in agitation. "Of course I have."

He flexed his fingers to ease the sudden chill that crossed his skin. "Right. Of course." He cleared his throat. "Have you ever wound one too tight?"

She frowned. "Possibly. I've attempted to wind clocks that had apparently been broken, but I would hardly know why."

"If you wind the spring too tight, it can snap or twist in on itself so that it can't drive the clock anymore."

She sat up straighter on the edge of her seat. "If you mean to call me uptight as Ambrose tends to do, I will leave this room."

Hugh winced. He was clearly making a mess of this conversation, but he couldn't stop now, especially not when he was right. "I didn't say you were wound too tight." He took a deep breath and plunged on. "But it's possible you are trying to keep winding a clock, hoping it will give you a different time."

"So I should stop winding the clock? I should stop trying to change things and just stand idly by while misguided decisions are made, and lives are left to wallow in the mire of the consequences of those decisions?"

She rose to her feet and began to pace the small room. "You would have me stand by and accept the outcome as I watch my cousin run himself to ruin, Mr. Pitt squander the shepherding responsibilities he is to have, and my name be given credit for efforts I have no part in?"

"I said no such thing." Hugh stood because it was either move his body or raise his voice. "Acceptance is not surrender, but you have to understand that no matter how much you influence or guide, you have no command over the will of others."

"I refuse to be a passive bystander in my own life."

"Yet you would have them passively allow you to steer their path."

"Well, someone has to step in because they are all doing it wrong."

"And who are you to declare that?"

"It is obvious to anyone who has ever listened to a sermon." She paced until she was standing directly in front of Hugh, eyes bright with the conviction of her stance. "Everything we do affects others. You don't just stick meaningless gears into a clock, do you? Everything has a purpose and changes something else."

He sighed. She had a point, and he had to concede it with a sharp nod.

"Then we owe it to the people around us to consider the weight of our choices and ensure that others are correctly impacted by our behavior."

He wanted to shove a hand through his hair or perhaps take his own turn eating up the floor with his paces, but she had him blocked into a corner between the chair and the door. "There is, perhaps, merit in your tenacity, but you cannot simply badger someone into accepting your view. I know little about Mr. Pitt's situation"—though he wasn't surprised to learn the man was less than honorable—"and I know even less of society ladies, but I've been spending a great deal of time with your cousin lately."

"Then you know the situation is dire."

"I know what you've set in motion is not directing his mind toward the thoughts you would like him to have."

"I will not give up on him."

Was she willfully misinterpreting him? "I never said you should."

"But you would have me simply accept his debauchery."

"I would have you accept his freedom of choice."

"He cannot be free when he is shackled by the consequences of his vices."

"And what of your shackles?"

"Mine?"

"You think you have none?"

She blinked at him.

Hugh was too caught up in the conversation to choose his words carefully anymore. As much as he knew he had a valid point to make, part of him was whispering that perhaps she had a valid point as well. The conflict robbed him of the careful control he'd used earlier.

"Pride is a vice, Clara."

She narrowed her gaze and leaned toward him. "As is apathy."

"You think I'm apathetic?"

"You seem to have nary a qualm that Ambrose spends his evenings . . ." She drifted off, clearly uncertain exactly how Ambrose was whiling away the night hours. "Coming home in a clearly disheveled state."

He didn't want to admit to her that he had indeed been apathetic about the choices Ambrose made in his personal life, as he'd given little to no thought to the condition of the man's soul. It wasn't a comfortable idea, and he refused to be the only one convicted in this conversation. "You would be satisfied with his proper behavior while you are here? Is it just that you don't want to see the indications of the state of his heart?"

She poked him in the chest. "Do not insinuate that I do not love my cousin."

"Then perhaps you should show that love a little differently. No one likes a beating, even if it is only a verbal one."

"You don't know everything about me."

"I never claimed to. But I've been in this home for a few weeks now, and I've observed an awful lot."

Their voices had dropped to a whisper. Somehow, they had edged their way closer and closer to each other. Hugh could see the flecks of blue in her eyes, make out the individual spikes of lashes still wet from her earlier unshed tears.

The agitation that had burned through him from the argument shifted, and his heart pounded for an entirely different reason. "Clara," he whispered.

Her voice was nearly silent as she answered, "Hugh."

And then they were kissing. Whether he moved or she did was unclear. All he knew was her lips were under his and her hands were gripping his shoulders while his fingers wrapped around the top of her waist.

The contact lasted but a moment until they both tore away, stepping back, chests moving with the effort to control their rapid breathing. His lips felt the chill of the separation, and all he wanted to do was step forward and take her into his arms again, though more firmly this time, and kiss her with predetermined intention.

"Good heavens," she whispered, one hand coming up to lightly trace her bottom lip.

"Indeed." Hugh shoved his hands into his pockets to keep them under control.

Silence stretched as they simply stared at each other.

"I should go," Clara said softly, though her feet didn't move.

"That would probably be best."

They stared at each other for a long while, until their breathing had returned to normal, until any remaining shred of dusk had disappeared from the window, until the clock in the corner struck the hour.

"I should go," she said again. This time she moved toward the door, but Hugh's stance in front of the chair made it difficult to open. He stepped to the side, trying to pull the door open for her, but that maneuvered him back into her space. She scrambled back as he nearly fell into the chair he'd vacated earlier.

Finally, he was able to open the door and step aside like a gentleman and she all but ran out of the room.

Several steps away, she paused and looked at him over her shoulder before fleeing into the darkened areas of the house.

It was a long time before Hugh was able to do the same.

TWENTY-THREE

Clara prodded her eggs with her fork, testing to see how many times she could graze the edge before the soft yolk broke, sending the inner yellow ooze sliding across her plate.

The answer was five.

She proceeded to sit in silence, staring as the river of egg drifted toward her untouched piece of toast.

Hugh Lockhart had kissed her last night.

Or had she kissed Hugh Lockhart? She honestly didn't know. Everything had happened so fast, and they'd been so invested in their passionate disagreement that one moment had seemed to slide seamlessly into another and then his lips had been on hers.

And she'd enjoyed it.

Hugh Lockhart was not the sort of man she intended to marry, so wouldn't it follow that he would not be the sort of man whose kisses she enjoyed?

Voices and footsteps beyond the breakfast room door gave her only a moment's notice before Ambrose and Marmaduke strode in, still dressed in their riding clothes and fresh from their gallop through Hyde Park.

Not wanting them to know she'd been staring at her breakfast instead of eating it, she quickly stabbed a bite of egg and shoved it into her mouth.

Then nearly gagged as the white glop of cold, congealed egg hit her tongue.

"Good morning, Clara," Ambrose said as he settled into his seat. "I'm not accustomed to having your company for the morning meal."

"Didn't you stay in last night so you could go to bed early?" Marmaduke smiled at the servants bringing in plates of food and a fresh pot of tea for the men.

One of the footmen gave Clara's plate a quick look before purposefully avoiding another glance in her direction.

Clara sighed. She was certain to be the talk of the kitchens in a few moments. Only girls with troublesome secrets had difficulty eating their breakfast.

Ambrose leaned over and ripped the corner from her toast. He held it up, inspecting it like a Bow Street runner. "How long has this toast been sitting there?" He looked to Marmaduke. "Cold enough to dip out a chunk of butter without melting it."

Clara rolled her eyes and snatched the corner of toast from her cousin. Resolutely, she bit into it. Cold toast was far preferable to cold eggs.

When Ambrose examined her face, the normal cover of easy charm was gone and true concern had taken its place. "Is everything quite all right?"

"Of course." She nibbled at the toast and her stomach turned. "I am simply not very hungry."

It was Duke's turn to frown at her now. "You haven't been not hungry in the morning since you were born."

"That isn't true." She dropped the toast onto her plate and gave her brother the haughtiest glare she could manage. "I hardly ate at all when I suffered that grippe last year."

"So you are unwell." Ambrose picked up his fork. "Should I send for the doctor?"

"I am not in need of a doctor." Not even the finest surgeon in London could produce a tonic to straighten out the mess in her head at that moment.

"A malady of the mind, then?" Ambrose nodded. "Perhaps a listening ear would be of help." He paused in the act of cutting a bite of his own eggs. "Holding everything in will not make it better."

Clara narrowed her gaze at Ambrose. She could simply abandon her plate and depart the breakfast room, but Ambrose was just stubborn enough to follow her. It wasn't as if he couldn't request another plate of freshly prepared food later.

"I am holding in nothing." The lie tasted bitter on her tongue. Might as well toss in another one to potentially quench his curiosity. "My mind is as clear as it has ever been."

Ambrose coughed out a laugh. "Your head is as foggy as a London morning." He took a bite and chewed slowly, his eyes holding hers the entire time.

Very well, if lies weren't working, she would simply cut the conversation off by force. She cleared her throat and sat up straighter in her chair. "I believe this conversation is over. As this month's Commander, I demand the subject of my dilemma be dropped immediately."

Marmaduke frowned. "So something is troubling you."

Ambrose smiled in victory as he set his fork down and sat back, steepling his fingers in feigned thoughtfulness. "I believe, dear cousin, you are forgetting the rules of engagement. A command may only be issued after a question is evaded or unsatisfactorily answered."

"Very well." She smiled, knowing that in this war of words, at least, she would have the upper hand. "Shall I ask about your exploits the other night? Or perhaps I should inquire of what troublesome thought you are keeping to yourself that makes you so aware of unease that arises from not discussing one's problems."

The strike felt victorious enough to allow her to pluck a berry from her plate and eat it without a revolt of her insides. She smiled sweetly at her cousin's dark frown. "Which shall it be?"

He slowly took a drink of tea, maintaining eye contact the entire time.

A trickle of unease wormed through Clara. Was he weighing the merits of revealing his own secrets in an attempt to gain hers? Would he sacrifice himself that way? He could pull some tale from thin air, and she would hardly be able to refute him, after all.

Duke looked from one of them to the other. "I am not usually a slow-witted man, but would one of you possibly tell me what I'm missing?"

"Clara, I'm afraid the mantle is to my back," Ambrose said, as he slowly lowered his teacup to the table. "Would you mind telling me what time it is?"

Heat flooded Clara's body as her gaze flew to the clock on the mantle behind Ambrose. He couldn't possibly know, could he? No. He was only guessing that it had something to do with Hugh. Or was her guilty conscious the only one associating any and every clock with the tradesman?

She cleared her throat and looked to the clock. "It is half past nine."

He pulled the watch from his pocket and frowned at it. "Seems to be a little off. I'll ask Hugh to set it when he is here next."

Drat the man. She still didn't know if he truly knew anything or was simply fishing around for information. Either way, she was finished with the discussion. "As you have refused to answer either question, it is my prerogative to issue a command, and I insist the topic be dropped immediately."

"You would use a game to prolong your own misery?"

Clara narrowed her gaze and leaned toward her cousin. "As you appear averse to discussing your own nocturnal pursuits, I must insist you refrain from poking into mine."

"But you were here all night." Marmaduke's fork hit his plate with a clatter. "What sort of nocturnal pursuits could you indulge in?"

Ambrose grinned in triumph as Clara sat back into her chair with a wince.

"I was home all evening." Not a lie. "And I did not pursue any particular activity of discussion." Also not a lie. She had not intended to kiss Hugh, after all. "I was merely making a point."

"The only point I am seeing is that both of you appear to be mired in your own problems and refusing to seek assistance in rectifying them." Duke picked up his toast and pointed it at Ambrose and then Clara. "You are both fortunate it is no longer my turn as Commander."

"My youthful discretions are years behind me and far too old for rectifying," Ambrose said. "Dear Clara, however, is clearly newly troubled and therefore ripe for rescue."

It was the first time Ambrose had ever admitted to a significant faltering in his past. The revelation was almost enough for Clara to completely forget her own predicament.

"It is never too late," she rushed to say. "One can always change one's ways. Just because you strayed from the straight and narrow as a young man is no reason to continue to dwell in a ditch of debauchery and sin."

Duke groaned and Ambrose sighed. Her cousin's gaze hardened toward her. "Clara, until you are willing to be transparent in your indiscretions, I would thank you to stay out of mine."

"I have no—" She cut off mid-sentence as Ambrose lifted a single brow in her direction.

"Perhaps the two of you could take a moment to recognize that you both had valid points?" Duke picked up his teacup and drank deeply, giving Clara and Ambrose time to consider his statement.

It was far too reminiscent of Hugh's comments to Clara. She might be too vulnerable to efficiently attack her cousin, but her brother was also fair game. "Pray tell us, then, what are you doing with your time? Should you not be off in Surrey, swinging a cricket bat? You hardly appear a paragon of responsibility."

Marmaduke met her gaze, unflinching. Then, ever so slowly, he grinned like the cat who had successfully lured a bird into its trap. "As it so happens, no. I should not be in Surrey."

As distractions went, Clara couldn't have asked for better. Both she and Ambrose declared shocked concern at the same time.

Duke held up a hand to silence them. "Not to worry. I am still being obnoxiously paid for my athletic ability." He shrugged. "I have moved to the club here in London, though. I've been paid for three different games already and asked to stay on as a regular participant."

He frowned as he looked from Clara to Ambrose. "Did the both of you not realize I've been here for nothing but a few hours of sleep the past three days?"

Clara's mouth dropped open. Ambrose was offering profuse congratulations, but she could not formulate the same sentiments.

"You are moving to London?" She swallowed. "Permanently?"

"As permanently as a cricket player can, I suppose." Marmaduke shook his head wryly. "I'm not foolish enough to believe such a career is forever sustainable. Here in London, I should be able to find the connections and opportunities to have a life after I've played all my good innings."

"What sort of connections?"

He shrugged. "Schools need coaches. The wealthy pay handsomely to train their sons. Many of the developers of bats and such have offices in London."

"You speak of business." She could not keep the bitterness from her words.

"I speak of provision."

Clara didn't know what else to say. There was, of course, a worldly wisdom to his words, but she'd always imagined him having a more virtuous plan for his future after cricket. He didn't have the schooling to attain a living, of course, but surely there was something he could do to better the lives of others in a noble manner.

"You disapprove," Duke said lightly.

"It is neither for me to approve or disapprove." Clara's voice was soft.

Ambrose snorted. "If only you had such an attitude toward me."

Clara narrowed her gaze at him. "You, cousin, cross the lines laid out in the Bible. He is merely betraying the teachings of our father."

It was Marmaduke's turn to scoff. "I betray nothing."

"Do you not?"

Clara and Marmaduke stared at each other for several moments before Ambrose broke the silence.

"Who do you think pays for those baskets you so nobly and sacrificially take to the poor?" He pushed his plate away. "Who pays for your father's living? Who is making it possible for you to have a Season with the luxury of picking and choosing who you would like to set your cap for?"

He pushed to his feet, sending the chair screeching across the floor. "You can disapprove of those who work to gain financially in life, but you have no problem allowing those ill-gotten gains to support your righteous deeds."

He threw his napkin onto the table. "If we all lived as you say we should, it would be the church who was in need of charity."

Clara's mouth dropped open, words and even full thoughts failing her.

"I, for one, am proud of you, Duke. The Marylebone Cricket Club is exclusive indeed. Should you wish to retire to my study with me, I would enjoy hearing more of your success and future plans. I might even have an idea or two for you."

Marmaduke considered Clara solemnly for several moments before he stood, gently easing his chair away from the table. "That sounds like a fine idea."

And once again, Clara found herself alone in the breakfast room, accompanied by quickly cooling tea and the unappealing remains of abandoned breakfasts.

Hugh's words last night had put a crack in Clara's view of the world and this morning Ambrose had sent words slamming into the same spot.

Both men were men of business, in a way, even if Hugh was in trade and Ambrose managed lands and investments. Of course they would formulate a view that protected the way they wanted to live life.

A quiet voice in her head nudged the idea that she might just be doing the same thing, and there wasn't enough noise in the lonely room to completely drown it out.

TWENTY-FOUR

Hugh arrived late to the townhome, hoping that he would have another evening of reprieve from his new friends. For the past several nights, Marmaduke had been unavailable or Ambrose had gone out early or both and he'd been left to his work.

He was hoping for one more such evening.

His hopes were not to be, though.

The butler directed him to the library instead of the billiard room and he walked in to find Duke and Ambrose sitting at a table playing piquet.

"You do not appear to be in need of a third." Perhaps Hugh could still get out of socializing this evening.

Ambrose scooped the cards into a pile and began to straighten the deck. "I was losing anyway. We'll switch to loo."

As it was one Hugh knew and he didn't think either man would believe him if he claimed otherwise, Hugh settled into the chair.

They'd played only one round of cards when there was a knock at the door.

All three men looked up to find Clara standing in the doorway. They stood as she stepped into the room, eyes darting from one man to the other until they stopped on Hugh.

"Hu—um, Mr. Lockhart. I didn't realize you would be in here." She shifted her weight from foot to foot.

"I can leave if you've a private matter." He stepped away from the table, but Ambrose held up a hand to stop him.

"Stay, Hugh. It should take her less than five minutes to become so disgusted with the sight of me that she departs the room herself."

"Ambrose, that isn't fair." Clara's mouth flattened into a tight line.

Hugh looked back and forth between the cousins. Granted, his knowledge of this family was limited—though far greater than he would have ever imagined it to become—but the biting derision in Ambrose's tone didn't seem normal for them.

Duke's groan seemed to indicate that as well. "Are the two of you going to fight again? Because if so, I'm leaving with Hugh."

Clara took a deep breath and let it out in a rush. "I actually came to apologize."

Ambrose gathered the just-dealt cards and shuffled them from hand to hand. "Is that so?"

She folded her hands in front of her. "Yes. You were simply showing that you cared. I shouldn't have held that against you."

"Does that mean you've decided to tell us why you were upset this morning?"

She'd been upset that morning? Hugh stared at her, willing her thoughts to become known to him. Had she been upset or merely thoughtful? Because he had barely slept a wink for all the thoughts racing through his head. He'd had to redo two balance plates at the shop because of his distraction.

"No." She studiously avoided meeting Hugh's searching gaze. "My secrets are still mine to keep, but that doesn't mean I should have attacked yours."

Ambrose set down the cards and picked up his glass of scotch. He swirled the liquid around and looked into the depths. "I didn't realize you needed provocation." He looked over at her. "I shall accept your apology, such as it is."

The timidity left her face. "Such as it is?"

"Well," he said with a shrug, "seeing as you'll likely be berating me for something else by tomorrow, my sense of relief is limited."

Marmaduke sighed. "Must you two always be like this? Why can't we all be friends like when we were children?" He scooped up the cards. "Come, let's play a game of Commerce."

Clara stepped further into the room and gingerly sat in the last chair at the table. The gentlemen all sat as well, but Hugh was having great difficulty focusing on the game. To his right sat Clara, looking like a skittish horse seeking a reason to bolt from the stables, and to his left was Ambrose, a man who seemed able to switch from charmingly distant to mysteriously tortured in the space of a breath.

Duke dealt out the cards and the hand played out in near silence. Only the bids and occasional remarks on the play order were uttered.

When Ambrose won the last trick, his grin was nearly boyish. "I believe the day is mine."

Clara groaned. "Only because I am out of practice. I've had no one to play with these past few years, and I've forgotten my strategies."

"We can try again. I have no issue with winning twice in a row." Ambrose sat back in his chair.

Marmaduke gathered up the cards. "You might want to remember that there are two other challengers at this table as well."

The smile Clara sent Hugh's direction made him lose any thought of joining Duke's playful outrage. "I don't believe Hugh is much of a threat."

His lips twisted. He never had been good at the game and if his inept playing made her smile, he'd consider that a win.

The thought made him glad he was sitting down as his knees went weak. Had a single kiss really sent him that far sideways? He was thinking about ways to make her smile instead of ways to grow his business. He was praying she would stay in this room a little longer instead of praying his chronometer would be the most accurate yet created.

He was caught up in his own thoughts instead of realizing that both of his new friends were now staring at him, and Clara's cheeks were red as cherries.

Ambrose quirked up an eyebrow. "Hugh, is it?"

She had called him by his first name.

"I, um . . ." Hugh cleared his throat. "I'm certain it's because the two of you have been using it as well."

"Is it?" Duke's smile was speculative but also . . . happy? Did he want Hugh and his sister to have such a close relationship?

"What have you been up to, dear Clara?" Ambrose asked.

She stuck her nose in the air. "I have been up to nothing. Yes, I have had a few conversations with Hugh, and he gave me permission to use his name. It seemed only natural, as you have granted him permission to use yours."

"Friendly intimacy over a game of billiards is rather different, don't you think?" Ambrose leaned forward. "One might say your behavior was even scandalous."

It was Hugh's turn to be embarrassed because the truth was, it would be scandalous if people knew about their late-night discussions in the back drawing room.

"Anything I've done couldn't even hold a candle to your indiscretions, so I do believe I'll wait to be concerned."

Hugh snapped his head in Clara's direction. Had she truly just said that to her cousin? The way Marmaduke and Ambrose were reacting, it wasn't the first time.

"Ah, there it is." Ambrose lifted his glass in a toast in her direction.

Clara sighed. "I don't mean to attack you, Ambrose. I just . . ."

"Wish I would be better, I know. Sadly, your expectations are higher than my ability to climb."

Clara crossed her arms over her chest. "That's nonsense."

"No, it's not." It was impossible to say who was more surprised that Hugh had broken into the conversation, but he had and now he had everyone's attention.

"Do you even know what you are condoning?" Clara's voice was soft, pleading. "Just because he has stepped into your business venture—"

"That has nothing to do with it." Hugh kept his voice calm, trying to sound like the uncle he'd heard placate many an irate parishioner. "It's just that people aren't capable of always doing the right thing. So if your standard is perfection, he's going to fall short."

"My standard is not perfection. No one is perfect."

"Except for Jesus." Ambrose pointed at Clara. "You see? I did listen to those sermons."

Hugh could almost feel Clara vibrating in the chair. He'd spent enough time with Ambrose to know that, for now at least, church was merely another social obligation to the man. There wasn't any personal connection to Jesus driving him to godly obedience. He might be battling with some form of regret or conviction, but he hadn't turned those over to God yet.

And Clara couldn't make him.

She stood up. "I will not be mocked like this."

"Which do you want, Clara?" Ambrose deliberately leaned back in his chair, making a show of not standing with her. "I do the wrong things and I am depraved. I say the right things and I'm a mocker. Do tell me which you prefer."

Two tears spilled from her eyes, and she ran from the room. Part of Hugh wanted to run after her, but Marmaduke was already up, and he had a feeling there was a more pressing need right here in this room. It wasn't one he'd have noticed before or felt a need to take care of, but now Clara had opened his eyes to it and he couldn't ignore it.

He sat quietly while Ambrose stared at the empty chair.

Eventually, the man spoke. "Are you a Christian, Hugh?"

"Yes." He kept the answer short and simple, waiting to see where this was leading.

"What sort of a Christian are you?"

Hugh's eyebrows lifted. "What are my options?"

"Whatever you want, I suppose. I see people in the pews on Sunday, saying their prayers and singing their hymns. Then I see them in the clubs on Monday. They're at the gaming tables with me on Tuesday." He waved a hand at Clara's vacated chair. "And then there's Clara. I'm sure there are other people like her as well, saying censorious things about my behavior." He gave a dry laugh. "If only they knew."

"I suppose, then," Hugh said thoughtfully, "I am the type of Christian that tries to live in God's ways but mostly minds my own business."

Ambrose nodded solemnly. "That's a good type to be."

Hugh winced. "I don't know that it is. I mean, you look more than a little bothered at the moment. If I don't tell you that God can help with that, I'd be a terrible friend."

Ambrose shook his head. "God can't help. No one can help." He picked up his glass and looked into the liquid again. "Did you know I tried to fix things? No, of course you don't, because you don't know what I did. But when Clara first came, the first time she lectured me like Uncle Paul used to do, I decided to try. What if I could right a past wrong?"

He shook his head. "It failed. I knew it would. There was only so much I could do, after all. A note. I sent a note because I didn't know what else to do."

Hugh prayed, knowing that whatever he said next needed to be God's words and not his own. "Nothing you do can undo what has already been done."

Ambrose frowned. "What do you mean?"

"I mean, if you pick up a quill, there's nothing you can write that will remove ink that has already been placed on the page." Hugh pressed on when Ambrose appeared to be listening. "That's why Jesus offers forgiveness."

"Ah, there's the catch. To accept it, I have to believe myself a man worth forgiving."

"And you don't believe you are?"

Ambrose said nothing and Hugh had a suspicion that the conversational door he'd never thought to try to open was soon going to close, and it was important he got a few more words in before it did.

"There isn't a person alive that God isn't offering salvation and reconciliation to. You have to accept it for yourself, though. It isn't a set of behaviors that make someone else happy."

"Perhaps therein lies the problem. I don't think I'll ever forgive myself." Then he lifted the glass and tossed the liquid smoothly down his throat, set the glass on the table, and left the room.

It was several minutes before Hugh departed as well.

Clara had been asked twice by Eleanor to help at the church since that first day she'd offered her services, but she'd never been happier to receive such an invitation as she was the next morning.

She hadn't seen Ambrose since their latest fight in the library. Marmaduke had run after her and asked why she felt it necessary to constantly push Ambrose. Clara had responded by asking why Marmaduke was constantly willing to endorse their cousin's bad behavior.

Her brother had chosen to avoid her after that as well.

With such turmoil in the house, she was more than happy to borrow the carriage and escape to St. Anne's, where she could do something that seemed right.

Eleanor took her to a room where they spent an hour sorting food-stuffs and other items into baskets to be delivered to families suffering from illness in the parish.

"I think I gathered a few too many flowers." Eleanor looked at the table still strewn with enough blooms for two arrangements and then at the baskets, all decorated with so many flowers one could barely make out the contents.

"We won't let them go to waste." Clara scooped up an armful. "There are vases in the porch. Let's go fill them."

"What a wonderful idea." Eleanor gathered up the rest and led the way to the entrance area.

They'd finished one arrangement and had started on the next when the door opened and Hugh walked in.

He stopped short when he saw them. After several moments, he gave them a short bow. "Good afternoon."

Eleanor's head swiveled back and forth as she looked from Hugh to Clara. "Who wants to tell me what's going on?"

Clara certainly didn't. What would she even tell Eleanor? They'd kissed? She'd been sneaking down to his workroom to have some of the more interesting conversations of her life? He'd taken Ambrose's side instead of hers, and she feared that might be the final encouragement her cousin needed to lose his soul completely?

Hugh cleared his throat. "I believe it is a simple matter of different perspectives."

"Perspectives on what?" Eleanor asked.

Clara would like to know what he was referring to as well.

Hugh shrugged. "Ministry, I suppose."

So he was assuming she was upset over Ambrose. It was a reasonable guess. Anything else would have her blushing instead of scowling.

"Do you need to . . . talk?" Eleanor shoved a few more flowers into a vase.

If Clara wanted to keep her friendship or whatever one wanted to call the relationship she had with Hugh, this was going to have to be addressed at some point. It might as well be now.

"I won't say what you do isn't necessary." She indicated his toolbox with a nod. "But perhaps you've forgotten that people must make changes in order to repent."

Hugh nodded and pulled a small hammer from his box. He examined it as he spoke. "Perhaps you have forgotten that the change doesn't start with the actions. You can't beat someone into loving Jesus."

"You act like I'm delivering sermons in the dining room."

"Are you? I confess I'm not there enough to truly know, but when I've seen you with your cousin, it's not a far stretch." Hugh took a few steps toward the doors to the nave. "Do you think he hasn't sat through hundreds of services? Ministry isn't just hymns and sermons."

"You think I don't know that? I've been here for an hour making baskets for people."

"Why?"

The question brought Clara's righteous indignation to a stop. "What do you mean, why?"

"Why are you making baskets for people?"

Clara was at a loss for words. No one had ever asked why. It was just understood that the church provided for those who could not provide for themselves. They were the hands and feet of God. "I don't . . ."

He leaned to the right to look past Clara's shoulder. "Eleanor, you can help her. I know Uncle Patrick has said it to you often enough."

"People have to know we care before they care what we know." Eleanor fiddled with the flowers. "If they think we don't care about them, they won't believe us when we tell them God does either."

"I know that." Clara turned to Eleanor. "Well, not in those words, though they are very good ones. But I know the idea."

Hugh nodded, giving Clara a considering look that had her dreading whatever he was going to say next. She had a feeling it wasn't going to be comfortable.

She was right.

"Perhaps," Hugh said, "your cousin needs a little of your care before receiving your correction."

Eleanor's breath blew out in a loud burst.

Clara stuck her nose in the air. "Perhaps if more of his friends wouldn't indulge his behavior, he'd feel the need to realign his life."

Eleanor sucked her breath in through her teeth.

Clara only had eyes for Hugh though. He stood for several minutes, watching her, saying nothing. She was silent as well, a tiny part of her knowing that there was some merit to what he said but also feeling certain that she was correct as well.

Of course, her time in London was proving she might not be the greatest judge of right and wrong. Finally, he moved up the stairs to take care of the clock.

Part of Clara wanted to follow him, but what would she say?

First, she'd been disillusioned by the character of a future leader of the church and now she'd been corrected by the tradesman she'd always thought had misguided priorities about life.

Clara picked up a flower with a broken stem and rolled it between her fingers. It wasn't lost on her that the betrayal of Mr. Pitt wasn't hurting her as much as the admonishment from Hugh.

Now if only she knew what to do about either.

TWENTY-FIVE

I t was finished.

There, in front of him, on the sheet-covered parlor table he'd used as a work surface, was his dream come to fruition. The wooden box had been polished until it gleamed. The dials and balance plates inside were brilliantly shiny. The winding key sitting on the table beside the box was free of scratches, as was the glass covering the intricate dial that would allow regulators and navigators to know precisely how long they'd been away at sea.

The rod running through the bottom portion of the box allowed the chronometer to function no matter the condition of the sea or the movement of the boat. He still needed to perform one more test on that portion by traveling around the city with the chronometer sitting on the floor of a carriage, but once the box left this room, it would no longer be a picture of perfection.

Life would soon mar the construction, which would in its own way be a form of beauty, as a clock or chronometer that never saw use was a waste of materials and design.

Still, he wanted to remember it like this. He wanted to remember that there was one thing in life he could get right. Because he'd certainly missed the boat in other areas.

The way Clara had looked at him in the porch of St. Anne's still haunted him. No matter how many discussions they'd had or how many arguments those discussions had devolved into, she'd never looked at him like that. Like he had failed her. Like she wanted nothing to do with him.

Not that he would change anything if he could go back. The discussion he'd had with Ambrose after she abandoned the library wasn't for Hugh to report even if he had thought through it so many times, he had it half memorized. Had he said all he should? There wasn't any way for him to know.

Would Clara's method have been more effective if she'd had Hugh's support? He doubted it, but only God knew for sure.

He'd had to make the best choice he could in the moment and trust that he'd made the right one. As he'd told Ambrose, there was nothing he could do that would undo his prior actions.

Which meant standing here, thinking through all that might have been wasn't helping anyone. It was time to move ahead.

He closed the hinged lid on the chronometer and scooped up the small box. He tucked it under his arm and went in search of his friend, host, and investor.

Ambrose was in his study, leaned back in the chair, staring at a small object he was rolling back and forth in his hand. Hugh knocked on the open door.

"Enter."

He stepped inside and set the chronometer on the desk.

With wide eyes, Ambrose set the object aside—a simple but elegant bishop from a wooden chess set—and sat forward to open the chronometer. "This is it, then?"

Hugh nodded. "I'd like to borrow a carriage and driver, if I may, in order to test the balance of the chronometer on the support rod."

"Of course." He stood and crossed the room to yank on the bell pull before returning to look over the device. "I'll go with you. We'll take it over to the shipping office. Perhaps they've a dinghy you can take it out on as well."

The Thames was hardly the rolling waves of the ocean, but the current would be a more accurate test than a carriage. "That would be excellent."

A servant appeared and the carriage was ordered. In less than fifteen minutes, the two men and the device were bundled into a carriage and driving across London.

The box sat on the floor, lid open so Hugh could observe the rotation of the balanced clock as the carriage changed speeds while navigating the busy streets.

"Will this do it?" Ambrose gestured at the box. "Will this be better than what they have?"

Hugh nodded. "I believe so. The trick is in the balancing, as well as the accuracy of the gears and the ability to have the chronometer continue functioning while the spring is being wound. There's an alternate spring that automatically—"

Ambrose grunted and held up a hand. "I consider myself an intelligent man, but I've already no idea what you are talking about. Your affirmation was all I needed."

Hugh grinned and nodded. "Fair enough."

When the carriage stopped, Hugh looked out the window and nearly gaped at the enormous house. London had crept up to the very edges, but it was obvious this home had once been an estate well outside the bustling city.

The footman opened the door and Ambrose bounded out. Hugh closed the chronometer and followed more slowly. Minutes later, they were climbing back into the carriage because, as luck would have it, Lord Northwick was at the shipping office that afternoon along with his father, Lord Prodford.

Once more the carriage set off, this time in the direction of the docks. Hugh settled in, knowing the ride would be longer than the trek across Mayfair.

"What you said two days ago . . ." Ambrose allowed the words to trail off, leaving space for both of them to remember the prior conversation. "Do you truly believe salvation is for everyone? I always thought it a line used by the preachers to keep as many pockets as possible in the pews."

Hugh shook his head. "My uncle is the rector for St. Anne's Limehouse. Sometimes he goes down to the docks."

"Rough place."

Hugh nodded. "I'll never forget the time one of the sailors came up to the rectory to help with a repair. He'd been talking to my uncle for years. Sometimes they'd go months between conversations, but that man loved Jesus. He looked rough, but I'd never seen anyone so happy to have the opportunity and ability to work with his hands."

"Interesting sort of man to take to the sea."

"He wasn't that way when he started, at least not according to him. Then one day, he was leaving port after having talked to Uncle Patrick and he was watching the sun rise over the horizon as he secured the rigging, and he couldn't deny God any longer. He became such a changed man, the other sailors thought he was possessed and threatened to throw him overboard."

Ambrose grinned. "I can picture that. People who are too nice are frightening."

Hugh nodded. "He became a sailor because he'd killed a man. It was flee the country and take to the sea or face execution."

When the man across the carriage didn't say anything, Hugh looked over at him. "I don't know what you've done, but I'm pretty certain it wasn't actual murder."

"Ah, no. I haven't that sin to lay at my door," the other man said quietly.

"Then I think God can handle it." Hugh shrugged. "And while you can't undo the action, sometimes you can do something about the consequences. Life isn't over until the breath leaves your lungs."

Part of Hugh wanted to keep talking, to press Ambrose to make a confession and allow the Lord to have control of his life, but Hugh didn't think he'd have been doing it for God. He'd have been doing it for Clara.

So, he watched the chronometer instead, pleased with the steady ticking of the timepiece and the steadiness of the device.

At the docks, they exited once more and took the chronometer into the building.

Lord Prodford and his brother, Mr. Fletcher, seemed impressed with the device. They didn't take it out onto the river, but they did traipse down to the docks to watch the chronometer on a rowboat that was bobbing freely in the current, held to the side of a ship by only a rope.

The small boat bobbed and swayed and still the chronometer stayed steady.

Soon they were back in the office, the two shipping men excitedly discussing how much time and money could be regained from even more accurate navigation and tighter routes.

The victorious feeling of success threatened to bloom in Hugh's chest, but he beat it back. Excitement wasn't enough to lease a storefront or fit out a large workshop. It wasn't enough to support him while he built up a reputation and a clientage.

"It will take a year for the Royal Observatory to declare a winner." Hugh hated to stop the excited chatter, but they needed to know that the piece they'd invested in wouldn't be declared better than everyone else's for a while. "That is the only way to test the accuracy of the timekeeping over an extended period."

"Are you confident you'll win?" Lord Prodford asked.

"I haven't seen the competition, but I know this is better than the ones currently available."

He'd sold and repaired many of the standard model, an ingenious design created in 1761 by John Harrison. At the time, it had been an incredibly innovative piece.

Hugh knew he'd improved upon it.

What he couldn't know was if anyone else had done it better.

The earl and the shipping magnate looked at each other. Finally, the earl said, "I want to be ahead of everyone else."

"Agreed." Mr. Fletcher nodded. "It's only an advantage if no one else knows about it."

They looked at Hugh. Lord Prodford nodded. "We've thirteen ships that sail waters we know can be traveled faster with better navigation."

Hugh's stomach tightened. These two men couldn't possibly be saying what he thought they were saying. A guaranteed investment of that size would give him funds to rent workshop space and provide for himself while he made the chronometers and possibly other clocks as well. It would be enough to get him started.

"That's a large investment in an untested entity." Mr. Fletcher scratched at his chin. "I'd take that kind of risk with you, Prodford, but you're family." He looked at Hugh. "I don't intend any disparagement, but our only connection to you is that Lord Northwick says you're a good sort. And he hasn't been the most consistent judge of good character."

"My son's been known to invest in scoundrels is what you mean." Lord Prodford shrugged his shoulders. "What are your plans for the future, boy?"

Hugh swallowed down the protest that he wasn't a boy. Everything he'd ever wanted was in reach. If they wanted to test his maturity first, so be it. "I'm going to have the finest clock shop in London one day. This order would just be the beginning."

"So I'd be investing in two businesses. A new one and the one I already have."

"Well, no sir." Hugh swallowed. He wasn't willing to let this one go. "My business would be mine. You'd be supplying the funds for the creation of a product you are buying."

Mr. Fletcher chuckled. "My brother likes having a say in the businesses he deals with. He says the connection keeps men honest."

Hugh swallowed. "I understand, sir, but I've already spent my life working under the direction of someone else. I can stay where I am and continue to do so."

The shipping magnate leaned back in his chair. "I might have a solution. Family is a strong tie. It's why we've not tossed Lord Northwick's business ideas out without listening to them."

Hugh didn't say anything, his mind churning with thoughts on where this could be going and not finding anything.

"I've a daughter. She's been asking for a Season, but that's a lot of money and time she wouldn't need to spend if she's already married."

Lord Prodford chuckled. "You'd probably buy chronometers for the entire fleet from a son-in-law."

"I would at that."

Everything thickened until it could barely move. The blood in Hugh's veins. The air sliding from his lungs. Even time itself turned into a sludge he could barely move through. He couldn't bring himself to clarify the offer out loud, but there was no confusing it.

If he married this man's daughter, a woman he'd yet to even meet, his every dream would come true. He'd have a family, a business, a name, and the chance to form a valuable reputation.

The man who would be his father-in-law pulled out a pocket watch. "Timing is just right for this conversation. She'll be bringing me dinner any minute now."

Hugh couldn't imagine not going home for dinner, but then he couldn't imagine using a daughter as a business investment. Then again, wasn't that what many marriages were? He'd heard of dozens of matches that were formed because they made sense for the people involved. In truth, until Clara, he'd never imagined his future marriage as anything other than another step forward in life's accomplishments.

The door opened and a pretty girl with bright blonde hair walked in with a basket. She smiled at the group, a tinge of pink on her cheeks. "Oh. Father, I'm afraid I didn't bring enough for your guests. Would you like me to get more from home?"

"No, dear," Mr. Fletcher said, his eyes watching Hugh watch his daughter. "They won't be staying. You can leave the food on the side table."

She nodded her head to the group and moved to the side to leave the basket of food.

Soon she was gone, and Mr. Fletcher closed the chronometer and handed it to Hugh. He wrapped both arms around it so that his nerveless fingers wouldn't drop it.

Mr. Fletcher winked at him. "You think about it and let me know. If that money doesn't go toward a Season's worth of gowns, I could easily invest it elsewhere."

Once they were back in the carriage, Hugh said nothing, even as Ambrose stared at him with considering eyes.

Finally, as they rolled back into the finer areas of London, the viscount spoke. "I can't say that was what I was expecting from this adventure."

"Nor I." Hugh's voice was rough as he spoke around the thick clog of confusion still lodged in his throat.

"Are you going to do it?"

Hugh opened his mouth, but *Of course not* and *I'm not certain* were both lodged in his brain, and he couldn't follow through with uttering either sentence. Finally, he managed to say, "I can't say that I will." He swallowed. "It was exceptionally unexpected."

"But not all that unconventional." Ambrose shrugged and looked out the window of the carriage. "Marriages have been made for less gain before."

That was true, but they hadn't been Hugh's marriages. And while he'd never given great thought to being married, now that the issue was pushed on him, he could think of little else.

And it wasn't a blonde woman in a simple green dress that he could picture.

TWENTY-SIX

Hugh had lived in these rooms for four years and, if asked, he'd have never been able to recall the pattern in the plaster on his ceiling. Until now.

Night had long since covered the city and there was barely a hint of light creeping through the gap in his curtains, but it was enough to keep the room from complete darkness.

It was enough for his eyes to focus on the slight dips and rises in the plasterwork of his ceiling while his thoughts swirled around the implications of Mr. Fletcher's suggestion.

When he stumbled into work, bleary-eyed and exhausted, it continued to fill his mind. Though he normally chafed against Mr. Johns' restrictions, that morning he was thankful to be confined to the back room. He wasn't certain he could hold his end of a reasonable conversation, much less an intricate discussion on the best clock for a particular room or purpose.

He selected the simplest of repairs to fill his time, ones that required only a fraction of his attention. Even those took three times longer than they normally would have.

Unfortunately, his afternoon duties required him to leave his workroom sanctuary. There was a long list of customers that paid for him to regularly come around to their homes and recalibrate the time on their clocks and watches.

Fortunately, most households weren't like Lord Eversly's and he could accomplish his duties with little to no conversation. He could enter via the servant entrance, go about his business, and leave without having spoken more than the most basic of greetings.

After he finished his rounds, he hired a hack to take him to St. Anne's. It wasn't his normal day to wind and set the clock, but perhaps a change of routine would help his thoughts land in some semblance of order.

After taking care of the clock, he didn't climb back down. Instead, he left his tools, climbed the rickety ladder several birds had left their mark on while using it as a resting place over the years, and let himself out onto the small ledge of the top of the clock tower.

From here he could see the docks. One of those ships could belong to Mr. Fletcher. In a matter of months, one of those vessels could be using Hugh's chronometer to calculate their navigational pathway.

He could also see the pale walls for the Tower of London and the beautiful dome of St. Paul's Cathedral. Beyond that would be Clara and her family and Mr. Johns' shop.

From the top of the church's clock tower, with the wind buffeting him and the birds protesting his presence, it seemed he was looking at his options. A life, ready and waiting, near to hand, accessible. Or the unknown. There was great potential, but no guarantee it would ever see true accomplishment.

He'd always said he wanted his own business. That had been his goal since he'd taken on his apprenticeship. There were notebooks full of ideas back in his rooms of the experiments he would do and the clocks he would make when it was his name decorating the dial.

There'd never been a time when he thought it would come easily, but he'd never guessed that the price to attain it might be more than he was willing to pay. He thought he'd be willing to give anything short of downright thievery.

It turned out reality was a little more complicated.

A few months ago, he might have been willing to trade his life for success, but now there was only one version of the future he could imagine choosing.

He climbed down the rickety ladder and through the maze of stairs. His clothing was covered in dust and grime and his hair was disheveled from the wind, but he didn't give it a lot of thought.

Until he saw Clara in the porch preparing to leave.

He dropped his toolbox and hastened to smooth his hair.

She smiled and reached up to pluck a feather from his messy locks. "Been making a few friends?"

His face smiled in return even as his insides curled up in embarrassment. This was not the picture he wanted to present next time he spoke to Clara, because now that the words had formed in his head, he didn't know how long he could keep from saying them aloud. If he voiced them now, this would be the image she would hold alongside that memory.

He cleared his throat and tried to consider his words carefully. "I was doing some thinking. Up in the tower."

"Oh?" Her gaze dropped to the floor. "What were you thinking about?"

Instead of telling her—because part of him hoped he could get cleaned up and present his pitiful case with some form of decorum—he looked around for Eleanor. "Have you been busy today?"

"Yes. We were mending some donated clothing, but I need to be getting home." She looked at the door. "There's a ball tonight."

Would Mr. Pitt be there? Would he hold her as they danced across the floor? Would this be the night when she finally decided she wanted a life Hugh would never be able to give her, even at the height of his success?

"Don't go." The words spilled out before he could stop them, and he simply couldn't wait any longer. No, he wasn't the picture of gentlemanly elegance, but that wasn't something he could consistently offer her, either.

She needed to know how he felt before she made a declaration she would feel honor bound to keep. Unlike him, she didn't have the luxury of refusing an offer that would provide for her future. He would have his own shop one day, even if he had to wait a year to receive his first large order of chronometers. His opportunity was coming.

But she couldn't wait that long. She couldn't wait for him to be ready.

She frowned up at him. "I beg your pardon?"

"Don't go to the ball. I—" A large clump of dust fell from his hair, rolled along his shoulder, and drifted lazily to the floor. Hugh winced. He could not declare himself like this. "I've finished the chronometer."

Her gaze fell. "Congratulations."

"But I haven't cleaned up my workspace yet."

"When do you intend to do so?"

"Tonight." He tossed his plans to stay with Uncle Patrick's family aside. This was more important. "I'd like to talk to you."

"You can talk to me now."

He glanced down. A smear of white that must have come from the bird droppings on the ladder ran across one leg. He could only imagine how the rest of him appeared. With a wry grin, he looked back up to meet her gaze. "I didn't really imagine declaring my intentions to someone while looking like this."

"You . . ." She stopped and looked everywhere in the church but at him. "You imagined doing so in my cousin's back drawing room?"

"Not originally, no. But now? Yes, I do."

Now that the door was open, he couldn't keep from laying all of it out for her. His thoughts, his feelings, his heart, they were all hers, and he couldn't hold them anymore. "I don't have a lot to offer you yet, and if we marry, it will take me even longer to build that, but . . ." He dropped the sentence he was forming because that was hardly what a woman wanted to hear.

He opened his mouth to try again. "I know I won't ever be able to give you what you've always dreamed of."

Honestly, could he make himself sound like a worse choice? Maybe. But the problem was he could not make himself sound like a better one. This was the reality he lived in.

Still, he pressed on because his other option was to give her up. "I'd like to think . . . that is, I hope . . ." He sighed. "Frankly, my dear Clara, I'm hoping you'll want to choose me anyway." In frustration, he looked down at his dirty hands. "I'd like to kiss you again, but I can't touch you like this."

Her eyes were wide as she looked up at him. Her voice was strained to the point of being barely louder than a whisper. "That's probably a good thing."

She stepped to the side, away from him, and put a hand on the door latch. "I . . . um." She swallowed. "I'll need to think about this."

He nodded. He knew he would be thinking of nothing else for the next few hours. "I'll be there tonight."

"Cleaning up."

"Yes."

"And taking your things home."

"Yes." The unspoken understanding was there between them. After tonight, she could be finished with him. He wouldn't be in her house, wouldn't be in her life. She could say no by simply never coming to see him again.

After giving him one sharp nod of understanding, she opened the door and walked out.

Hugh departed soon after to go home, get a bath, and go to his temporary place of work in his best Sunday suit of clothing. If anyone else saw him tonight, he'd be a laughingstock, but if it gained him a chance with Clara, it would be worth it.

"There you are." Aunt Elizabeth met Clara in the front hall. "Did you go off to that church again?"

Clara blinked several times as she handed her spencer and reticule to the maid. "I, what? Oh, yes. I was at the church."

"I suppose it keeps you out of the gossip papers. Come along, you've barely time to get dressed for the ball tonight." Aunt Elizabeth joined arms with Clara and led her up the stairs. "We had several guests yesterday, and I would like you to keep a particular eye out for them when positioning yourself for dance partners."

There had been only three guests to their drawing room the day before and Aunt Elizabeth had made sure all of them were out within the customarily accepted twenty minutes. When Clara had asked why, she'd been told they didn't want to lose the mystery that was driving her popularity.

In other words, Aunt Elizabeth didn't want them to get to know Clara too well because then they would stop coming around.

But Hugh knew her, and he didn't want to stop being around her.

What on earth was she going to do about that?

The truth was, she didn't have to do anything. He'd all but implied that he would stop coming around if she weren't here tonight.

But how could she know? Yes, she'd been horrified by what she'd learned about Mr. Pitt, but what if her mother and aunt were right? What if he could be a changed man? What if he hadn't been the man those girls were talking about? What if they'd been lying? The man they'd described wasn't the one she'd conversed with for the past several weeks.

Or was it? Was she the one who was lying? To herself?

Clara's mind was spinning as she dressed in her favorite ball gown and sat for her hair to be done.

She'd never been a woman who made quick decisions. It had taken more than a year for her to agree to come to London and have a Season. When she'd been a child, she informed her mother she couldn't possibly choose a favorite color until she was nine because, to a four-year-old, her nine-year-old brother had known everything about life.

Part of her wanted to convince herself that staying and listening to Hugh wouldn't be her making a decision, but she knew, in reality, it would be. She would be either staying in London forever or leaving it as soon as possible. It was likely both options would leave her with fewer prospects than she'd arrived with. Her future would be all but determined, even if she tossed it all aside and determined to live as a spinster.

It wasn't just a question of if she loved Hugh. She rather thought she might, though she wasn't entirely convinced she knew what love really was yet. But was that enough for her to change everything she'd thought? How could she possibly be a woman of charity if her husband was a man of business? No matter what everyone tried to tell her about the church needing funds and that being as necessary as the work, she wasn't certain she was meant to be on the more monetary side.

Could she be the woman he thought she was? London was already making her say and do and think things she never would at home. Did that mean she was changing or that the person Hugh knew wasn't the real her?

She went downstairs and made her way to the small drawing room at the back of the house. The box that had sat in prime position on the table was gone. Only the tools and extra springs remained.

He would be there tonight to retrieve these items.

And she wouldn't be here when he did.

Hugh risked Ambrose's displeasure and entered the house through the kitchens. The servants gave him a few concerned looks, but he ignored them. He might return to this house a time or two if the cousins chose to continue socializing with him, but in time, that connection was likely to fade.

Unless Clara was waiting for him.

Hugh tried desperately to assume she wouldn't be there, but he couldn't possibly eradicate the hope his heart pumped through his veins.

He made it to his drawing room with minimal interactions.

It was empty.

She wasn't there.

Still, his hope refused to die. She would hardly want to be caught waiting for his arrival in this private room. It was more likely she'd wait in a reasonable location, like the front hall or the main drawing room.

Hugh should have come in the front door as he normally did.

As quietly as possible, he moved through the house. She wasn't in the front hall, the drawing room, or the billiard room. Desperate, he looked in the library, but it, too, was empty.

He didn't dare to check her rooms, but the lack of servants on the private floors—indeed the lack of servants much of anywhere—indicated the family had vacated the home for the evening.

She'd gone to the ball.

She'd chosen Mr. Pitt. Or perhaps she'd chosen to wait for a man she hadn't yet met or return home and find a match in the country.

What was certain was that she hadn't chosen him.

He didn't blame her. Mr. Pitt was truly the better choice. Yes, the man was a third son, but he was still of aristocratic lineage. He had a fine living lined up for him, thereby securing his future, and until then he had an allowance that was enough to keep him in high fashion and social connections.

Hugh didn't know much about the man, but his reputation must not have been too bad, or Ambrose and Duke would have been angry about her choice instead of merely disgruntled about it.

What he did know was Mr. Pitt couldn't love Clara like Hugh did. Clara might not know that, though. Hugh hadn't exactly been eloquent that afternoon.

Clara didn't know that Hugh craved her conversation because her view of the world and understanding of faith challenged his own and made him think. She didn't know that she'd made him a better person in the past weeks of their acquaintance. She didn't know that his first thought in the morning was not about clocks and shops and ledger books, but about whether or not she'd come by his workroom that day.

What she knew was that he thought she wouldn't help his business and he'd never be able to give her what she'd always wanted.

Was it any wonder she wasn't here tonight?

He'd never been a man who followed his feelings, and it would seem there was a reason he didn't. Feelings weren't something a man could plan and work toward, like a business.

Now the business was all he was going to have. Did that mean he was willing to marry Mr. Fletcher's daughter? The idea sent a shudder through him, but he had to entertain the idea. He could court her, get to know her, see if they would suit. He refused to marry someone for money or have them feel like they'd been bought and sold, but he was willing to see if she would make a decent wife.

The question was, could Hugh be a decent husband?

Back in the workroom, he began gathering his tools. He should be prouder of the work he'd done within these walls. He knew enough about the industry and who was working in it to know that there wasn't going to be a better chronometer than his submitted to the Royal Observatory. Even if he had to while away his time working for Mr. Johns for another year, his life would change eventually. His opportunity would come.

It would seem he'd lost his opportunity to win Clara, though. Not that he'd ever had much of a chance.

He'd had his moment to dream, and now it was time to go home and be practical.

TWENTY-SEVEN

The frenzied clamoring for Clara's attention that had accompanied her last ball seemed to have faded, but she still never spent more than a moment or two on the side of the dance floor.

Every turn around the room, every glass of lemonade, every conversation seemed to clog Clara's lungs until breathing was thick and difficult.

Mr. Pitt was standing at her aunt's side, smiling and waiting for her after the fourth set of dances.

This was it. She would have to decide for herself if he was the person of integrity she thought him to be. After years of caution about gossip and hearsay, it didn't sit right for her to allow such things to determine if she needed to abandon the man she'd spent weeks intending to marry.

But perhaps there was another reason to change her plans?

Her mind recalled a man with light brown hair, grinning at her over a partially finished project, scowling at her as he questioned her thoughts, and sighing before helping her find exactly what she needed to survive London with her sanity. He'd helped her find what she needed to make her days better, to give meaning to her life stuck in the city.

Was it possible she'd done the same for him?

Wasn't that what Mother had said love was?

It wasn't fair to Mr. Pitt for her to be thinking of another man while she was supposed to be weighing his merit. She was here, so she needed to cease all consideration of Hugh Lockhart.

Giving Mr. Pitt what she hoped was a soft, inviting smile, she asked, "How long have you been staying in London?"

Her dance partner appeared surprised by the question. "Four years, perhaps. I moved here after I finished my schooling."

"That is a long time to be without purpose."

He laughed and his hand tightened on hers as he led her in a circle. "I can see where you might think so, but I have a purpose."

The air whistled into her lungs a little more freely. She hadn't been completely wrong about him. "I'd love to hear about it."

"There are many preparations that must be considered before I take up my living."

This was why Father always told her to make up her own mind about people. "Such as?"

"A good shepherd needs to learn about the vices his people will face so that he can safely guide them away from them. No one wants to follow a man who has no idea what he's talking about." The wink he gave her made her stumble through the next three steps.

She'd never had a gentleman wink at her. She'd never had anyone wink at her.

"And, of course, I need to find a wife to stand by my side."

"Of course." Clara made herself stop to think about what the man was actually saying. Ever since she'd met him, she'd been taking his answers to mean something good, but was he actually saying anything of merit?

Perhaps the problem was that she wasn't asking the right questions

"Mr. Pitt," she said resolutely. "Are you a man of honor?"

The man looked so stunned by her question that it was his turn to stumble. "I beg your pardon?"

"It is a valid question."

"But a very impertinent one."

So it was. But Clara didn't much care that she was being impertinent. This was her future on the line. Much better to be slightly off-putting than married to a wretch of a man.

"Why would you think I was anything but a man of honor?" His voice was low, ensuring that no one would overhear him. If anyone saw them, it would look like a scandalously intimate conversation was being had on the dance floor.

"I have heard rumors about you, and I wish to ascertain for myself if they are anything to be concerned about."

His mouth hardened into a flat line. "It is rather bold of you to assume you've reason to be concerned at all."

Wouldn't a virtuous man understand the need to have such virtue verified? Especially if a woman was considering whom to trust with her future wellbeing. Clara was inclined to think his lack of an answer was all the confirmation she needed.

This entire business was ridiculous. She shouldn't be here. She should be in a tiny drawing room listening to Hugh, a man who had shown more than once that he was indeed virtuous and noble and all the things a woman wanted in a husband.

Aside from being financially solvent.

Clara frowned up at Mr. Pitt, not caring who noticed. "I consider it rather bold of you to prey upon women too desperate to tell people that you play with affections and steal kisses for a thrill."

His eyes widened, his shoulders straightened, and he glanced furtively around to see who was close enough to have heard her. Guilt was written across his features.

When his gaze dropped back to her, he looked down his nose at her. "You question whether I am a gentleman?"

"Yes." She lifted her chin. "I, however, am a lady, so we shall finish this dance and then part ways."

She ignored him as much as possible as they completed the required figures. Instead of grasping his arm whenever possible, she allowed her hand to simply hover over his sleeve.

Despite his manners, his upbringing, and his social position, this man was not a gentleman. How long it had taken her to realize that actions meant far more than honorifics and monikers. She'd thought she'd understood that, but she hadn't truly.

Now it was nice to know that while she didn't want to spend the rest of her days traipsing through ballrooms, didn't want to dress in fine satins or purchase three identical bonnets, she did have the qualities of an actual lady. Aunt Elizabeth might be exasperating at times, but in these nearly two months in London, she'd helped Clara see what it meant to be a lady in the important sense of the word.

After the dance, she begged her aunt and mother to take her home early. Once there, she made her way to the back drawing room.

But he was gone.

It appeared he'd been gone a while, because the servants had already been in the room, cleaning and dusting and rearranging furniture.

The pang in her heart was the only remaining proof he'd ever been there at all.

Clara couldn't seem to settle into her own company the next morning. Mother and Aunt Elizabeth had left to go calling on friends. They had, of course, invited her along, but Clara was too restless to pretend she didn't mind sipping tea and having the same inane conversations over and over again.

That was not a part of being a lady that she was ready to embrace. It was probable that she never would. How many times could Aunt

Elizabeth truly enjoy discussing what everyone was wearing at last night's ball? Or trying to put together a list of everyone a particular suitor danced with? The answer was apparently at least four because she'd already done it once over breakfast and she intended to make three visits while she was out.

Clara shuddered at the thought as she wandered through the house, desperate to find something to do with herself that didn't make her insides itch.

She needed to talk to Hugh. Without his gears and springs and tools in residence, though, she didn't know how to make that happen. Likely not today, as Marmaduke had left the house early this morning for a cricket match. Those could last for days. Clara didn't want to wait days.

Ambrose was still around, though. Did she dare approach him?

She had to admit, their relationship this Season had not been what she'd hoped. Why had she thought that living for an extended period under the same roof again for the first time in years would remove the contention that had grown up between them over those years?

Restless and unsure of what else to do, she went in search of her cousin. His study door was partially open, so she stuck her head in to see if he was inside.

He was.

It was a picture she'd actually seen numerous times while living in his home. Ambrose, seated behind his desk with a serious expression on his face. Normally, a ledger of some sort was open on the desk in front of him, but today it was a chessboard.

No pieces.

Just the board.

"Ambrose?" she asked, suddenly concerned by the dark, pensive expression on his normally jovial face. He had his serious moments, of course, but had she ever seen him look like this?

Yes, she had. In the breakfast room, when she'd tried to pry his secrets from him, this same tortured look had briefly crossed his features.

He didn't look up when she called but used one hand to beckon her into the study.

She slid in, pushing the door back to its position of almost closed, and crossed the room. "What are you doing?"

He glanced up at her then, the crooked smirk she'd seen so often on his face, but this time it looked sad instead of arrogant. "Contemplating my mortal existence, you'll be happy to know."

Clara almost fell into one of the chairs near his desk. "You're what?"

He opened the top drawer in his desk and began setting out playing pieces on the board. He stopped before there was a full set. After closing the drawer, he scooped up a piece and set back in his chair.

Clara leaned forward to examine the set. The pieces were elegant in their smooth simplicity, the wood grain seeming to flow along the lines.

Chess had never been a popular game in their family. Her father had a chessboard, but she hadn't seen anyone use it since they'd been children.

Ambrose placed the piece he was holding back down on the board. It was a bishop. He pressed one finger top the pointed top of the piece and began tipping it to one side and then the other, tilting it onto its rounded base. "Have you ever made a mistake, Clara?"

"I, well, yes, of course I have." Who hadn't made a mistake in their life?

"I don't mean like putting too much salt in the pie crust or wearing the wrong shoes with a dress. I mean a real mistake. With consequences that changed someone's life?"

Clara started to toss off the question with a dismissive assurance, but something in his tone made her stop and reconsider. Had she ever made a hugely significant mistake? Life-changing consequences were rather drastic to consider.

He snorted a humorless laugh. "I didn't think so."

"Give me a moment. I'm still thinking."

He shook his head. "If you have to give it that much thought, you've never stepped that far off your precious, perfect path."

Clara screwed up her face in a fierce frown. "What do you mean?"

"What's the worst thing you've ever done, Clara?"

She knew the answer to that because guilt still plagued her on occasion when she looked at the poor box at a church. "I once nicked money from the alms box to buy a doll. I'd been saving for months, and I had more than half the funds, but it seemed like it had already been forever to me as a child and I couldn't wait any longer."

His smile held a touch more life to it as he looked up at her. "Were you caught?"

"No, well, not that I knew of. I found out later that Father knew, but he didn't do anything."

"Where is the doll now?"

"I ended up giving it to a little girl in the family's Christmas basket. I couldn't stand the guilt anymore."

"Uncle Paul had the right of it then."

"I suppose." Clara frowned. "What's going on, Ambrose? You've made some type of mistake, I'm assuming."

"A long time ago. Like you, I was young and foolish."

And he was still thinking about it? "Did you make amends?"

One shoulder lifted. "I didn't have to. Someone else offered to take care of it. All it took was money."

What was Clara supposed to say to that?

"You see, that's the thing of it, Clara. You can lecture me all you want about the right way to live, but the truth is, I haven't seen anything that couldn't be fixed with a coin in the right palm or a whisper in the right ear. Even your discretion was fixed indirectly by money and favors. None of your righteous piety was needed."

"It isn't righteous piety—"

"Isn't it?"

Was it? She could see how maybe it would look that way to him, but she'd only wanted to save him from his own actions. "Perhaps if you'd heeded my warnings earlier, you wouldn't be sitting in your study contemplating consequences from old actions."

It was the wrong thing to say. She knew it the moment the words left her mouth. What had Hugh said? Maybe Ambrose needed a little of her care and concern?

Before she had a chance to correct herself, though, Ambrose was responding.

"Perhaps you are right."

His agreement threw the thoughts from her head.

"But there's nothing I can do that undoes what has already happened. I can't remove the writing from a page with a quill."

"Well, no." Clara frowned. "Did you come up with that?"

One side of his mouth tilted up. "No. I heard it from . . . a friend."

"Oh." Clara lapsed into silence. He was correct, of course. No one could change what had already happened, but if he was considering a realignment of his behavior moving forward, wasn't that a good thing? Wasn't that what she'd been asking him to do for years?

She leaned forward a little in the chair. "It's true you can't undo the past, but you can do better today and create a different path for the future. That's what—" She snapped her mouth shut mid-sentence, Hugh's views of righteousness playing through her mind, but it was too late.

Ambrose blew out a breath as he raised his eyebrows at her. "That's what you've been telling me? I am aware, believe me."

Clara sat back in the chair, stunned at the bitterness threaded through those words. Her voice was small as she said, "I just care about you."

He bit his answer out harshly. "Did you care about me or your comfort in being around me?" With a deep sigh, he carefully slid the bishop into its place on the chessboard. "Apologies."

Clara swallowed. "For what?"

He raised an eyebrow at her.

"What are you offering apologies for?"

"A gentleman does not speak to a lady as I just did, Clara. You may think me utterly devoid of manner and responsibility, but I have been raised with a certain level of decorum."

That it wasn't the words he wanted to take back, but the manner in which they'd been delivered, hit Clara in the chest, driving the air from her lungs. Was that truly how he saw her care and attention? She'd been thinking of him, not herself. She'd been concerned about his relationship with God, the sin in his life, the path he was moving down. Why hadn't it seemed that way to him?

She cleared her throat. "So, why are you contemplating your mortality now?"

"Because that's rather important, don't you think?" He picked up a queen and rolled it from hand to hand. "Do you know the last time I actually had a conversation with our esteemed Prince Regent?"

Clara couldn't answer, as she couldn't begin to follow this conversation.

"I am an aristocrat, a peer of the realm, and it's been weeks since I had a face to face conversation with the man and even longer since we discussed anything of great import. If I had something I wanted to discuss with him, I would have to send requests, wait, and hope for an answer."

His gaze met Clara's. "But the idea that I have an immediate audience with God because He sacrificed His son to make that pathway is rather worth a little examination of what is truly important in life."

Tears rushed to Clara's eyes. What conversations had Ambrose been having? What sort of revelations had gotten through to him? She couldn't fool herself into thinking it had been her words to make him start thinking like this.

"I thought it didn't matter anymore." His voice was quiet as he lined up the chess pieces on the board. The gaps in the pieces were strangely disconcerting.

"Thought what didn't matter?" Clara's voice was a similar, reverent whisper.

"What I did. I heard you all those times, you know. Heard your admonishments and corrections." He shrugged. "It seemed too late to begin living by them, though."

Clara frowned. "Why?"

He nodded toward the chess set as if that would provide all the answers. "Because I'd already broken the rules. By the time I realized that came with consequences, it was too late to live by them."

"No, it's not." Clara clasped her hands in her lap. "There's forgiveness for all past indiscretions. Future ones, too."

He shook his head. "So I've heard. You might want to lead with that next time."

Clara felt cold and her skin seemed to tighten around her body. Had she never told him that? She had to admit she'd stopped telling him that. Especially in the past few years, when he'd seemed to mock her every attempt at correcting his wayward behavior.

Perhaps she should have been more concerned with his inward faith than the outward appearance of it. She'd just assumed, since he'd grown up with her father's lessons, that he believed the same as she did. What if he didn't? What if he'd thought church was merely a social obligation, like going off to school or visiting Almack's?

Her throat tightened and her eyes burned with unshed tears.

He cocked his head to the side. "You might be interested to learn that I intend to conduct an experiment of sorts." He lifted a folded piece of paper from the desk beside the chessboard. "If there's forgiveness to be had from the Lord, one has to wonder if there is redemption to be had as well."

"Of course, there is." Clara swallowed. "God can change the path of any life, provide a way to right wrongs, and lead anyone into a brighter future. He doesn't leave us where He finds us."

He tapped the paper against his desk and then tossed it across the surface to land in her lap.

It was the invitation to the charity musicale. The words she and Hugh had so carefully worked out had been underlined.

"Remember that," Ambrose said dryly as he rose, gaze fixed upon the chessboard, "because I have a feeling I know what you're actually raising funds for." He opened the drawer and swept all the chess pieces back into it. "I'm afraid I won't be here for your grand party. I've made a donation, of course, but I find myself fully compelled to see if there could, indeed, be a way to redeem my past mistakes."

Clara's thoughts swirled into a dozen different directions, unable to clarify a single fact other than Ambrose seemed to be leaving. "You are departing from London?"

"I am." He picked up the chessboard and tucked it beneath his arm before walking toward the door. "I've an eight-year-old child I believe it's high time I met."

And then he was gone, leaving Clara staring at an empty doorway, her mouth hanging slightly agape. He had a child? An eight-year-old child?

How was it possible she didn't know that about a man who'd been like a second brother? Did Marmaduke know?

"Oh, and one more thing." Ambrose's voice preceded him sticking his head back into the room. "You should know that Hugh received an offer of marriage a few days ago. It comes with enough business connections and chronometer orders to open the business he's always wanted."

Clara's fingers went numb and the invitation in her hands fell to the floor. "H-Has he accepted?"

"I don't know." He shrugged. "It's not my month as commander, but I rather think you should do something about that."

And then he was gone again.

Off to meet a child he hadn't seen in eight years.

Her eyes dropped to the invitation. A child he thought was somehow connected to the charity Eleanor was protecting.

Suddenly, everything Clara thought she knew about her life and how it worked, and even how God worked in it, seemed as useless as Ambrose's partial chess set.

The assured steadiness she'd stood on all her life was gone.

And she wasn't certain she'd ever get it back.

TWENTY-EIGHT

Clara wasn't sure what she'd have done with herself over the next week if it weren't for the charity musicale. Not that she had much to do for it, but it at least gave her something to think about, to talk about, to blame her constant preoccupation on.

Prior to the morning of the event, she'd assumed it would feel just like any other party or dinner or soiree she'd attended in London.

It didn't.

Perhaps it was knowing that every person in the room represented money that would be helping someone else fulfill their needs. Perhaps it was the way some of those same people were deferring to her as if she was someone important.

Perhaps it was that she'd sent Eleanor an invitation and was somehow hoping the women would bring Hugh along with her.

The party spread through several rooms, and the atmosphere was interestingly divided among the groups congregating in each area. As this was a ticketed event in the name of raising money to help the less fortunate, anyone with enough pounds in their purse was welcome. Now everything from wealthy businessmen to powerful aristocrats grouped into the rooms' various corners.

The evening was also different because it was the first one where Marmaduke had joined them. He stood to her left, looking about the room with wide eyes. "So, this is what you've been doing."

Clara laughed. "Yes. A lot of standing around and talking. At least tonight there will be entertainment."

As Duke had not been with her at the other events, there were many speculative looks in their direction.

"Honestly, Marmaduke, don't you have any friends you can go visit with? You're scaring away the potential suitors." Aunt Elizabeth pulled her fan out and flipped it open to hide her frustration.

"Tonight is about helping others, not myself." Clara cast another look around but had yet to see Hugh. "A night away from the marriage mart would be a nice break."

"That isn't what you are meant to be doing."

"Perhaps it's what I should be doing."

Mother stepped up to Clara's right and took her hand. "Perhaps it is." The smile she gave Clara was a little too knowing. "We'll let tonight take your mind off of things."

Aunt Elizabeth sighed and declared she was going to speak with the rest of the Virtuous Ladies Society.

Soon Lady Grableton was moving through the rooms, directing people to the chairs in the music room and connected drawing room. It wasn't until Clara was seated near the front that a group in the back corner caught her eye.

Hugh was here.

But he wasn't with Eleanor.

Instead, he was talking to a petite blonde in a simple but elegant dress. Two older men were on either side of the couple and Ambrose's friend Lord Northwick was with them as well.

This had to be the woman Ambrose had warned her about.

If this woman could connect him to the well-dressed men flanking the talking couple, then she could obviously provide Hugh with something Clara never could. Money. Business. Credibility.

Clara didn't continue to stare, didn't want to catch his eye, didn't want to alter this possibility for him. Turning in her seat, she kept her gaze on the piano at the front of the room and the man situating himself at the keys.

Lady Grableton welcomed everyone and asked the society members to stand. When Clara didn't move from her seat, the countess gave her a curious look. She didn't stumble over her words, however, as she introduced the opera singer for tonight's performance. A lovely woman with a soft smile and kind eyes joined the pianist.

Clara was certain her singing was breathtaking. At least the reactions around her and Marmaduke's rapt expression seemed to indicate it was such. She barely recognized it. All Clara could think about was the fact that she didn't belong here. She didn't belong in London, didn't belong in this drawing room.

High society wasn't a world she knew, nor one she wanted to know.

It was time for her to go home.

Clara's determination to go home was not as easy as she'd hoped. None of her family was willing to entertain the idea, even though Mother seemed to understand why she'd lost her determination to find a marriage that would please her parents.

As she'd never talked about Hugh with her mother, she had to wonder if the house had been more aware of her time in the back drawing room than she'd thought.

Still, she was determined to go home. If her family wouldn't help her, she had a feeling she knew who would.

As she'd been granted use of the carriage on multiple occasions, no one questioned her request to be taken once more to St. Anne's Limehouse.

No one was in the church when she entered, and Clara made her way toward the front to stand prayerfully in front of the altar. The Lord had not granted her the successes she'd wanted when she came to London, but she was certain she was going home having gained what He knew she needed.

An older man entered from the door behind the vestry. Clara had met him once before and knew him to be Eleanor's father.

"Miss Woodbury." The man slid his spectacles from his face. "Was Eleanor expecting you today?"

"No." Clara shook her head slowly. "I'm afraid I'm here to receive solace rather than give it today."

He picked up a hook and opened one of the front box pews. Clara entered and gratefully sank on the padded bench.

"What is it you need from our church today?" The pastor sat on the other end of the bench, looking forward to the altar instead of staring down Clara.

"I was hoping Eleanor would know how I could find transportation home."

"Are you running toward or away from something?"

"Both, I think. I'd like to think I'm running toward the rest of my life and away from what I thought it would be." Clara took a deep breath and let it out slowly. "And perhaps there's a person I need to leave behind as well."

"I see." He cleared his throat.

The door from the vestibule opened behind them, and Mr. Porter looked over his shoulder. "Ah," he said. "I believe God is in the mood to answer prayers today."

He stood and slid out of the box as Clara turned to see who had come in. It was Eleanor, but she wasn't alone. Lady Grableton was walking beside her. Both women stopped their conversation and rushed down the aisle.

"Clara," Eleanor gasped out as she joined her in the box. "What's wrong?"

"Your charity—" Clara turned to Lady Grableton. "Or I suppose it is your charity, isn't it?"

The older lady sat gracefully on the bench and smiled. "Not really. I'm just honored to assist with it. We raised a lot of funds last night, which is fortunate as they have recently chosen to make a change to their financial structure."

"What is this charity does, exactly?"

Eleanor sighed. "I can't tell you. I've been sworn to secrecy."

"What do you think it does?" Lady Grableton asked.

Clara put together everything she'd learned from Eleanor, Hugh, and Ambrose. "I know it has something to do with the ton. And children."

"Yes, it does. Eleanor is correct, we have been sworn to secrecy, but I do believe I can tell you that it helps ladies who find themselves in a treacherous position."

Clara's shoulder had been cried on by enough women who found themselves with child and without a husband to guess the sort of people they helped. The particulars were not important.

What was important was that women like that frequently needed to get out of town.

"Can you help me get home?"

Eleanor gasped. "Why? I thought . . ." She sighed. "Well, I thought you and Hugh were creating something special, but I should have known there was a problem when you seemed to want me to be the one to get him there last night."

Clara nodded.

Eleanor winced and clasped Clara's hand. "I'm sorry I didn't come. I just . . . well, I don't know what to wear or how to act at those things. It simply seems a waste of everyone's time to try to change that."

"Was he there?" Lady Grableton asked Clara after giving Eleanor a questioning look.

"Yes. And he was sitting with someone else. Someone who can help him get everything he wants."

"What about what you want?"

What about what Clara wanted? "I'm not even sure what that is now."

Eleanor didn't look happy with that answer. "You aren't?"

What Clara wanted was another chance to see if she and Hugh could have made it work. She wanted to have gone down to that drawing room instead of to a ball. But as Ambrose had said, nothing they could do would undo things that had already been done.

Lady Grableton took Clara's hand. "I can get you home, my dear. And I will pray that you find peace there."

Eleanor still wasn't happy. "I don't understand this. I worked so hard to get you together."

Clara and Lady Grableton both looked to Eleanor whose cheeks turned a light shade of pink. "Well, I did. Hugh is always so . . . practical. You made him feel something."

"Unfortunately, that doesn't build him a business."

"There's more to life than business."

Lady Grableton laughed. "Spoken like a woman who doesn't know what it's like not to have provision."

Clara grinned. "I don't think you've experienced that either."

"No, but I was born to an aristocrat. We are well aware of the tug-of-war between desire and practicality."

Clara knew this conversation was at its end. She couldn't let them convince her to try to stop Hugh from making the best decision for his future.

Her mother was nearly beside herself with worry when she got home, worried Clara had done something desperate, like take the stage to the nearest large town.

Even Aunt Elizabeth couldn't argue with Clara's plan to ride home in Lady Grableton's personal carriage. With Clara definitely going home, Mother decided to pack her trunk as well. There wouldn't be room for everything in the carriage, but they made arrangements for the rest to be sent later. Clara didn't need a lot of ball gowns in Eldham.

Her first night back in her own room was a bittersweet feeling.

But she knew it was the first day of the rest of her life.

TWENTY-NINE

I t took Hugh three dinners, two outings, and one week to realize he couldn't do it.

First, Mr. Fletcher sent him an invitation to join his family for dinner. Apparently, the man was willing to return home for the meal if it meant he might not have to take time away from work to launch his daughter into society. Hugh had accepted because, well, broken heart or not, he still had a future to consider.

There was a possibility this opportunity was from God, another pathway opening up when the one he'd wanted to take was closed. Until Hugh knew for certain that wasn't the case, he needed to learn more about it.

That first dinner had contained nothing but talk of business while Mrs. Fletcher and Miss Fletcher sat quietly, eating their food.

The second dinner had been just as awkward, with Mr. Fletcher peppering his daughter with question after question to force her to expound upon her accomplishments.

In an effort to give her a true chance, he'd asked her on a walk and taken her to Gunter's for ices. She'd been pleasant enough, but the way she agreed with every opinion he had made him want to run far away and not look back.

He knew what he needed to know now, and he knew he couldn't do it.

As the date of the charity musicale had approached, he'd considered removing a large chunk of money from his bank account to contribute to the cause. It didn't make sense, as he might need every pence and pound soon. Mr. Johns would not be happy when he learned that Hugh had submitted a chronometer under his own name instead of Mr. Johns', and there was a chance he'd lose his employment over that choice.

If Mr. Fletcher also pulled away when Hugh admitted he couldn't marry the man's daughter, well, Hugh might be the one relying upon the mercy of his uncle.

Unfortunately, when it came to Clara, he didn't always think straight.

Fortunately, God had another plan. When Ambrose left town suddenly, he'd sent his ticket to the musicale to Hugh. He would be able to slide in, sit in the back, and at least see Clara in her triumph.

Hopefully, he wouldn't have to see her with Mr. Pitt, but maybe such an occurrence would help him stop thinking about her so much.

Mr. Fletcher also had a plan and an abundance of money. He purchased tickets for his entire family, and Hugh's plan to quietly sneak in late and slip out early was foiled. Lord Prodford and Lord Northwick joined the party as well, and Hugh was well and truly stuck.

It was the most animated he'd ever seen Miss Fletcher. She was enthusiastic about hearing the popular opera singer. It was enough to convince Hugh to wait one more day before giving up on the proposed match.

Until he saw Clara. More to the point, he saw Clara ignoring him. Had she seen him? She had to know he'd find a way to be here, to support this event.

Even without her blue eyes on him, just looking from her to Miss Fletcher made it clear once and for all that Hugh could never use marriage as a business deal. Perhaps people whose hearts were not engaged could form a solid marriage on practical grounds, but that wasn't Hugh's situation anymore.

He spent the night in prayer, shoring up his resolve that his dreams were still alive, but his integrity and faith were as well. Somehow, God would provide. It wasn't as if Hugh would go hungry and homeless. The worst possible scenario found him on the settee in the St. Anne's rectory parlor at night.

He knocked on Mr. Fletcher's office door. As his heart pounded, he reminded himself he was making the right decision. This was what God would have him do.

It would be awfully nice, though, if God made it so that Mr. Fletcher wanted to make a life-changing business deal that didn't include bartering for the future of his daughter.

"Mr. Lockhart!" Mr. Fletcher closed a ledger and set it aside. "Come in, come in."

"Do you have time to talk now, sir?"

The satisfaction on the other man's face made Hugh's stomach churn. To think he'd even for one moment considered accepting this man as a father-in-law.

"For you, I'll make the time. Have a seat."

Hugh sat and took a deep breath, determined to dive right into the situation. "Mr. Fletcher, I will not be offering for your daughter's hand in marriage."

The shipping magnate frowned. "I thought we had an understanding."

"No. You made an offer, and I was contemplating it, though I think it shows a significant lapse in character that either of us did so." Hugh was willing to toss himself into the pit if it made the other man a little more amenable to hearing his words.

"I am a businessman. If you're going to be successful, you'll learn that everything is business."

"If that is what it takes, I will never be successful. But I believe there is more to life than business, and people matter more than profits. One day, I will have the best clock shop in London. because I make the best timepieces and I refuse to quit moving forward on that path."

"Such nobility will cost you."

"Perhaps, but it will cost only money and not my soul."

"What are you implying?" Splotchy red patches appeared on Mr. Fletcher's face.

Challenging the man's character had not been Hugh's intention, so he changed the subject. "You are a businessman. Better chronometers and tighter shipping schedules are to your benefit. Should you choose to move forward in that goal, I'm certain we can work out a deal. If you wish to spite yourself, then I'll be certain my availability is known to your competitors. There are likely other captains who want early access to what will soon be the best chronometer in the world."

Hugh was laying it on a bit thick, perhaps, but he was truly confidant in his abilities and his design. He was going to change navigational timekeeping.

His integrity might not be up for sale, but his pride and reputation were free to be tossed on the line.

The other man sat for a long while, staring at Hugh, willing the man to break.

But Hugh didn't move. He sat in silence, using the anxiousness created to remind him that he could indeed, feel things. That there was more than logic in decisions and the way he behaved could affect people's hearts and ways of thinking.

Finally, the man sat forward in his chair. "Very well. Let's talk."

"Did you go all the way up the tower again?" Eleanor stood at the base of the church steps, arms crossed over her chest and a frown on her face. "You're going to ruin all your clothing."

Hugh finished descending the stairs before putting his toolbox down and leaning against the newel post. "As it so happens, I'm smart enough to wear the same set of clothes that I wore last time."

"Well, there's that, I suppose." She sighed. "What are you doing up there?"

"It's a good place to think. There's a certain perspective one gains when looking at the world from up high." Hugh tried to put into words what had drawn him up to the top of the tower three times in the week since he'd turned down the offer of Mr. Fletcher's daughter.

"Up there," he said slowly, letting her know he intended to answer but still buying himself time to think, "it's hard to see the small problems."

"I suppose that's true. Although I don't know how you escape worrying about the big problem of not falling off. That ledge is not very wide." She shuddered.

No, it wasn't very wide, which was why Hugh always crawled out the door and sat with one arm tucked inside the wall opening. The feeling of the wind and the freedom to look out at the world like a bird were worth it.

"Perhaps that is why it works." Hugh shrugged. "When I'm up there, I can only consider things that impact the whole of my life."

"Like whether or not you should go after Clara?"

Hugh shook his head sadly. "No. I'm afraid I know the answer to that one."

"Then you're wrong, because I've never seen a woman so sad to be leaving a man behind as she was."

"That's because you're usually talking to women who wish the man in question hadn't come into her life in the first place."

Eleanor nodded her head with a wince because she couldn't deny that was true. More than once, the women she assisted in departing London wished some sort of harm would befall the man who'd recently affected their life.

Hugh could at least take comfort in the fact that he hadn't made Clara's life any worse. At least, he didn't think so. When Eleanor had told him Clara had gone home without securing an engagement to Mr. Pitt, Hugh had been hopeful that he'd maybe even helped her make life a little better.

"There is more to life than love," Hugh said. "As difficult as it will be to remain a spinster in her father's home, Mr. Woodbury can provide for her better than I can until I gain a reputation. I'm at least a year away from being able to start my own business."

It was clear by Eleanor's mutinous expression that she didn't want to admit he had a point, but he also knew she didn't want to be making up a poor basket to deliver to her own cousin.

"It's a good thing, then, that Father and I have prayed every day for you to have an opportunity sooner rather than later."

Hugh had to admit he'd been praying the same thing. Were he solvent or even potentially soon to be so, he'd probably have already purchased a ticket on the next stage north. While it was all well and good to understand that life had to be lived with both the heart and the mind, there was still a time when practicality ruled the day.

He almost turned right around and climbed back up to the tower to pray some more. Did prayers reach God faster if there were no buildings or trees in the way? Probably not, but it made Hugh feel better to think so.

The next morning, he was working in the back room of Mr. Johns' shop when Mr. Fletcher flipped back the curtain and strode into the workroom.

Hugh set down the balance plate he was filing and leaned back in his chair. "I don't think customers are meant to come back here."

"And I didn't think you intended to work for someone else."

Hugh sighed. Didn't people understand that change took time? "It's a work in progress."

"How quickly can you progress it?"

A flickering flame of hope flared in Hugh's chest. "With the right incentive, I've enough savings to try to make a go of it." Once more, the integrity that had him turning down Mr. Fletcher the first time rose up to thwart him. "At this moment, though, I'm working for Mr. Johns. Should you wish to discuss other business, I'll be happy to meet with you after the shop closes."

Mr. Fletcher looked like he was going to protest but then he sighed. "At least I can be confident you won't be cheating me when you quote a price."

Satisfaction replaced the trepidation in Hugh's stomach that had formed at the thought of losing out on a business opportunity again. This was what Uncle Patrick meant when he said to work as unto the Lord. When he did business with integrity, even when it wasn't to his benefit, people would notice.

And what was noticed could eventually change lives.

They made arrangements to meet in the evening, and Hugh struggled to concentrate the rest of the day.

Finally, he walked to the shipping office and knocked on the door.

Once he was seated in front of Mr. Fletcher's desk, the man jumped right into it. "I'll order three. If my captains report a noticeably better experience, we'll consider more."

Three was far fewer than thirteen, but Hugh was ecstatic. If there was one thing he knew about London, it was that they liked to talk. No matter the class, no matter the occupation. When word got around that Mr. Fletcher was trying a new style of chronometer, other people would have questions. Knowing it was currently being trialed by the Royal Observatory would only add to the intrigue.

Three chronometers. It would be enough to pad his pockets some, even after purchasing supplies and paying back Ambrose and Lord Northwick. Was it enough to truly step out on his own, though?

Possibly. Some of Mr. Johns' customers knew it was really Hugh behind their repairs and favorite devices. Would they follow him? He wouldn't be able to start as big as he'd wanted, and it would be a long time before he could afford anything remotely considered a luxury, but he could do it.

Maybe, just maybe, that would be enough.

Hugh couldn't remember the last time he'd left London, but he was certain it hadn't been for a small village the size of Eldham. It had taken him two days and three stages to arrive, but here he was.

It was easy enough to find the church and the rectory behind it.

Clara was correct in saying that the air out here in the country was fresher, the sky clearer, and the space more freeing. Beyond the village streets, he could see rolling hills and patches of trees.

The confidence that had propelled him to sit atop a mail coach for two days began to wane as he got closer to the house.

Was he enough to compete with all this? Because he had to be. As much as he wanted to tell her that he would give her everything she ever wanted in life, Hugh was a clockmaker. There wasn't enough business in a hamlet like Eldham to keep him in food and lodgings, much less provide for a family.

No, he couldn't give her this, but maybe what he could offer would be enough.

He had to at least try. If her answer was no, his heart would break all over again, but he would be able to return to the city knowing he had tried everything.

Heartbreak was something he could learn to live with. Cowardice was not.

Would she be home? Would she want to see him? There was only one way to find out.

He was preparing himself to see Clara again with so much concentration that he hadn't given a thought to the fact that he was about to meet her father. The man who opened the door couldn't be anyone but the one who'd raised her and instilled such strong faith within her.

Hugh tried to swallow but his mouth was dry, and he ended up making a sort of scratchy gagging noise.

The man's eyebrows lifted. "Interesting greeting. I'm afraid all I have in return is a standard good afternoon."

Hugh finally got control of his tongue and answered with a gravelly, "Good afternoon."

The man smiled, his kind eyes those of a pastor who knew what it was to have his day disturbed and didn't mind in the least. That might change when he learned who he was.

"Would you like to come in?" Mr. Woodbury stepped aside and held the door open wider.

"Yes, sir." Hugh followed behind the man, saying a quiet prayer.

"Miriam," Mr. Woodbury called as they entered the front hall. "Put on the kettle, please. We've a visitor."

"Oh, how nice." The woman entered from the drawing room with a smile and froze when she saw Hugh. "Mr. Lockhart."

"Oh." Mr. Woodbury dragged out the word as he turned to look at Hugh. "You're Mr. Lockhart."

Was it a good thing this man had heard of him?

Hugh gave a stiff nod. "Yes, sir."

"Clara isn't here."

No other information was offered, so Hugh had to assume they were deliberately leaving him unaware of whether or not she was away from the house, away from the village, or had hopped on a ship and sailed away from the country.

Hugh nodded. "I should probably talk to you first anyway."

"Wouldn't be a bad idea."

Mrs. Woodbury gave a shaky smile. "I'll just . . . go put on the kettle."

Hugh followed Mr. Woodbury into the drawing room and sat. Twenty minutes and two cups of tea later—constantly talking about his plans and his heart and his future left a man's throat more than a little dry—Hugh sighed and spread his hands wide. "And that's all I have to offer."

"You say that like you don't think it's enough."

"I'm not certain if it will be. There's no guarantee I'll ever have more to offer her than I have now."

Mr. Woodbury gave his wife a thoughtful look. "What you're offering now is rather beneficial. You know what my daughter wants more than anything, don't you?"

Hugh nodded with a laugh. "She wants to change the world, or at least her little corner of it. With her passion and faith, I believe she can probably do it."

Mr. Woodbury nodded. "All I've ever wanted for my children is for them to chase the dreams God gave them and follow the Lord as they went." The man grinned. "That they've both been unconventionally inspired has only made it interesting."

"That's one word for it," Mrs. Woodbury grumbled.

Mr. Woodbury reached across the settee and took her hand. "I trust my daughter, Mr. Lockhart. If you head out of town on the south road, I do believe you'll learn where you stand in her eyes."

That wasn't exactly comforting. If her father was telling him that leaving town and walking in the direction of London would tell him Clara's mind, well . . .

Still, Hugh did the only thing he could do. He thanked them for their hospitality and for hearing him out.

Then he asked which direction was south because he was so turned around in his mind, he didn't trust his own sense of direction.

The stones of the narrow country lane crunched under his boots as he left the village behind and strode in the direction he'd been sent. The grating noise combined with the rush of the pounding blood in his ears to block out any other sounds. Were there birds chirping? Children laughing? Peddler's wagons in danger of running him over? He hadn't a clue.

There was still the possibility that he wasn't being sent away, and he would actually find Clara as he walked in this direction. Then again, there was also the possibility that he was being sent into the grisly hands of a pack of known highway robbers.

Not that they were all that close to a highway, so if there were a group of robbers living in that distant wood, they were sure to be lousy ones.

Hugh paused and took a deep breath to clear his racing thoughts. His eyes slid closed as he imagined Clara's smile, the look in her eyes when she thought he was ridiculous, the laughing sigh she gave when he got her to see life a little differently.

Then he opened his eyes and continued up the small rise topped with a twisted tree growing out of a cluster of broken rocks.

At the top, he paused and leaned against the tree as he quietly laughed.

He'd found Clara, all right. She was in the wide, flat clearing beyond the rise, surrounded by four children in various conditions of clothing.

And she was flying a kite.

THIRTY

C lara did not realize how much she'd missed the sound of children until she'd spent months in London, separated from anyone not yet out of the schoolroom. She laughed at the antics of little Susan chasing the tail of the kite, as if she could somehow reach more than a dozen feet above her head to grasp the trailing ribbons.

It was nice to be back in the country. She knew what to do here, knew where she belonged, knew the people she encountered. It was what she'd been wanting to return to ever since leaving for London.

And if she reminded herself of that often enough, she would be happy again. She would stop wondering about the children she and Eleanor had packed baskets for. She would stop wondering how Lady Grableton's group was doing. She would stop listening for the busy life of London outside her windows in the middle of the night.

She would stop missing Hugh.

"Miss Woodbury." A little boy named Charlie tugged on her skirt. "How do I attack a person?"

Clara laughed softly. Charlie was always coming up with outlandish scenarios. Yesterday he'd contemplated what it would look like if a large cow broke into their house and ate all the pudding before dinner. Given the crumbs clinging to his cheek and shirt, Clara had been fairly certain he was the large cow in question.

Last Sunday, he'd wanted to discuss the possibility of giving the church a roof that could roll back so that he could enjoy the sun while sitting through the boring sermon.

"Well," Clara said as she gave the kite a tug to keep it aloft in the light breeze. "We don't typically attack people. It isn't how God wants us to treat each other."

He puffed up his little chest. "But I'm the man of the house. I have to defend you."

She bit her lip to keep from laughing. He was, indeed, the oldest male in their little group today. "That's a noble idea, but we are quite safe out here. We aren't even a mile away from the village." It was debatable if they'd even completely left the village, given they were in sight of two cottages.

"But what if, Miss Woodbury?"

She gave him an indulgent smile as she kept her eyes on Charlie's little sister Marie and another younger boy named Michael who had joined Susan in running around beneath the kite.

"It's admirable that you would want to protect me, Charlie."

"That's right." He gave a nod and pressed his mouth into a firm line. "It's my job to protect you. And the girls."

"What about Michael?"

"He's too little to help me. I'll have to do it myself."

And then, to Clara's absolute shock, he took off at a run, screaming at the top of his lungs.

She spun around to see him charging toward a man who was indeed walking toward them from the village.

A man Charlie would not know.

A man that looked an awful lot like Hugh.

Her heart climbed into her throat, choking out her breath as she tried to call out for Charlie to stop.

Unfortunately, his screaming caused the other children to start screaming and crying as well. Clara turned toward them, swallowing multiple times before she managed to call out that everything was all right.

Susan calmed her cries to a sniffle. "Are you certain?"

"Yes, that man is a friend of mine."

Michael gave a chest-jarring hiccup. "You tell Charlie." Then he stuck his little thumb into his mouth.

Clara turned back around to see that Charlie had made it to Hugh and was still yelling, arms outstretched and hands curled into claws as if he were pretending to be a bear.

Hugh knelt down just out of arms' reach of the boy, talking and pointing.

Charlie stopped screaming but didn't lower his arms.

"Is Charlie going to eat the man?" Susan asked.

Clara turned to look down at the girl. "No, of course not."

"Is the man going to eat Charlie?" Marie's eyes widened.

"No, children, no one is going to . . . eat anyone." The words were so ridiculous she could barely say them, particularly as the only thought that could stay solidly in her mind was the question, *What was Hugh doing here?*

She turned back to Hugh. Charlie's arms were lowered now, and both of them were turning toward the little group.

His gaze met Clara's for a moment. Then his eyes widened, and he was running her direction.

The children started yelling again, though it was an excited, laughing sort of yell. Clara turned to look at them and found herself nearly nose to tail with the kite she'd all but forgotten about.

In all the twisting and turning, she'd completely trapped herself in the kite string still clutched tightly in her hand. The kite had yet to plummet from the sky, but when it did, her head was doomed to be its destination.

Then Hugh was by her side, catching the string and pulling the kite gently to the ground. He grinned at her. "I do believe you and kites should not be in the same vicinity."

Clara licked her lips twice before her mouth could manage to form words. "I do believe you are correct."

With the kite safely on the ground, Hugh set about lowering the string to the ground so she could step out. The assistance of four very excited children made the process long and complicated, but eventually Clara stepped free of the encumbrance and handed the remaining bits to Charlie.

"Your freedom has been attained," Hugh said, his voice barely above a whisper as he rose to stand beside her.

"So it has."

Clara heard the children's chatter, their questions about Hugh mingled in with their immediate retellings of the event they'd all just witnessed, but she couldn't tear her gaze from the man. Why was he here?

His brown eyes watched her, assessing her as he would the inner workings of a clock, yet the confidence she'd seen him display in front of those gears and levers was missing. Had he come for her?

Of course he had come for her. The man had no reason to leave London unless he was coming for her. No one from Eldham would be contacting London's premier clockmaker for themselves.

The question she couldn't answer was how she felt about his arrival.

"Miss Woodbury." The insistent tugging on her skirts finally drew Clara's attention. Michael was pressed to her side, gaze fixed on Hugh, mouth pressed into a firm determined line. "Do you want me to call a bear on him?"

Clara sputtered. "Call a bear?"

"Like the story in the Bible. I can ask God to send a bear out of the woods to protect you."

"I believe that won't be necessary. Mr. Lockhart is an, er, acquaintance from London." Clara noted an intention to discuss with her father which stories were being used in the Sunday children's lessons. It wouldn't do to have Michael running about praying for God to smite people with random bear attacks. Not that she'd heard of many bears in the local woods, but should someone actually encounter one, Michael's calling for it wouldn't go over well.

"An acquaintance?" Hugh gave her a crooked grin.

Clara shifted her feet. "One could go so far as to say friend, I suppose."

"I see."

The space between them, which had felt so intimate only moments before, suddenly seemed cavernous. His gaze lowered from her, and he turned to face the children. She immediately felt the loss of his complete attention.

His voice was tight as he addressed the children. "And what has brought you lot out to this field on such a fine day?"

"Mama says I little menace," Michael said.

"Oh?" Hugh's mouth tilted into a grin. "Is that so?"

He nodded. "Miss Woodbury made me disappear."

Clara smothered a laugh with her hand. "I'm giving their mother a moment to air the house without assistance. Their father was recently ill and caring for everything has been difficult."

That was an understatement. Clara had offered to do the actual cleaning, but Marie's mother had nearly cried at the idea of a morning of silence to work in peace, so Clara had brought Marie and Michael on a walk.

Charlie and Susan had been collected on the way, along with Charlie's kite.

"I'm certain she appreciates the respite."

"As am I." Clara cleared her throat. This man had come all the way from London. She would be a fool to think he hadn't come with intentions of declaring himself or the hope of reciprocated feelings. A man didn't travel one hundred miles just to tell a woman that he'd been right to let her go.

Perhaps she should tell him that their time apart had given her time to reconsider things as well? She had, after all, given him the impression that she'd chosen another. Had Eleanor told him otherwise? Was that why he'd come now?

Clara licked her lips and kept her gaze fixed on the children who'd grown bored with the statue-like adults and were now attempting to get the kite aloft once more. "This was a ministry I could offer their mother this morning."

"Oh?" Hugh nodded. "There are quite a few verses about rest and peace that would apply."

"Yes." She swallowed. "But I didn't recite any of them."

Somehow, he grew even more still, as if he'd decided to not even breathe until he knew where she was going with that sentence. She rushed on. "Ministry is more than hymns and sermons, you know."

He turned to look at her, a bit of hope back in his golden eyes. "Is it? I don't believe I'm aware of a story where Jesus gave a woman a rest from her rambunctious children."

She shrugged. "He kept their attention by telling them stories at least once, but that isn't the point."

"It's not?"

She shook her head. "No. A wise man once told me that people had to know I cared before they would care about what I know." She gestured toward the children. "A tender touch on the scraped knee of a child is needed before the admonishment to not run along the top of the field wall."

Hugh looked at the ground and shoved his hands into his pockets. "It sounds as if you have been reconsidering your goals in life."

She shook her head. "No. But I have been reconsidering by what means I can best achieve them."

He gave a nod. "I have been doing the same."

"You have?"

"My uncle taught me that doing something for God meant giving my best effort to the task. Somewhere along the way, I twisted that to mean I had to be the best. I had equated success and acclaim with honoring God with my work."

Clara snorted. "By that token, only one clockmaker in London would be able to serve God at a time."

Hugh nodded. "A ludicrous idea when taken to its end, I agree."

"Have you decided to give up clockmaking, then?"

The look he gave her nearly made her break form and laugh. "Hardly. Nor have I given up the goal of owning my own shop and achieving success with it."

"Oh." Any desire to laugh left her. Perhaps the assumptions she'd made earlier were wrong. Perhaps Duke or Ambrose had sent him on some phony clock mission, hoping they would reconnect.

She had to know. The time for plain speaking had come. "If you've not changed your goal, may I ask why you are here? I can't aid your cause. My father cannot guarantee you an order of chronometers large enough to establish your shop and reputation."

"I never asked him to."

Clara curled her hands into fists, a renewed stab of misery slicing through her chest. "Yet that is what you rejected me for."

"May I remind you that you rejected me first? Perhaps I should save myself some embarrassment by asking if you still intend to hold out for a man bound to the church. For while I will never stop assisting my uncle, I will still be a man of trade."

"Seeing as I have no control over what offers will come my way, I could not possibly make assurances as to what my future's husband's occupation will be."

She swallowed and gave him the confession she'd been unwilling to utter in London. "I admit I was rather blinded by Mr. Pitt's situation in life, and I did not see his character. I can assure you that I have no intention of allowing such a mistake to happen again."

"Are you saying that character now matters more to you than position?"

"I am saying—oh, blast, yes that is what I am saying." Tears pooled in her eyes. "It's hopeless, isn't it? You and I? We can't even apologize to each other, or whatever it is we seem to be doing now, without turning it into a battle of wits and contentions."

His smile was soft as he extended a hand toward her. "Clara."

Silently, she placed her hand in his without thought. Only after his fingers tightened around her own did she question the wisdom of the move.

"I would rather spend my life fighting with you than agreeing with any other woman. Even at our most heated, we have never been cruel."

She squeezed his hand in agreement since there wasn't a chance words would get past the lump suddenly in her throat.

"Some might call that passion," he continued with a wide smile. "You make me a better man, Clara. You make me think, make me care, make me come alive when I was finding it easier to numbly chase someone else's goal."

His free hand lifted to brush away the curl that had blown into her face. "I would rather spend a lifetime arguing with you than a single day with a simpering miss. You show me parts of myself I would never have dared to confront before, would never have thought to question. Perhaps, if you continue to do so, I may one day turn into a man worthy of you."

Clara sniffled and realized warm tears were slowly tracing down her cheeks. "That sounds awfully close to a proposal of marriage, Mr. Lockhart."

"That's because I'm working toward one, Miss Woodbury."

"I do believe a lifetime with you would be a challenge I never thought to seek out."

His eyes widened, and Clara rushed to say the words that would let him know she had no intention of rejecting him a second time. "But it is an adventure I now know I will not be complete without."

They stood for a moment, grinning stupidly at each other.

"Miss Clara Woodbury," Hugh said gently, "would you do me the great honor of—" His eyes suddenly widened and his hands tightened around hers. "Run!"

"What?" Clara's mind spun off in bemusement as he attempted to jerk her to the side, just as the kite, followed by all four children, rammed into her back.

Epilogue

H ugh looked up and up and up. One hand was wrapped around the top of the cane he leaned a little heavily on these days. The other hand was wrapped in both of his dear Clara's. In a few seconds that large, black piece of gun metal was going to shift and point straight up to the sky. Then the bells would chime across London, telling everyone it was exactly 12 o'clock noon.

"It looks amazing, Father." The supportive hand of Hugh's oldest landed on his shoulder and gave it a strong squeeze. "You made a beautiful clock."

"You both made four beautiful clocks." Clara beamed at them before turning her face up to the sky again.

"It's only one clock," Hugh said gruffly. "It has four faces."

Her grip on his hand tightened. "We're here to celebrate today. I refuse to have an argument with you."

He let his gaze leave the clock so he could smile at the love of his life. "But it makes life ever so much more interesting."

She chuckled and bumped his shoulder with hers before nodding toward the clock that deserved his attention.

Seven long years it had taken them to build the Great Clock. Hugh and his two boys, Denton and Edward. The clock company he'd founded all those years ago had indeed grown into London's finest. They'd been at the forefront of new designs for clocks, chronometers, and watches, but being selected to build the clock for the tower of the brand-new parliament building was a crowning achievement.

They'd expanded the company until there were three shops in London. One run by Hugh and the other two by his sons. He'd never stop thanking God that they'd inherited his love for timepieces. Their wives and children were gathered around as well, though chasing the littlest ones and convincing them not to jump into the Thames was occupying some of their attention.

Finally, the hand on the clock face shifted to point straight up. The sun sparkled off the surrounding opal glass and the golden spires of the tower. The rich sound of the newly cast Big Ben bell rang down through Westminster.

The twelve deep tones mingled with the cries of triumph and joy from his family. Those squeals and laughs were more precious to him than any contract he'd even been granted.

To think he'd almost given this up all those years ago. Yes, it had taken him a little longer to get there than it might have had he been alone, but he could never have built a better life.

"It's the most beautiful thing I've ever seen," Clara said softly.

"Then you've never looked in a mirror, because frankly, my dear Clara, there isn't a clock in existence more beautiful than you." Hugh's gaze roamed over her face, and his eyes burned with unshed tears. "I love you."

She smiled and rose on her toes to give him a light kiss. "Well. I don't suppose I can argue with that."

Curious about how Marmaduke and Ambrose will find love? Their books will be coming soon! Be sure to sign up for Kristi's newsletter at kristiannhunter.com/newsletter to stay up-to-date on the latest releases and information.

HISTORICAL NOTES

Hugh Lockhart's skills, accomplishments, and career are very loosely based on the life on Edward John Dent. The timeline is shifted by a couple of years, and certain events have been condensed for the sake of the story. This horologist was indeed a pioneer of design when it came to the accuracy and construction of timepieces.

His journey was more complex and his life far different from Hugh's, but he did create an award-winning chronometer, as well as the regulatory clock at the Royal Observatory in Greenwich and the clock in the tower at the Royal Exchange. The true first chronometer trial did not happen until later in the 1820s, but Dent's work was being used by the Royal Observatory for several years prior. His 1815 chronometer is on display in the Clockmaker Museum within the Science Museum in London, UK.

While Dent was chosen to build the Great Clock in the tower of the parliament building, he was not the original designer. Nor did he live to see it installed or hear Big Ben chime. The project was completed by his two stepsons, who took the name Dent and carried on his legacy.

Today Dent is still a maker of luxury watches, stunning clocks, and architectural centerpieces.

Acknowledgements

Frankly, this book would not have happened without Leslie DeVooght being willing to spend hours upon hours helping me understand Clara. Some characters are just slipperier than others and Clara proved quite elusive. Wrestling with them often helps me understand God and people better, so it's always worth it.

I also couldn't have done this without support from my family. Thank you to the Hubs for reading every word I write and being a willing and able sounding board for my brainstorming and insecurities, and thank you to the Blessings for being the best cheerleaders an author could have, even when you have no idea what's going on.

To my writer friends who chit chat about life and study crafty craft together, you make this a less lonely profession, even if you are disembodied voices on an app.

For Angie, Laurie, and the other professional fans and friends who have come alongside me on this indie publishing adventure, I could not do this without you.

And finally, but perhaps most importantly, to my loyal fans, my dedicated readers, and my real-life encouraging supporters, thank you for believing in my ability to do this even on the days when I'm not so sure of it myself. Your continued reassurance means everything to me.

ABOUT THE AUTHOR

Kristi Ann Hunter is the Christy Award winning author of Regency-set romances and contemporary romantic comedies. A graduate of Georgia Tech, she has always enjoyed exploring how life, love, and faith work in people's lives. She lives with her husband and three children in Georgia where she supports her family, serves at church, and makes way too many visits to Chick-fil-A. Find her online at www.kristiannhunter.com.

Also available from Kristi Ann Hunter

A Defense of Honor
Haven Manor, Book 1

Miss Katherine FitzGilbert knows life is unfair, but she's spent her adult years trying to make its consequences a little less detrimental for some stumbling innocents. When her path crosses with Graham, Lord Wharton, her heart may be in just as much danger as her secrets.

Pixels and Paint
Trinket Sisters, Book 1

Emma Trinket thinks she's finally found a way to impress the family that has always seen her as a little odd. When it requires the assistance of Carter Anderson, an artist immersed in a world she's always avoided, they both learn a new way of looking at themselves, love, and relationships.

Prayer and Practicality for Parents of High School Seniors
A Devotional Journey

If you have a student graduating high school soon and would like a guide to help you pray for and support them, look no further. This book is available for purchase or can be downloaded for free at kristiannhunter.com/devotionals.

Made in the USA
Monee, IL
19 December 2024